AF437919

"I devoured this book. From heartbreaking to joyful, *Greater Expectations* is relatable and beautifully written; I couldn't put it down."

— ANASTASIA RYAN, AUTHOR OF *NOT BAD FOR A GIRL* AND *YOU SHOULD SMILE MORE*

Praise for *Charming Falls Apart*

"From the very first page I was hooked on this tale of heartbreak, self-discovery, and one woman's charming determination to turn lemons into lemonade. Fans of Emily Giffin and Lauren Weisberger will love this engaging and entertaining debut!"

— MEG DONOHUE, USA TODAY
BESTSELLING AUTHOR OF *YOU, ME, AND
THE SEA*

"*Charming Falls Apart* is the perfect comfort read. A smart and heartfelt ode to the healing power of friendship and the strength in reinvention. Fans of Sophie Kinsella will root for Allison James as she rebuilds her life on her own terms."

— ALLIE LARKIN, INTERNATIONALLY
BESTSELLING AUTHOR OF *SWIMMING FOR
SUNLIGHT*

"In addition to being a well-woven story about second chances and trusting your own instinct, *Charming Falls Apart* is also a love letter to the city of Chicago. One of my favorite things about the book was experiencing the city through Allison's eyes. This book belongs at the top of your list of summer reads."

— MARY CHRIS ESCOBAR, AUTHOR OF
NEVERENDING BEGINNINGS

"A breezy read perfect for a summer day. So many young women rush to make a plan for how they think their lives should go without stopping to think about what will make them happy. We can all cheer for a heroine who loses it all and comes to realize she never wanted it anyway."

— MARIA MURNANE, BESTSELLING AUTHOR OF THE WAVERLY BRYSON SERIES

ALSO BY ANGELA TERRY

Charming Falls Apart

The Trials of Adeline Turner

The Palace at Dusk

GREATER EXPECTATIONS

A NOVEL

ANGELA TERRY

Published 2026

ISBN (paperback): 979-8-218-88786-5

ISBN (e-book): 979-8-234-02973-7

Cover Design by Katarina Prenda

For my parents,
Catherine & Richard Terry

PROLOGUE

Beep, *beep, beep.*
The monitor shows her heartbeat. Her body is small and frail. My heart swells with love. This is life. Precious life.

1

Beep, *beep, beep.* The monitor shows my mother's heartbeat. My father squeezes my hand, and I squeeze back. We've been up since before dawn and are exhausted as we sit quietly in my mom's hospital room in the ICU at Northwestern, waiting for her to wake from emergency heart surgery.

* * *

AROUND THREE A.M. I woke to my phone ringing and saw my dad's name lighting up the screen. He never calls me, only my mother.

"Allie, honey." His voice trembled. "It's your dad." He took a shuddering breath. "Your mom and I are at Northwestern. She had a heart attack and is going into surgery."

My own heart raced. "Is...is she okay?"

My boyfriend, Eric, was awake now too, and sat up beside me. My parents lived in the Chicago suburbs, but they had gone to the theater downtown that night and had been staying at my condo in the Gold Coast rather than driving home, while I stayed over at Eric's.

"She's having surgery," he repeated. "We'll know more soon."

My hand clenched my phone, and I squeezed my eyes shut. Even my sleep-addled brain knew that was a non-answer. *She's obviously not okay if she had a heart attack and is having surgery*, I thought.

"Okay. I'm on my way. Where do I go?"

"Come to the Feinberg Pavilion and take the elevator to the check-in desk on the eleventh floor. They'll give you a guest pass."

"Thanks. See you soon," I croaked.

Eric had been rubbing my back while I was talking to my dad. Now, I turned to him, my voice shaky, and said, "My mom had a heart attack. She's in surgery at Northwestern. I have to go."

"Oh my god!" He hugged me quickly, and not missing a beat, said, "I'll drive."

He threw off the covers, and I threw on a pair of sweats. I grabbed my purse, and he grabbed his car keys, and within minutes we were headed from the West Loop to Northwestern. It was only a ten-minute drive with barely any traffic, but it felt like it took forever. Eric dropped me off at the front entrance, and then he left to find parking.

I raced through the doors and to the elevator, pushing the up button over and over, willing it to come faster. Finally, the elevator swooped me up to the eleventh floor, and the nurse at the desk directed me to the ICU family waiting room, where I found my dad.

Seeing him in his rumpled clothes, his head in his

hands, elbows on his knees, made the lump in my throat even bigger.

At my approach, Dad looked up. When he saw me, he stood. "Hey, honey."

I fell into his arms, giving him a hard hug, and felt all the weariness of his body seep into mine.

Once we pulled apart and sat down, I asked, "What happened?"

"Your mother woke up in the night and got out of bed for a glass of water. But when she stood up, she felt lightheaded and a sharp pain in her chest." He winced as he put his hand to his own chest to show me. "She woke me and told me to call 911. Luckily, the ambulance came quickly. She was conscious when they arrived, but she was in a great deal of pain and had trouble talking."

His voice wobbled for a second before he continued. "The EMTs said it was a heart attack, and as soon as we got here, she was rushed into the cardiac unit. The doctor said there was a blockage in her heart and that she needed an emergency bypass. They prepped her right away, and she's in there now."

I knew my mother took high blood pressure medication and watched her cholesterol, but I didn't think it was anything too serious; I thought it was just the norm for people in their sixties.

"Did they say whether she'll be okay?" I asked again, my voice shaky.

His shoulders sagged. "She's at one of the best cardiac hospitals in the country," was his reply, as if he had been repeating that to himself. "We just have to wait. The surgery can take several hours."

I nodded, and we sat down to start the interminable wait.

My phone buzzed in my purse, and I took it out.

Eric texted: *I parked the car, but the front desk won't let me come up. They said the ICU waiting room is for family only.*

I texted back: *It's okay. My mom will be in surgery for the next few hours. I will call you when she is out.*

Sorry I can't be there. I know how hard this is. Tell your dad, I'm thinking of you guys, and I hope she recovers quickly.

Will do. Thank you for the ride. Love you.

Love you too. I'm going to head home and then into work. I'll keep my phone on.

"That was Eric," I said to my dad. "They won't let him up. He told me to tell you, he's thinking of us and wishes Mom a quick recovery."

"That's nice of him," my dad said absently, his mind clearly in the surgery room with Mom.

My dad and I tried to distract ourselves and made small talk here and there, but we mostly spent the next few hours in the waiting room in silence. On the wall, a muted TV played the news. There was only one other family besides us, also sitting staring at it and past it. There were magazines on the table in front of us; I picked one up to read, but the words and images blurred before me, and I gave up. I was unsure whether I could use my phone, but it wasn't like I could focus on anything. Mostly, I used the longest hours of my life to ruminate on my relationship with my mom and tried to remember our last conversation.

My mother and I had always had a close but difficult relationship. She was smothering and yet overly critical. She always believed she knew what was best for me, even if I disagreed. Which made me feel I was lacking by not living up to her standards. For example, throughout my mid-twenties and early thirties, she wanted to see me married and settled down. But a few years ago, when I had what could lightly be called an early midlife crisis at age thirty-five, we finally had our come-to-Jesus moment.

After I'd been fired from my PR job and unceremoniously dumped by my fiancé Neil on the same day, my mother's first response was, "How did you let this happen?" She actually suggested couples' counseling and called Neil to apologize for me, still hoping we could work things out. But when she saw me much happier without Neil and thriving in my new consulting startup, we finally understood each other, and our relationship began moving toward an adult one.

We've only just come to a truce and understanding. In her own way, she was a self-made woman, working with what she had at the time, marrying my dad and "moving up" in her world, and so didn't quite trust that my world and my path are different. She still tells me what she thinks of my choices, but lets me live my life rather than trying to control it. I'm thirty-eight now, and I can make my own decisions.

Around seven o'clock, a nurse came in and said Mom was out of surgery, and everything went well. They were waiting for her to wake up so the doctor could assess her. In the meantime, we could sit in the room with her.

* * *

NOW MY DAD and I sit here holding hands, watching and waiting for her to open her eyes. We don't know how to act. Each needing consoling, while feeling we need to console the other. Her body looks so small and frail under the sheets and with various tubes attached to her. I've always seen my mother in charge, a petite powerhouse. Now there's a ventilation machine helping her breathe, fluids and medicine being dripped into her, monitors everywhere, while she silently lies in bed.

Suddenly she wakes with a jolt; her eyes fly open wide. Her hands go to pull out the intubation tube, but they're tied down, and her eyes widen further in fear and panic. My heart stops. The nurse in the room rushes over and another medical team member enters the room. They try to calm her down and after a quick look at all the monitors, they begin the process of taking out the tube.

My mom looks so frightened and confused that I have to hold back my tears. I realize I have never seen her helpless. The nurse in the room focuses on my mom, checking everything, while my dad and I sit here. Relieved, but still scared.

"The anesthesia is wearing off," the nurse explains to us. "So she's going to be confused."

It takes several minutes for her to come to. My mother is still confused as the nurse asks her questions, and she doesn't seem to know who we are. When she can't answer a question, and my dad tries to step in, she shoots him an angry look, as if he's a stranger speaking for her. But after twenty minutes, she is smiling dazedly and talking to us in a loopy voice. The nurse explains to us again, "Painkillers."

We wait until after the doctor checks on my mom and assures us everything went well. They tell us that she's going to sleep for the rest of the day while they monitor her.

"You're free to stay, but it isn't necessary," the primary nurse says.

We're reluctant to leave, but then another nurse tells us it's a good time to go home and take a break. My dad and I both need a shower and fresh clothes and probably a long nap as well, so we take their advice.

As we make our way out of the building, my dad asks, "Should we get some breakfast?"

In response, my stomach growls. After being in a knot for the last several hours, I feel like I can finally eat.

"Sounds good. But I'd like to shower and change first," I say, looking down at my sweatpants that double as pajamas. "What if we share a cab, and then I'll meet you back at my place? We can go somewhere in the neighborhood."

My dad agrees, and we hail a waiting taxi at the hospital entrance.

When I walk through Eric's door, I see a note on the counter with a big heart on it. There's also a sticky note with a heart on the coffeepot, meaning that Eric set it up, so all I have to do is hit brew, which I do.

Thanks for the coffee! I text him. *Mom's out of surgery and will be sleeping the rest of the day. I'm back at yours, but meeting Dad for breakfast near mine.*

Wish I could join you, but we're short-staffed this morning! I'll swing by for a quick hug and moral support.

Though I think my dad and I could use some outsider company, I tell him not to worry about it and that I'll fill him in on everything tonight.

I unofficially moved into Eric's loft in the West Loop since it's more spacious. But we still toggle between our two places, and sometimes Eric stays at mine since it's closer to his coffeehouse, The Cauldron. But lately my parents have been using my place for when they come downtown for dinner or a theater night. My dad is semi-retired, and I think they've been testing out downsizing from their large Colonial-style house in the suburbs to a condo, something that requires less maintenance. Or, as my mother likes to say, "I don't know why we have this big house if there are no grandchildren to run through it." Which has become more of a running joke between us than a passive-aggressive remark (or so I choose to believe).

After listening to her lament my declining fertility, I finally froze my eggs in my mid-thirties, hoping that would shut down the conversation for a while. And though Eric and I have been dating for a couple years now, they've been some hard years and not particularly ones where I would have wanted to put a baby into the mix.

Eric and I met in the spring of 2019 when I first went to his coffeehouse, and by fall of that year we started dating. Then, when the COVID-19 pandemic happened, early 2020 had us as a pod of two; and since his place was larger, we mostly stayed there. My other option was staying with my parents in the suburbs, but I had to consider my mental health as well as my physical health. My other "pod" person was my best friend, Jordan. If Eric and I weren't already living together, I think Jordan and I would have reignited our college days and probably moved in together to stave off the loneliness of the lockdown.

While the pandemic stay-at-home orders had Eric and me living together sooner than we expected, we weathered the storm, and our relationship survived. Our fledgling businesses, not so much.

When we met, Eric owned three coffeehouses in Chicago. The Gold Coast location was the only one that survived that year as it had enough neighborhood foot traffic and was close to an El stop—and most importantly, didn't have a greedy landlord. After being fired from my big, fancy

PR firm the year before, I had started my own consulting business, matching corporate sponsorships to various charity endeavors. My new venture stalled to a sputter in 2020, but with no debt and no real overhead, I was able to make it through. But poor Eric—his entire business counted on people walking in and staying a while. We tried different things, such as a coffee bean subscription program and some Zoom events, like a coffee tasting and an online book club, to keep the community aspect going. But the subscription program wasn't sustainable, costing us more money than it was worth, and eventually people were "Zoomed" out. Some neighbors tried various grassroots efforts like GoFundMe, but it wasn't enough. The rent on three stores was draining Eric's finances, and so he kept the one that was the most profitable. Now he puts all his energy into it—opening at five in the morning and closing at ten at night. Honestly, if we didn't live together, I would probably never see him.

The adrenaline from the last several hours is starting to fade, and I know I need to hurry and shower, so I head to the bathroom and shake out of my clothes. With the water running over me, and realizing I'm alone, I finally allow myself to cry all the tears of dread and exhaustion and what-ifs I felt at the hospital. It seems like my mom will be fine. *Thank god.* But it's a harsh reminder—nothing in this life can be taken for granted. Even when you think you've survived one catastrophe, there will always be something new lurking around the corner, another shoe to drop.

Once I've cried it out and feel like I can be human again in public, I turn off the water. I dress in a sweater and jeans, and pull my damp hair into a bun, and then head out to meet my dad.

2

____

After parking my car in my building's garage, I head into the lobby.

"Hi, Robert," I greet my doorman.

"Hello, Allison," he says, standing behind the large front desk with a protective plexiglass shield. "Your father told me to let him know when you arrived, and he'd come down if you just wanted to wait here for him."

"Oh, okay. Thanks." I take a seat on the lobby's leather sofa and listen to Robert on the phone with my dad.

"Yep, she's here...You're welcome."

When he hangs up, he comes out from around the desk. "I'm so sorry to hear about your mother. She's such a wonderful woman. I've been praying for her."

Somehow my mother has spun a spell on Robert, and he not so secretly has had a crush on her ever since I moved into the building.

"Thank you. Yes, it was scary, but she got to the hospital at the right time and the doctors did an amazing job."

"You tell her I'm wishing her a quick recovery."

"Of course. She'll be happy to hear that."

"And what about you? How are you doing these days? I haven't seen you around lately, or that young man of yours."

I chuckle inwardly. Robert is the nicest, and nosiest, doorman on staff, and I know he's looking for a scoop.

"I've been well. Spending more time at Eric's these days since he has a bigger space."

Robert regards me carefully. "You're not looking to move out, are you?"

"No immediate plans. It's nice having my own place still, and my parents seem to be enjoying it. Maybe if Eric and I decide to do something more permanent, my parents will move in here."

By the big smile on Robert's face, I can tell he's delighted. Before he can respond, the elevator doors open and my dad comes out.

"Here he is," Robert says. "Hello, Mr. James. Allison and I have been having a catch-up."

"Hi, Robert. Is that so? It's been a long morning." My dad sounds tired. He turns to me. "Hey, honey, ready for breakfast?"

I stand and wobble for a second, still feeling a little light-headed from the early wake-up call and the adrenaline crash later. "Yes, I can definitely eat now."

We walk down the street to a restaurant that serves all-day breakfast. My dad opens the large wooden door to the entrance, and we step inside. It's ten in the morning on a Thursday, and the place is surprisingly busy with a mix of retirees, young people, and mothers with kids. We're seated immediately and handed menus. Since we've been here several times before, we order quickly: the ham and cheddar omelet for my dad and the house coconut oatmeal for me and two coffees, and my dad says, "And keep 'em coming."

After the server takes our menus, my dad sits back and rubs his face. "I hope your mother is getting some sleep."

"I'm sure she is." I picture her in the hospital bed, the machines humming around her, and grimace. "How are you holding up?"

As I sit across from my father, who is three years older than my mom, he suddenly looks so much older to me, as if this morning's emergency has knocked some years off his life as well. He's only a couple of years away from fully retiring at his law firm, and I can't imagine him going alone on all the trips they have planned for that time.

"Tired, obviously, but okay. After we eat, I'll go back to the hospital and see how she's doing."

"I just still can't believe it," I say.

"Well, high blood pressure and high cholesterol run in her family. Both her parents died within a year of each other from sudden heart attacks."

I never knew my mother's parents because I was only an infant when they died in their early sixties. Even though in photos my grandmother was small and trim like my mother, I assumed her heart issues were from smoking and a bad Midwestern diet, not something hereditary.

"Your mother was lucky. I don't want to think about what would've happened if she hadn't woken up."

I gulp. She could have died in her sleep last night. I hadn't let myself think about that.

My dad's phone rings before I can respond.

"It's your brother," he says and then answers while pushing back his chair to stand. "Hi, Jake. One second, I'm at a restaurant with your sister. Let me go outside." He nods at me and then heads outdoors.

I watch him stand on the sidewalk in front of the café's beveled glass windows, though I can't hear what he's saying on the phone. I use the opportunity to text Jordan.

Hey, so...my mom had a heart attack and surgery this morning. Everything went well, and she's recovering. Just wanted to let you know.

I don't have a sister, but my relationship with Jordan is what I imagine it would be like if I did. Ever since we met in college, we've spoken or texted almost daily.

Oh my god! she texts back. *I'm so sorry to hear that. Sending love. Can you talk?*

Not right now. I'm at a restaurant with my dad.

Okay. How are you? Can I do anything?

I'm still shocked, but okay. She's at Northwestern in the ICU. Having breakfast with my dad and then we're going back to the hospital to learn more.

I'll meet you there.

That's okay. They're only allowing family in the ICU. I'll call you later and fill you in. My dad is coming back now.

She sends three hearts in response.

My father sits down. "Jake is flying in tonight. He's on a six o'clock flight, so he shouldn't get in too late."

I haven't seen my brother since last Christmas, and he was only in town a few nights before turning around back to New York for a New Year's Eve party. And even though he had been here, staying at our parents', he wasn't really "here" in the sense that he was always tied to his phone or laptop. He's a partner at a prestigious law firm in New York and loves his job. And, clearly, his coworkers love him too, since they made him a partner.

But despite all this distance and no hope of grandchildren, Jake is still my mother's favorite.

After breakfast, which neither of us finishes, my dad and I head back to Northwestern. They are still running tests, and my mom will stay in the ICU overnight and then be transferred to a hospital room in the morning. My dad brought a book and stays in her room. I have my laptop with me, which I'm not allowed to use in her room, and so I camp out with it in the waiting area. It's not the most comfortable setup, as there aren't any free tables, and I have to balance my laptop on my actual lap to work. I put on headphones to drown out the sound of the television and try to ignore the other anxious visitors around me. There's no reason for me to stay in the hospital, but after almost losing my mom, I don't want to be too far.

I receive a text from my brother also letting me know he's flying in from New York to be here and what time his flight lands. Any communication from Jake is as rare as a phone call from my dad. It's not that we were never close, we just had little in common after he moved away. Now we'll go to the gym together when he's home or roll our eyes at each other when our mother is in major micro-managing mode, but we don't make special trips to visit each other; we reserve our catch-ups for the holidays and family events.

He wants to know how my parents are *really*, and I text him that Dad is still shaken up, but he's putting on a good show.

He tells me he's been tied up in a negotiation, otherwise he'd be on the next plane.

Don't worry. You'll see her tomorrow...and you'll still be her favorite, I write, inserting a smiley face emoji.

At age forty, my brother remains single, and I'm grateful

he now gets some of the, "When are you settling down?" pressure from my mother that I've been hearing since my mid-twenties. While he's had girlfriends, none last, and he doesn't seem too bothered by it. Not that he's out sowing his wild oats; he just doesn't seem to want to settle down, and deal with the responsibilities and compromises that come with a long-term relationship. He's a serial monogamist, but once women realize they won't be getting a ring on their finger, they move on. And after being led on by a fiancé for five years, I've always sympathized and related more to those women than I do to my brother. So while he continues to be our mother's "favorite", this makes me feel like we're on a more level playing field.

Ha! Keep me posted on any changes. See you tomorrow, he writes.

I spend the rest of the afternoon trying to respond to emails and not crash out until the hospital staff kicks us out at five o'clock.

As we left the hospital, I asked my dad whether he wanted me to stay at my place with him. "I can sleep on the sofa," I offered. He said it wasn't necessary, and we made a plan to head back to the hospital together in the morning when visiting hours started.

When I get to Eric's, he greets me right away in the hall-way. Every time I see him, I still get goosebumps. He's barefoot, just wearing a T-shirt and jeans, and with his wavy blond hair and blue eyes that always sparkle when he sees me, I still think he's the best-looking guy out there.

"Come here," he says.

I fall into him, resting my head on his chest. His strong arms squeeze me, and I feel safe and warm, and finally let some of the stress of the day evaporate off me.

"I'm sorry I couldn't be there today," he says. "How's she doing?"

I fill him in. "She pretty much slept all day. They have her on a lot of painkillers. And she'll be moved to a regular room tomorrow."

"That's all good news."

Eric's mom had a stroke a few years ago, and he quit his finance job to take care of her full-time. It changed his entire outlook on life. When she was fully recovered, he started rethinking his career choices and decided to go the entrepreneur route and open a coffeehouse. He's been through this, and so he's able to say all the right things and ask the right questions, and promises to get away from work to visit her in the hospital.

He makes us dinner, and immediately after eating, I crash into bed and fall into a deep sleep.

* * *

IN THE MORNING, I meet my dad at my condo, and we walk over to the hospital. It's a little over a mile away, but after being cooped up indoors in small rooms yesterday, we're both craving the fresh air. The weather is in the upper forties with no wind, mild for this time of year, and we move briskly to stay warm. Jake is staying downtown at a hotel and will meet us there.

When we enter the new hospital waiting room, Jake isn't there yet. So my dad and I head to my mother's room. She's sleeping peacefully, with much less machinery attached to her than yesterday. After about twenty minutes, my dad whispers, "I'm going to stay here, if you want to go out and check for Jake."

I nod and head back to the waiting room. I immediately spot Jake, who waves to me, and he's talking to a woman with long curly hair whose back is to me. She turns around.

"Jordan?" I say, doing a double take while my hand flies to my heart.

"Hey, girl," she says, coming up to me and giving me a big hug.

Mid-hug, I wave with one hand to my brother. "Hey," I say.

"Hi, Al," he greets me with my childhood nickname. Growing up, I used to hang out with him and his friends, running around the neighborhood, playing basketball, and I grew up feeling like one of the guys rather than the little sister, and the shortened nickname stuck.

Jordan releases me and steps aside so Jake can come up. He gives me a light, polite hug with a kiss on the cheek. I always joke that my mom gives "air hugs," and she must have passed those genes onto my brother.

"So continental of you," I joke, despite the circumstances. But he's the more sophisticated and successful sibling, so he can take a little ribbing. He rolls his eyes, and then gives me a much heartier hug that almost knocks me over.

"How is she?" he asks, releasing me.

"She's good. Sleeping. Dad's in there. They're only allowing two visitors at a time. If you want to go back there now, it's the first room on the left."

"Okay. I will," Jake says to me. "Nice seeing you again,

Jordan." He briefly touches her shoulder. "Thank you for coming." He then nods at me and leaves to find the room.

Jordan reaches out for my hand and squeezes it. "How are you doing?"

We sit on two empty chairs in front of us, and I take a deep breath.

"I don't know. I'm still in shock, I think. The time between my dad's call and waiting for my mom to get out of surgery was the longest five hours of my life." I tell her how the anxiety was so intense that I couldn't read, watch television, or make decent conversation with my dad, and then the utter relief I felt when she was out. I don't mention how I cried in the shower when I went home, but it's probably assumed. "But what are *you* doing here?"

"Well, other than, you know, living a few blocks away," she shrugs nonchalantly, "I have an appointment this morning with my advisor and thought I would head over here a little early."

Jordan used to be a corporate litigator, but she quit her high-powered law career to become a therapist catering to unhappy lawyers. Because she's a brainiac, she finished her coursework for her master's degree in two years, and is now seeing clients with her supervisor to fulfill her experience requirements before she can apply for her license and become a full-fledged therapist.

"Aw, thank you. Good surprise," I say, leaning over and resting my head on her shoulder, and she gives my shoulder a little squeeze. I lift my head back up. "How did Jake seem?"

"I was already here when he arrived. I could detect some stress in his stoic facade, but I'm sure once he sees her, he'll be relieved."

"Yeah. Though I'll feel better once she's out of this

place." I sigh. "But, god, Jor, she's only in her sixties. And my dad is retiring soon...or so he says." I give a little eye roll because my dad can be as much of a workaholic as Jake. "And these are supposed to be their golden years. She's always seemed so healthy." A tear I wasn't expecting rolls down my cheek. "Sorry. I think it's all catching up to me now."

"Awww, I'm sorry, sweetie." Jordan hugs me. "She's going to be fine. The surgery went well, and she's at one of the top hospitals in the country, getting the best care. If your mom was going to have a heart attack, she couldn't have planned it better."

"I know, I know." I take a deep breath and smile a little at her comment. "And I'll be fine too."

"In other news, your brother is looking fine these days." Jordan grins.

"Eww..." I give her a light punch. "Don't be checking out my brother during our family crisis." Though she totally makes me laugh.

Even though he's my brother, I can admit Jake is attractive. He takes after my mom with his dark hair and blue eyes, and has my dad's height at over six foot two. He keeps in shape with regular gym workouts, and any wrinkles on his face seem to make him more handsome. It's bad enough he got the brains in the family, but somehow he also got the looks. At five foot seven, I'm not short, but I'm also not super-model tall. Like my eyes, my hair is brown, and not an interesting brown, so I have it highlighted. And my figure can be described as average, though I run and hit the gym too. At least I clean up well.

"Just calling it like I see it," Jordan says.

Because Jordan is the closest thing I have to a sister, it

would be amazing in some ways for her to get together with Jake so that we could be sisters-in-law. However, I would never wish my commitment-phobic bro on my bestie.

"So what's going on with Sean?" I ask. Sean is a fellow student Jordan met in her master's program, and they went from study buddies to dating. Sean is "fine" too, but not in the way that Jordan thinks Jake is. He's okay-looking and seems to be a decent guy, but Jordan started dating him only because of shared interests and proximity. I think she's already tiring of him, and I get it—he's kind of a bore.

"Nothing new. We're both busy these days, especially now with working with clients, and so we haven't been hanging out as much. And when he's not working, he's gotten into pickling, so his place smells like vinegar all the time." She makes a sour face.

"Gross." I wrinkle my nose. "Yeah, I could imagine not wanting to spend much time there."

"That, and it's all he wants to talk about. It's a total yawn. Though his last batch of zucchini pickles were pretty tasty." She shrugs. "How's Eric?"

"Crazy busy, as usual. It's a good thing we live together now, otherwise I wouldn't see him at all."

"Poor guy. Things will turn around for him."

"Yeah. I know that. You know that. But he doesn't know that yet, so it's hard to watch him." I tap her on the knee. "Tell me some good news."

"Hmm, I'm not sure I have any good news here. But I do have some juicy 'loud neighbor' gossip." Jordan can hear her new neighbors through the vent in her kitchen, and she's taken to listening like it's the next best reality show. As she recounts their latest antics (a bird cam feeder that has attracted an influx of pigeons, much to the consternation of the other neighbors), I'm so grateful for her company and to take my mind off everything for a while. We chat until she needs to get to her appointment.

Jake comes out to the waiting room. "Did Jordan leave?" he asks.

"Yeah, she had a meeting with her advisor. How's Mom?"

He sits next to me. "She's awake now, and she seems okay. A little tired, but not like someone who just had heart surgery. I mean, *wow.*" He shakes his head. "That call from Dad really scared me."

"I know. Me too."

We look at each other and exchange worried frowns. That's about as far as we're willing to get in to being emotional with each other.

"You should go back and see her," he says. "I can watch your stuff."

"Okay. Thanks."

When I return to her room, my mother greets me from her bed. "There you are, darling." She pauses, then says, "Did you brush your hair today? You shouldn't wear it pulled back in those scrunchies. You'll get a bald spot there."

Aaaaand she's back.

"Hi, Mom." I ignore her question and walk up to her bed. "You gave us quite the scare yesterday. How are you feeling?"

"I've been better," she says.

I lean in to give her a hug, but she waves me off. "Oh, no. Don't, darling. You'll mess up the wires."

Theresa James may have had a heart attack, and we may finally have an adult relationship, but she's still the same woman—and she will continue to boss her daughter around.

* * *

IN THE AFTERNOON, Eric swings by to visit my mom. As soon as he walks in, her eyes light up. If Jake is my mom's favorite, Eric is her second favorite.

"Eric! Come here." She pats the side of the bed.

"How are you feeling?" he asks, as he approaches her.

"I've stayed in better hotels," she jokes. "The Ritz-Carlton, this is not."

"I'm sure." Eric laughs. "Glad to see you're in good spirits."

And when he bends down to give her hand a light squeeze, suddenly she has no concern for the wires.

For the rest of the visit, I'm forgotten as my mom fusses and flirts with Eric, and he plays it up, bantering with her.

When he says he has to get back to work, she is visibly disappointed, but says, "Of course, of course."

I walk him out and then head back to the room. My dad is out running an errand, so it's just my mom and me.

"So when are you two getting married?" she asks.

"Should we be having this conversation? You're going to raise my blood pressure and yours," I say, lightly.

"Fine. But even if you don't get married, you two can give me some beautiful grandbabies."

"I thought we agreed not to talk about this," I try again, rolling my eyes jokingly. But she's not wrong. I, too, think Eric and I would make adorable babies. He knows I want children, but we haven't discussed it recently.

"Yes, but that was *before* I had a heart attack. I'm not going to live forever, you know."

Her words punch me. "I do know, Mom," I say. "Thank you for sticking around."

This time I reach out, not caring if she protests, and hold her hand without the IV needle.

She gives mine a light squeeze and her eyes soften as she says, "I'm not going anywhere yet."

* * *

ERIC HAS BEEN TEXTING and checking in with me all day. At five o'clock, when visiting hours are over, my dad, Jake, and I head back to the Gold Coast to meet up with him for an easy dinner. When a cab drops us off in front of Eduardo's Enoteca, Eric is already sitting at an outdoor table in the heated patio with a beer in front of him. He spots us and waves.

"Hey, James Family, is this table good? After being inside the hospital all day, I thought you'd appreciate some fresh air."

"Thank you, babe," I say, giving him a kiss.

After hugging me, he then shakes my dad's and Jake's hands.

As we sit down and pick up our menus, Eric says, "Dinner is on me tonight. You've all had a rough couple of days."

And I thank my kind, wonderful boyfriend.

* * *

AFTER DINNER, Eric returns to The Cauldron, and I head to his place with the intention of trying to get some of my own work done. I set up my laptop on the kitchen table. When I go to the fridge for some water, there's another little post-it on the fridge with a heart. I pull it off and sit down at the kitchen table with it. Looking at the heart, I sigh, thinking about what my mother said in the hospital.

I was in my last relationship for five years, five years in which Neil—my boyfriend, then fiancé—promised we would have children. And I believed him, right until he called off our wedding because he was in love with my maid of honor, Stacey, an old high school friend turned frenemy. Making his announcement even worse, it was the day before my thirty-fifth birthday, and I had just been fired from my job of twelve years at PR Worldwide, my only place of employment since college. Looking back now, I realize he did me a favor. I'm much happier with Eric. We have enough shared interests, communicate easily, and he challenges me to be my best self. With Neil, I was too focused on catering to his needs, his interests, and our relationship. What I thought was compromise was really a misplaced sense of people-pleasing.

The same was true of my career. I just kept focusing on the next rung on the ladder at my PR agency, and while I was good at it, I fit myself into the job, never questioning if it was actually a right fit for me. Getting fired made me reevaluate what was important to me in my work, which was the community service outreach programs. So I founded a startup that matches corporate sponsorships to worthy causes, and it's turned out to be my dream job. Though I had to pivot some, the pandemic brought new opportunities, and, oddly, my company did even better with the rise of at-home learning, and matching students with the necessary technology.

I turn on my computer and check my work email and respond to some clients. Since I'm on my computer, mulling about life and counting my blessings, I drift over to social media and Facebook. Neil's page is public, and while I defriended him, I'm a little insulted he hasn't blocked me.

Stacey too. Not that I think they want me to spy on their life, but I clearly matter so little to them that they couldn't even be bothered to block me. His page is filled with photos of their son. I'm not sure why I'm doing this to myself. It used to make me angry, but now I'm resigned, and in my current circumstances, a little sad. While Neil's photos are more natural, and interestingly don't involve his wife, Stacey's photos look like a trying-too-hard mommy influencer, when really she's just a garden-variety narcissist. I click off.

My backup plan was to freeze my eggs, and knowing they've been sitting there waiting for when I was ready made me feel like I had time. But after my mom's heart attack, I'm feeling the clock start to tick again. I never knew my grandparents, her mother and father, because, as my dad reminded me today, they passed away before I had a chance. And so if I want my future children to be able to meet their grandmother, I need to start taking some action sooner rather than later.

3

———

I work out of the hospital's visitors' lounge for the next few days. Luckily, I don't have any big work events scheduled, so it's mostly emails and keeping up with my current projects. My dad spends most of his time in my mom's room. After the third day, she is restless to get out of here. She complains that the nurses don't let her sleep through the night. "They're constantly waking me up to poke at me. How am I supposed to recover?" She complains about the menu, asking my dad and me to get her something from the outside. "Let's just see what the doctor says," my dad always answers, and she always huffs in response. When she starts in on the curtains and paint colors in her room— "Those checkered curtains are so depressingly eighties. And is pea-soup green meant to be soothing?"—we know she's on the road to recovery.

On the fifth day, her head nurse gives us instructions for her home care. My mom is supposed to work up to walking a mile, and they've been taking her on short rounds in the hallway. Because they had to break a rib to perform the surgery, my mom has to blow into a tube several times a day to strengthen her lungs. And she's on a low-sodium, low-fat diet, which is why she has been complaining about the tasteless food.

She is to be released later this week, and we decide that while she recuperates, she and my dad will stay in my condo, as it's closer to the hospital, rather than going back to the suburbs. And this way, I can be easily available to come over, cook them meals, and help out.

The day before my mom is discharged, she gives me a detailed list of items she wants from home, from clothing to toiletries. "The blue robe on the back of the bathroom door, not the green one." "The Ivory soap, not the gel face wash sitting in the cabinet." "The white sheets with the scalloped border on the third shelf in the linen closet."

"I got it, Mom." Though I'm insulted by her request for the sheets, I keep my mouth shut. She's been helpless in the hospital for almost a week, and I understand her wanting to exert some control over her life...even though my cotton sheets are very nice.

That afternoon, I drive to my parents' house in the western suburbs. Since I spent my high school years there (we moved when I was in eighth grade), I guess it's my old house too. But I've always felt a bit of a disconnect with it. My mother remodeled and redecorated it so frequently that it never felt familiar. And walking inside with no one home makes it feel even emptier, in a soulless way.

After finding my mother's suitcase in the basement, I go through her list, checking off items, packing them quickly, not wanting to linger, and not wanting to get stuck in rush hour traffic back to the city. I leave the sheets for last. I head to the upstairs hallway linen closet and look through the bedding. Not seeing the requested sheets right away, I carefully take out a pile of folded blankets and set them on the floor to search deeper in the closet. Behind them is a basket that seems full of folded items, so I pull that out as well. But it's not sheets in the basket, it's clothes.

I set it on the floor and plop down beside it.

On closer inspection, I realize it's filled with baby clothes. *Weird. Are these my old clothes?*

I pick up the first item, a onesie, which still has tags on it. *Guess not.*

Behind it is a bright floral matching set with a soft bow headband, also with tags. I rub the velvet bow with my fingers and imagine setting it on my future daughter's downy head. Next is a mini cable cardigan and plaid bottoms, and an image of Eric holding our son at one of our family's Thanksgiving dinners pops into my head. Then there are pairs of tiny penny loafers and sweet little ballet slippers, and I can almost see one of those first footprint impressions hanging on the wall in our baby's nursery. I continue pulling out and holding each item one by one while my eyes water.

Since my mom doesn't seem to have any secret doll collection, I know she's been buying these hoping for grandchildren. Maybe it's a shopping disorder, maybe she's a hoarder, but with each little onesie, a wanting grows in my chest. While my mom's heart attack has made me realize I need to move up my family-planning timeline, her desire for grandchildren, manifested in her buying these clothes, has awakened my own longing to be a mother. To have children; to nurture them as infants; to watch them grow into little people with their own personalities, thoughts, and dreams; to shepherd them to adulthood; and then to stand back as they make their way in the world.

But a different ache tells me I'm not quite emotionally ready to revisit this conversation with Eric and face the potentially difficult choices that lie ahead.

* * *

I MET Eric the morning after Neil and I broke up. After my first run, pounding the pavement, wishing it was Neil's and Stacey's heads, I literally ran into the sign advertising Eric's coffeehouse. So I went in, and Eric took my order. I appreciated the warm vibes of the space, with its exposed brick walls and fireplace, vintage lighting, and comfy, worn leather sofas and chairs. The Cauldron soon became my go-to after not wanting to talk to the overly friendly barista at my old Starbucks. A new identity, and a new coffee place.

Eric and I started chatting more and became friends, and the fact that he was easy on the eyes wasn't lost on me. But I was fresh off a breakup and any sort of attraction was not on my mind. He was the calm in the storm, and his Zen view of life, combined with some tough love advice, was what I needed to hear at the time. We bonded further when I learned how he had weathered the storms that had led him to start a new business. And while it wasn't easy (I've realized he's a workaholic, and he simply went from stressed-out finance guy to stressed-out entrepreneur), he gave me the push to start my own.

Once I finally got enough closure on Neil, Eric and I started dating. We were constantly together—I helped with marketing for The Cauldron and worked out of there on my new consulting business. Plus, I lived nearby. I didn't expect to get into a full-time relationship, but it seemed my breakup helped me finally find my soul mate. We had first met in the spring, and in September we started dating, and by October, we were officially a couple.

With that time of year and the holidays, we met each other's families, attending two Thanksgiving dinners and Christmases. My parents loved him right from the start. "Quite the upgrade," my mother commented to me when Eric was out of earshot; and Jake and Eric hit it off right away—Eric even got Jake into CrossFit. And I immediately adored his mom and two nephews. While I wanted to love his sister, Elaine, she was a little standoffish on that first meeting, and I couldn't discern whether she was territorial or assumed I wouldn't last. For my contribution to dinner, I had brought a harvest-themed salad with roasted butternut squash and pecans. When his mother complimented me on it and said, "You'll have to bring this again next year," Elaine gave a quick snort and eye roll. I wasn't sure if it was a reaction to her mother's presumptions or disbelief that I would last until next year; but then her son Liam referred to me as Auntie Allison and she corrected him, "Just call her Allison. She's not your aunt," with a tone so definitive that it made me feel she could have easily added, "And she never will be." But over the years, and with Eric's and my help babysitting, she's come around.

For our first New Year's Eve, Eric and I decided to stay in and celebrate at his place. He made us dinner, and we popped champagne. While dinner was cooking, we sat on the sofa with our drinks.

"Any New Year's resolutions?" I asked.

"Yes, I want to grow The Cauldron. The Lakeview and Lincoln Park locations have finally been holding steady, and now with the Gold Coast location doing so well, I'd love to expand to a new neighborhood. Maybe explore Wicker Park or Bucktown?" he said. "And, of course, spend more time with my gorgeous girlfriend." He leaned over and kissed me.

I laughed and clinked my glass against his. "Both worthy goals," I said.

"What about you?"

"Well, I would also like to spend more time with my sexy boyfriend." I grinned. "But on a more serious note, there's still some unfinished business I need to take care of from last year."

"What's that?"

I took a deep breath. "My resolution this year is to freeze my eggs."

"Oh?" He shook his head a little, looking surprised.

"Yeah. It was something I meant to do last year when Neil and I broke up, but then with getting my consulting business started and us," I pointed between us, "and the holidays, I didn't get around to it. But this year, I'm doing it!"

Eric swallowed, pausing before saying, "Well, good for you."

Normally he was my biggest cheerleader, so his somewhat lackluster response wasn't what I was expecting. Granted, talking about eggs wasn't the sexiest conversation, and we'd only been dating for a few months, and so I nervously wondered whether I just killed the mood.

"Sorry if that was too much information." I patted his knee to break any real or imaginary tension. "Don't worry, I'm not planning our future kiddos yet, just buying myself some insurance." Though, truth be told, I had pictured them in my mind with hopefully his curls and big eyes.

He gave me a small smile. "So you definitely want kids," he said, and I couldn't tell from his tone if it was a question or a statement.

Now I swallowed. We'd had some deep conversations, but this felt different. "I do. That's why I mistakenly stayed with Neil for so long. I thought he wanted us to start a family, but he kept putting me off...until he started one with Stacey." I rolled my eyes.

"His loss." Eric set down his champagne glass. "I'm going to check the oven. It smells like dinner is almost ready." And just like that, he dropped the subject.

A week into the New Year, Eric asked if he could come over after he closed The Cauldron. He texted, *I have something important I want to talk about.*

The formal tone of his text set my nerves on edge for the rest of the afternoon. And when I opened my front door and saw the serious look on Eric's face, my skin prickled. I offered him a drink, which he declined, and we went into the living room. Eric sat on the edge of the sofa cushion and then stared at the floor for a couple of seconds, rubbing the back of his neck before he spoke.

"I don't know how to say this, so I'm just going to come out with it." He then looked up at me solemnly, his eyes steady on mine. "I don't want kids."

"Okay," I said, feeling my stomach turn. *Why did I bring up my eggs? We've only been dating a few months.* "I'm not ready to have any right now either. I mean, we've only been together for a short while. And so I wasn't propositioning you or anything when I told you I wanted to freeze my eggs. It was something I thought about before we even started dating seriously."

"And you should do that. You would be an amazing mother." He took both my hands in his and squeezed them, holding them gently but tightly. "But what I'm saying is, *I don't want kids.*"

The room started to tilt.

"Ever?"

He nodded. "I thought I should let you know now. On New Year's Eve, when you said how you stayed with Neil for too long because you thought he wanted a family, I didn't want to be that guy and lead you on."

His revelation was a kick in the gut, or more like a kick to my ovaries.

Here was this guy who had started a business and yet used his free time to volunteer with kids at CrossFit, who encouraged me to work on a nonprofit with kids, who was amazing with his nephews, and frankly all children...yet didn't want children of his own?

"But you're so good with your nephews. And your kids at CrossFit..." My voice cracked.

He shook his head remorsefully as he explained his reasoning. When he was twelve, his dad died of brain cancer, leaving him, his sister, and mom. Growing up, and even now, he always felt responsible for his mom and sister. His fear of cancer running in his family meant he couldn't imagine having children and leaving them. He shouldered so much responsibility, taking care of others, that I could understand not wanting to add to that load. But knowing that he would love his theoretical children so much that he already feared leaving them, it hurt my heart. I could imagine the scared little boy he had been, trying to be the man of the house while grieving for his father.

The truth is that Eric was always trying to chase away those frightened feelings. He turned to finance because he thought that would give him a secure future; and he turned to sports instead of drugs to fend off his anxiety. In coaching all these at-risk youth, he learned that kids growing up without positive parental supervision were statistically more likely to abuse drugs and alcohol. And so he tried to give them the same outlet he had found for himself when he was fatherless.

This wasn't just jitters about being a dad; this was a full-on, well-considered life decision.

"And maybe this is something I should've said earlier, but the reason I've stayed single for so long is that the kid thing has sometimes been a deal breaker in the past. Also, I've never met anyone before I wanted to get married to. But with you, I know it's early, but you're someone I can see a future with."

Oh? A quick surge of hope ran through me. "Do you think you'll change your mind about having a family?" I asked.

He shook his head. "If there's anyone I would want to have a baby with, it's you. But it's not something I can do."

His words left me speechless.

When I didn't say anything, he continued, "When you brought up freezing your eggs, I knew that you were thinking about the future too. And I think that's totally awesome and empowering and smart of you. If you want a baby, you should have a baby. You should have everything you want." He swallowed. "And I wish I could be that person for you, Allison, but I can't. And I understand if you don't want to take things further knowing this about me."

My insides felt hollowed out, and I couldn't believe that here I was on my sofa, brokenhearted again in less than a year.

I managed to say, "Thank you for being honest. I...I do want kids. It's important to me. And so I think we should take some time apart to consider what this means for us."

* * *

So, in January, after only a few months of dating, we broke up.

Since I had already been researching fertility clinics while we were together, I decided to make good on my New Year's resolution and made an appointment to start the egg-freezing process right away. Eric had called my decision "empowering," and I needed to feel in control of something while nursing my broken heart. I went alone to my initial visit to learn more about the process and to be set up on a plan. For moral support, Jordan came with me on the follow-up visit where they explained how the shots worked, and she stayed at my place the night I had to take the first one.

"Next time you ask me out for shots, they better be tequila," she quipped after my first jab to my stomach.

For the next two weeks, I felt more confident giving myself the jab, but I cried myself to sleep, the hormones amping up all the rawness of my broken heart. I went to all my checkups alone, but my mom came with me to the egg retrieval surgery and took care of me afterwards. Even though I had the support of my family and friends, I still missed Eric every day.

Then, in March, news of a deadly virus started spreading. Cities like San Francisco and New York were going into stay-at-home orders. When lockdown started in Chicago, Eric called me and said, "I miss you. Where are you?" And suddenly, when we didn't know what was going to happen next, it seemed stupid to break up for a future baby I didn't know. The one thing I *did* know was—I was still in love with Eric, and I wanted to be with him and so I "moved in" with him during the shutdown. But then our relationship accelerated with the pandemic, and a few years later, here we are.

* * *

THE ONLY RELATIONSHIP advice my dad has ever given me is to marry someone you can talk to, and for me, that someone is Eric. And I didn't want to have another person's baby when I had this incredible person in my life. While I didn't plan to change Eric's mind when we first got back together, I figured I would wait to see where the relationship took us. I knew the risk and took it anyway. But here I am again, almost three years later.

Freezing my eggs gave me a sense of reassurance. Plus, we were both so busy; I was building my business and Eric was trying to salvage his. Theoretically, if there was a bad time to start a family, this was it. Still, I was secretly jealous of friends who announced pregnancies during that time. Looking at my social media feeds, it seemed everyone I knew was expanding their family (all that togetherness, I guess).

Maybe I'm so scared of the possibility of losing Eric again that I've been people pleasing to keep the peace and avoid a Big Talk. But as I fold and put back these tiny clothes, I know I want to be a mother, and the time is now.

While setting the basket back on the closet shelf, I finally spy the sheets with the scalloped edges my mother requested. They had been hidden behind the basket, and I sense some ulterior motives. I consider leaving them, pretending I couldn't find them. But being the dutiful daughter, I take them out and pack them into the suitcase.

I also text Jordan, *Any chance you're free for a drink in the next few days?*

If I want to seek Eric's support, I need hers first.

4

____

"Oooh, that Theresa. So crafty!" Jordan says, with a hint of admiration in her voice, after I regale her with the story about the sheets and the baby clothes.

After I texted Jordan, she said she was free tonight and could meet me up in my neighborhood at the wine vault in the 3 Arts Club Café. Back when I was going through my breakup/firing/existential crisis, Jordan had paid for all my drinks with her large attorney salary. Now that she's a trained therapist, I pay for my "sessions" in wine, and she throws around fancy psychology terms like "boundaries" and "conditioning", so I feel like I'm getting my money's worth. Also, since she already knows my mom, I don't need to tell her all about my mother to determine that, yes, our relationship is the source from which many of my "issues" originate.

"Yeah, while I would like to think it was an accident, I know my mother and her ways," I say. "But the last few days have had me thinking..." I pause. "And I think I'm ready to have a baby."

"Oh?" Jordan was about to take a sip of wine, but instead lowers her glass. "What does Eric think?"

She's also already familiar with Eric's backstory and reasons for not wanting children. I know she would love to set him up with a therapist to explore these fears, but she also wants to respect his wishes. (The tug between being a best friend and a mental health expert.) Also, I try not to bring up the topic that often. While she can relate to career strife and relationships, the desire to have children, not so much. As long as I've known Jordan, she's had no wish to be a mother, and so she's avoided settling down. Whenever one of our mutual college friends had kids, she'd always say, "Guess that's the last we'll see of her." Often, Jordan was right, as our once-close group slowly migrated to the suburbs; but also, Jordan didn't try to stay in touch because tales of horror birth stories and screaming infants gave her the shudders.

"I haven't talked to him about it yet. And while it's been on my mind since my mom's heart attack, it didn't really hit me until today when I touched those clothes."

"Baby clothes are super cute. Even I like those." She gives me a sympathetic smile. "But this is big, Al. What if he hasn't changed his mind about kids? What are you going to do? What do you *want* to do?"

"Well, my hope is maybe he's changed his mind. We haven't talked about it since our early days of dating, but now we've been together for over two and a half years. So maybe he'll be more open?" I say.

Jordan nods. "Do you want to marry Eric?"

"Yes, no, maybe?" I shrug. "To be honest, the marriage stuff isn't a big deal to me anymore. I mean, I've already experienced planning a big wedding only to watch it all fall apart with Neil, and eloping would probably upset both our parents. But I *do* want to spend my life with him. I can't imagine life without him. Next to you, he's my person."

"For your sake, I hope he's come around. But I also think you need to be prepared if he hasn't, and what that would look like." Her serious eyes bore into mine.

I take a large gulp of wine, and sigh.

"Do you think you'll ever want a kid? What would get you to change your mind?" I ask.

"No, and nothing." She shakes her head. "Of course, I hope Eric will change his mind. The difference between us is he actually *likes* kids. Honestly, I can't stand them." She pats my hand. "I'll love yours, of course," she says, correcting herself.

"Ha! That's good because I'm already making you its godmother."

She laughs, breaking the tension. "That I can do." Then she raises her glass. "And I want to be the first to take them out when they're twenty-one."

I clink my glass against hers. "Though now I'm starting to wonder if you're going to be a good godmother or a bad influence?"

"Yes, and yes!" She grins.

My phone buzzes. To my surprise, it's my brother.

Just finished working for the night and can use a break. What are you doing? Want to meet up?

"It's Jake," I say.

"Oh yeah?" Jordan's eyebrows shoot up.

"Yeah, he says he's done working for the night and wants to hang out."

"Tell him to join us," she says.

I text back: *I'm having a glass of wine with Jordan at Restoration Hardware by my place. Come on by!*

Jake writes back: *On my way.*

I put my phone down and pick up my glass. "Okay, our therapy session is over. Thank you for listening."

"Of course, but before we table this, just one last thing." She leans forward, gazing at me intently. "No matter what happens, if this is what you really want, you know you can do this with or without Eric."

"I know. Thanks, Jor."

"And, let's be honest," she grins, "your mom will probably move in with you."

"True, but that's not a particularly comforting thought." I roll my eyes and then grimace. "Sorry. And now I feel guilty for saying that right after her heart attack."

"Love is complicated. Get ready for that with your own kid." She raises her eyebrows, looking at me over her wine glass.

"Don't I know it?" I snort. "Anyway, enough about me. What's up with you?"

"Ugh. Have I told you the latest with Lauren?" Lauren is Jordan's supervisor who oversees her sessions with patients.

"*No*. Now what?"

Jordan's years in Big Law taught her well how to deal with and soothe big egos, which apparently Lauren has. She fills me in on Lauren's latest condescending remarks until something catches her eye behind me, and she waves.

I turn around to where she's looking and spot Jake.

He approaches our table and takes a seat. "Hey, sis. Hey, Jordan. Thanks for letting me crash your party."

"It's good to see you again," Jordan says. "So, you're done with the workday, I hear?"

"Yeah, the beauty of the one-hour time difference between here and New York." He smiles and picks up the menu on the table.

"I'm sure the majority of lawyers in your office are still working. *Ugh*. You couldn't pay me enough to go back to that lifestyle."

Jake taps her arm with the menu. "Yeah, about that. After I order, I want to hear more about this big leaving-the-law career change of yours."

After the three of us order a bottle of wine, I invite Eric to pop over, and we end up having dinner in the restaurant. It's probably the most relaxed I've been, and the most fun I've had during this long week. I forget all about the basket of baby clothes and the difficult conversation that I'm going to have to face in the near future.

* * *

THIS AFTERNOON, after a week in the hospital, my mom is finally being discharged. My dad and Jake are taking care of her there and bringing her to my place, while I'm here getting everything ready. I've already made the bed, hung her robe on the bathroom door, and unpacked her clothes, clearing out one of my dresser drawers to place them in there. I've also stocked up my kitchen with heart healthy groceries. The doctor had told her no red meat or pork, and instructed her to be on the DASH diet, which is basically low-fat, low-salt, semi-vegetarian fare. Eric gave me some cookbooks he used when his mom had her stroke, and he marked her favorite recipes. I decide on a vegetable soup with low-sodium broth.

As I'm putting in the last ingredients, I hear the key in

the front door, and voices. "Hello, hello," my dad says. "It smells good in here."

I quickly wipe my hands on a towel and set the pot lid on the soup to let it simmer, before stepping out.

"Hey, guys," I say. "Mom, you're free!"

My mother smiles weakly and shuffles into the living room, holding onto my father's arm. He helps her into the closest armchair.

Once she's settled, a look of relief passes over her face. "Oh, it feels good to be out of there," she says. "I don't think I could take another day."

My brother slyly shoots me a look as if to say, "the hospital couldn't handle her for another day either."

"I'm glad you're out, too, Mom," I say. "Can I get you anything? Some water?"

"I would love some hot tea, darling. And use the kettle, not the microwave. The microwave doesn't get the water hot enough."

"Sure. And what type of tea would you like? I have chamomile and mint."

"Do you have any black tea?"

"Theresa, you're not supposed to have caffeine yet, remember?" my dad says.

"Then mint, I suppose." She sighs.

"You got it," I say.

I head to the kitchen to boil the water and check on the soup. By the time I bring her tea out, she's already asleep in the chair, so I just set it next to her.

"What's in the pot?" my brother asks as he follows me back into the kitchen.

"A low-sodium minestrone soup. I made enough for all of us."

"Thanks, but I should get going. I have some work I need to take care of."

"Okay. I'll see you tomorrow?"

"Yep. The doctor said she's probably going to sleep a lot. But if you need anything, call me."

Once my brother is gone, my dad reads in the living room next to Mom, and I quietly set the table, and then use the break to finish some work that I've been behind on this week.

There's an email from my former colleague and now client, Kate, asking me about our latest project, which is coming up with and coordinating community outreach programs where her client's employees can select from a list of volunteer options. When I was offered another agency position at my friend Suzy Weitzman's firm, I realized that agency life wasn't for me, and so while I turned down the interview, I suggested Suzy contact Kate. And it's been a perfect match. When Kate and I worked together at PR Worldwide, she hated organizing these types of programs, whereas I loved them; and so now she outsources all these requests to my consulting business.

I respond, apologizing to Kate for not getting back to her sooner, and tell her about my mom. I also request a few more days to complete the list. She must be checking her email right when I hit send, because she responds immediately.

I'm so sorry about your mom! And, of course, you can take another week or two to finish up. Whatever you need. Can I do anything? Need to talk?

I let her know that I just need a week, and we agree to grab lunch or something soon to catch up.

Before I can get to my other messages, I hear rustling in

the living room and look over to see my mom waking up. My dad helps her to the bathroom, and then to the table. Despite the bravado she's been showing, her face is paler than usual, and I can see that she's in pain.

Once we all sit down, she asks, "Where's Jake?"

"He had to go and take care of some work stuff. He said he would come by tomorrow."

"Your brother," she says, shaking her head. She picks up her spoon. "He's married to his career. I feel sorry for any woman who ends up with him."

This is one of the rare instances I've heard her say anything critical about Jake; and I worry that maybe she was discharged too soon, or I should check my hearing.

"But, you know," she continues, "that's why he's so successful. And, honestly, I think a family would hold him back." When I hear a note of pride in her voice, I realize she's not actually criticizing Jake (and has a double standard for her children). So my relief that she still has her mental faculties is now tinged with annoyance.

"Thank you for the soup, honey," Dad says. "It's delicious. Is this spinach?" He points to a green leaf in the soup.

"It's kale. It's like a stronger-tasting spinach," I tell him. "This is one of the recipes Eric's mom liked when she was recovering from her stroke."

"Tell Eric thank you." My mom smiles at me. "And look at you, cooking soup for your father and me. Your brother wouldn't do this, and your father wouldn't either. He can't heat a can of soup without me."

My dad laughs good-naturedly, and I smile at him. It's funny because it's true.

She smiles at him too, and then turns back to me. "And it's not because they're men, it's because they don't have that caretaker instinct. You're a nurturer, darling, and Eric is too. You're made for each other. And I know I joke about grand-children, but I couldn't imagine two people being a better set of parents." The soup seems to be giving her energy. "Did you find the sheets with the scalloped trim?" she asks with a mischievous glint in her eye.

Oh, well played, Mom.

"I did," I say, looking down at my soup, not giving anything away. "And I already made up the bed for you."

"Good girl," she says, and innocently takes another spoonful of soup.

She has no idea, and I could never bear to tell her, that Eric doesn't want children. I don't want her to think badly of him or our relationship. Even more so, I don't want her to accost him to change his mind every time they're in the same room.

In some ways, Eric reminds me of my brother. While my brother wears suits with a tie and Eric wears a T-shirt and jeans, they still have that same drive, that intense, dedicated focus on work. It gives me a little shiver and an ick feeling that I'm dating a version of my brother. But Eric's hours are necessary, since he's an entrepreneur and small-business owner. And unlike my brother, Eric has always still made time to volunteer and spend time with his family, whereas Jake would rather donate to causes and spends the bare minimum of time with us required during the holidays. Eric really would make a great parent.

After dinner with my parents, when I return to Eric's place, he's already asleep. So I quietly crawl into bed next to him. He wakes up anyway, his voice sleepy, "Hey, how is she?"

"Good. She was tired, but okay. She wanted me to thank you for the soup recipe. It was delicious."

"That's great. You know, I think I'm going to make a special batch of heart-healthy muffins tomorrow for work. I'll try to stop by with some."

"She would love that. Good night, babe."

Eric rolls toward me, and I spoon up against him. As I feel him fall back asleep, his breath steady, a lump rises in my throat. My mom is right that Eric is a natural nurturer. And Jordan is also right that I need to think long and hard about my choices.

5

As I run south along the lakefront from Lincoln Park toward Oak Street Beach and Navy Pier, I can see my breath puff in front of me. The low gray clouds threaten either rain or flurries, while a brisk wind blows off the equally steel-colored lake. There are only a few of us diehard runners out here, which leaves me even more alone in my thoughts than usual; but these last few weeks, I've had to remain in constant motion to keep my nerves in check. I'm still spending every night at Eric's loft while my parents stay at my place. Once they leave, I know I need to bring up the talk with Eric, and to say it's had me on edge is an understatement.

With each step, I play the imaginary conversation in my head, and with each version, map out a decision tree. Plan A is the obvious best-case scenario, where Eric has had a change of heart about having kids. I throw out my birth control, he throws me on the bed, and we immediately get down to business on baby-making. Plan B is somewhere in the wishy-washy world of he'll consider it, which may buy our relationship some time, but then we're relying on a deadline and probably a dreaded ultimatum. And I'd be walking on eggshells the entire time, waiting for his decision, which isn't much different from where I am now. But if Jordan has never changed her mind on kids, it's very possible Eric hasn't either. If he's still firm on not wanting children, then it's on to Plan C, which is the breakup of our relationship, and I'm on my own for this adventure.

I watch my breath dissipate in front of me, my lungs burning with the cold air and this last thought.

Emotionally and mentally, I'm ready for a kid, but not so much for the heartbreak involved in this last possibility. I remember how devastated I was breaking up with Eric after just a few months of dating. And when we got back together again, it seemed crazy to me that I had chosen a baby over him; but today it doesn't feel so crazy. These feelings never went away, they have just been dormant. If anything, I could be accused of leading Eric on all these years, and I don't want to face that betrayal.

The wind whips at my face, and I turn around to begin the loop back home. The gust now at my back propels me forward as I ponder this worst-case thought.

In case it is Plan C, I need to be prepared, which means moving back to my condo (something I can't do while my parents are still using it). Also, my support system would be my family. Even though my parents are still in the younger stages of senior citizenry, they're getting older, and it's clear I need to worry about their health now. My workaholic brother lives in New York, and while he can probably be counted on for generous cash gifts, not so much for babysitting. I know Jordan would be supportive, but only up to a point. She'll be starting her own practice, and her time will be limited. And then there's my business. I'm a sole proprietor. Plus, I have to pay for my own health care. Unless I'm actively working, I can't exactly afford to give myself maternity leave. While I make just enough to cover my costs of living, it's only thanks to my prior savings and severance at the time that I've managed this far. Would I have to get an employee to fill in for me? What would my clients think? Would they move on? My book of business isn't huge. My primary source of business comes from Kate's clients, and so I'd like to think she'd keep me on...especially considering she kind of owes me for getting her current job. But the others are new, and I don't feel like we have that kind of loyalty yet. And with everything going on with my mom lately, I haven't been totally on the ball with client matters or seeking new business.

I stop before the Lincoln Park Pedestrian Bridge and take out my phone. Just in case I need to implement Plan C in my near future, I message Kate to ask if she'd be up for a coffee or lunch today.

She immediately replies, *Sure. Is this for work or fun?*

Both. Let's talk about the United program.

Okay. Meet at The Cauldron?

No. Let's do near your office.

I feel like the change of neighborhood scenery will do me good.

Most days either I've been working out of my condo or The Cauldron, when I need to avoid getting distracted by my parents at home. But being at The Cauldron has me typing with jittery hands and losing focus every time I catch sight of Eric, reminding me that the poor guy doesn't know what's going to hit him. Though lately, The Cauldron has been so packed that we've had only brief interactions. Despite my anxiety about our imminent conversation, I'm happy for this uptick in customers. The worry lines on his forehead seem softer, and he's been more energized.

* * *

KATE and I decide to meet at a popular Italian restaurant on the riverfront downtown. When I arrive, the cloudy skies have cleared, and the sun is shining, making the space bright and cheerful, with a view of the sparkling water. As the host leads me to a table by the windows, I not only spot Kate but also Suzy.

When I reach the table, Suzy jumps up, gives me a big hug, and says, "I hope you don't mind, but Kate and I were in the elevator, and when she said she was meeting you, I couldn't help but crash."

"Of course! So good to see you!" I hug her back.

While I always love seeing Suzy, I know right away that this will be more of a professional lunch; I'll have to update Kate on my ready-to-have-a-baby news another time.

Mid-embrace with Suzy, I look at Kate and say, "Hey."

"Hey." Kate stays seated. She's not a hugger. "I figured you wouldn't mind." She gestures to Suzy. Kind of bold, considering Suzy is her boss and my client. But that's typical Kate. She's not one for hierarchy. And, funnily enough, for someone in PR, she doesn't always have the best people skills; but behind the scenes, she's a spin-and-strategy wizard.

At the beginning of my career, Suzy and I had been acquaintances who always bumped into each other at PR events and ended up hanging out together. Then, when I was fired, she was a sympathetic ear and later a lifesaver at a time when I needed it, even though I passed on her job offer. Over the years, we've become real friends.

With Suzy, Kate, and Jordan, and all of us being very different personalities, I have my little Sex & the City quartet. As a former lawyer, Jordan is the Miranda, but a fun one. A petite brunette, Kate is a snarky, untraditional Charlotte. And Suzy has the energy of a Samantha, but if Samantha was married with three kids. I guess that leaves me as Carrie, the one constantly analyzing her love life, which, fair enough, though I wish I had her wardrobe.

As soon as I sit down, a server arrives with a bottle of wine and three glasses. "Your Pinot Grigio," he says with a flourish.

"Oh!" I say, looking over to Kate and Suzy. "It's going to be that kind of lunch."

"Kate told me about your mom," Suzy says, "so I figured maybe you needed this." After the server leaves, she tilts her head, giving me a sympathetic look. "How is she doing?"

"Thank you. She's doing okay. The surgery went well, and she's been recovering at my place, and so far so good. She was really lucky."

"Glad to hear that."

"So, are you staying at your place too?" Kate asks carefully, knowing my relationship dynamic with my mom, heart attack or not.

"No. My dad is with her, and I'm around during the day to run errands and get her whatever she needs. Then at night I make them dinner and Jake joins us. But after that I head to Eric's and sleep there."

She nods.

"Well, here's to your mom's health and a speedy recovery." Suzy raises her glass, and Kate and I pick up ours to clink.

"And here's to your sanity," Kate adds.

After we all touch glasses and take our first sips, she says, "Jake's in town?" Kate has met my brother a few times during his holiday visits.

"Yeah, he flew in the night of our mom's surgery and has been here since. I think he's waiting until our parents are back in the 'burbs before he heads home to New York."

"That's..." she pauses, "unlike him."

"Yeah, he always plays it cool, but this shook him up, too. It was such a shock. And having him here has boosted our mom's spirits. Anyway..." I shake my head, not wanting to be a downer at lunch, "what's good here?"

After ordering our meals, Kate says, "Should we get the work talk out of the way?"

"Good idea," Suzy replies. "Then we can gossip about what's happening over at PR Worldwide, and the latest I heard about Paige." Paige was my old boss. Even though she totally sabotaged my career back then, I don't have any ill will toward her. But I'm not above listening to some good dirt.

"Yes, well, I'd love to know how the United project is going?" I ask, referring to the volunteer program where employees can choose from a list of various opportunities, such as literacy programs to packing items at a food bank to litter clean-up in the city and suburbs, based on their interests. "This was the first time I've done something like that. How was the feedback?"

If the feedback is good, I'm wondering whether it's something I should offer to other clients. Coordinating it required a lot of emails and phone calls, but I didn't have to physically set anything up or go to an event. Programs like this could be great to manage when I'm also taking care of a baby.

"United loves it," Kate says. "They've been doing more of a hybrid work environment, where people only come to the office three times a week. So their employees appreciate the autonomy and working within their schedules, rather than one big event where everyone feels pressured to participate."

I laugh. Kate is one of those people who hates attending such events.

"Great! Okay, then—we're onto something," I say.

"Yes," Suzy jumps in. "And we just had Abbott ask us about setting up something similar. Could you put together a presentation and proposal for them?"

"On it," I say, and make a note on my phone.

We also talk about how a volunteer tutoring program is going for another client, and that they'd like to expand the kids' program outside of tutoring. I make another note to research this.

"We don't want to overload you though, with everything going on with your mom," Suzy says.

I shake my head. "It's no problem at all. I can handle it," I say, while thinking, *please overload me*, and I imagine cartoon-like dollar signs floating above my head.

And, really, between my dad, Jake, and me, we've been able to tag-team on anything my mom needs. She typically sleeps or watches television during the day, and my dad has been fine to get her to and from appointments. I mostly run errands for them, like picking up her prescriptions, shopping, and cooking. Per the doctor's orders, my dad reminds her to blow into her tube and helps her walk the length of the hallway and back to increase her stamina. He assists her with getting in and out of bed and chairs in the proper manner. We have to measure her blood pressure every day, and my dad records it in a notebook the hospital gave us. I think my mom might have to eat her prior words that my dad's not a caretaker, because I have to say, I'm impressed.

Once the three of us have exhausted talk of work projects, our meals arrive, and Suzy asks for another glass of wine. Somehow we've already finished the bottle we ordered.

"Anyone else?" asks the server.

I wasn't planning on it, but it's a Friday, and why not?

We end up ordering another bottle of Pinot Grigio, and I notice that Kate barely sips hers and declines any top-offs. Suzy can handle her alcohol; Kate not so much.

"Sorry, you two," Kate says, "but you need to finish that. I have a Zoom call with Hector at three this afternoon, and I can't take a nap."

Suzy's phone buzzes in her purse. "Sorry, I have it on do not disturb, so this is either a kid or my husband." She pulls it out. "Kid. I'll be right back."

She gets up from the table and as she walks away, we hear her answer, "Hi, honey. What's up?"

When she returns in a few minutes, she huffs, "Not an emergency. It seems Ben and Abel got their lunches mixed up, and so I just got an earful from Abel about how dare I put jelly in his peanut butter sandwich. *Expand your palate, kid.*" She shakes her head. "You two are smart. Don't have children. They're the worst."

Without meaning to, I let out a long sigh.

Kate looks at me. "What's up?"

"Oh, Allison, are you okay?" Suzy says, putting her phone back into her purse with a dramatic zipping up.

"I am. I just..." I start, and another accidental sigh

escapes as I internally debate whether to say anything. The wine decides for me. "Well, lately I've been thinking a lot about having kids."

"Oh? I'm sorry," Suzy says. "I wasn't serious about my comment. I love my kids, even though they drive me crazy."

"And they drive you to day drink," Kate says.

Suzy guffaws. "Yes, and that."

"You've always wanted kids, that's not news," Kate says to me. "So what's up?"

"Oooh, are you and Eric planning on starting a family?" Suzy asks.

"Well, we haven't really talked about it yet. My mom's heart attack just reawakened the idea. But things feel a little tenuous with Eric's business, even though he's making good progress..." I drift off.

Kate, though ever sharp, says, "Does Eric want kids?"

I look at her and give a slight, *I don't know*, shrug. "We haven't talked about it in a long time. And the last time we did, we broke up."

Kate knows all this, of course, but this is news to Suzy. "*What?*" she says, and I fill her in.

"Oh, honey, but now you two have been together for ages and are practically living together. It's totally different," she says.

"But if not, then I need to be prepared for what that looks like. Cause this baby fever isn't going away."

"*If not*, you can always go the Stacey route," Kate says, giving me a look. "Seemed to work for her."

Neil and Stacey had been having an affair behind my back. And when Neil said that he was breaking up with me because he was in love with Stacey, the true catalyst for his confession was that Stacey was pregnant. I've always wondered if Neil would have still gone through with the wedding if that didn't happen. It's all for the best in hindsight, though it didn't feel that way at the time.

"Well, that's Stacey," I say. "And a good life rule is to do the opposite of whatever Stacey does."

"Truth." Kate snorts. "But, hey, these things happen?"

Suzy raises her eyebrows. "Better to ask for forgiveness than permission?"

"Oh my god, you guys, I'm not going to secretly go off birth control. I'm going to assume that's the wine talking."

Suzy giggles. Kate shrugs.

"Ben wasn't planned, you know?" Suzy says of her firstborn. She then takes a sip of wine while looking at me pointedly.

"Wow, I didn't realize you both had such dubious moral codes. I wouldn't do that to Eric." I shake my head, knowing they're just trying to lighten up a serious topic. "Anyway, I've been thinking about the worst-case scenario, and I need to come to terms with the possibility of raising a kid by myself, and what life would look like as a single mom." I take a deep breath. "My business is doing fine, but it's just me. And getting pregnant might be expensive. And then if I get pregnant, it's not like I can give myself maternity leave."

Suzy waves her hand. "You just come work for us. We'll create a position for you, and you continue to do what you do now but in-house."

"And getting pregnant doesn't have to be expensive," Kate says. "I think a lot of guys would take you up on the offer."

Suzy laughs. "Good one, Kate."

"You two are the worst, and also the best. And we should probably cut Suzy off."

Kate catches our server's eye and makes a subtle hand gesture for the check.

* * *

THAT NIGHT, I look at my pills in the bathroom. I could never do that to Eric. Yet, I can't help but think an accidental pregnancy would make things easier...or maybe that's Suzy and Kate's bad influences. As I swallow a pill and place the packet back in the medicine cabinet, I hope this will be the last pack for a while.

6

A month has passed since my mom's surgery, and she's eager to get back to her house, friends, and, most importantly, hair salon. She's still not allowed to lift her left arm above her head, and neither my dad nor I have blown out her bob to her satisfaction. So tomorrow my parents move back to the suburbs, and Jake flies out in the morning.

Tonight we're all having dinner, and Eric is joining us. I'm making them a chickpea pasta dish with kale and mushrooms since it's been my mom's favorite meal during this time. I tried some alternative grains like a quinoa bowl, which didn't go over too well with my parents, and a vegan dish with tofu, which made my mom comment, "Darling, why are you serving us sponges?" After that, I was bumped from menu planning. My mom commandeered the cookbook Eric gave me and has been placing her order the night before.

With my parents vacating my place, tomorrow I will finally talk to Eric. After our lunch, Suzy reached out to assure me that if things didn't go the way I hoped, the job offer stood. So, really, if it came to Plan C, the only thing left to do would be to find a donor. While it all makes logical sense in my head, it still doesn't comfort me.

As I drop pasta into the pot of boiling water, some splashes onto my bare arm. "Ow!"

"Careful!" my mother admonishes from her armchair, even though she can't see what I'm doing.

"I'm okay," I say. I turn on the sink faucet and run my arm under cold water.

My mom says something that I can't make out.

"One sec," I call out. I set the pasta timer, and then step into the living room. "What can I get you?"

"Nothing, nothing. Just come here where I can see you."

Dad went out for a pre-dinner walk, so it's just the two of us here. I stand in front of her chair. She peers up at me and says, "What's up with you? You've been dropping things, forgetful, and a nervous wreck lately."

Oh. "Nothing. Just tired, I think."

"I'm fine, and I'm going to continue to be fine by following the doctor's orders. So what else is it?"

Nothing escapes her notice. I've already unloaded to Jordan, Suzy, and Kate, but since I can't stop thinking about it all, I give in to my need to keep talking about it. We have at least seven minutes before the pasta reaches al dente, so I plop down on the sofa.

Next to me is the heart-shaped pillow the hospital gave my mom that she is supposed to hug to regain her strength. I pull the pillow to my chest and wrap my arms around it, hoping it will do the same for me, emotionally. "There is something on my mind, but I don't want to worry you."

"When you say that, you know I'm going to worry." Her voice trembles. "And that's not good for my heart."

"It's nothing *bad*. But if I tell you, you have to promise not to mention it to Dad or anyone. Okay?"

Her eyes widen. "Of course, darling. What is it?"

I take a deep breath. Once the news is out, there will be no ignoring it, and she will bring it up with me every time we're alone. But my pressure cooker needs a little release, so I just have to tell her.

"Over the last few weeks," I begin carefully, "I've been thinking it might be time to start a family."

She gasps, obviously thrilled. "What does Eric think?"

"We haven't talked about it in a while, and I'm not sure when to bring it up. And it might be best to wait until you're fully recovered."

"Way to motivate your mother to get better!" She laughs at her own joke.

I roll my eyes. "Well, it's all part of a bigger conversation with Eric. You know he's still bouncing back from the coffeehouse closures. And I need to think about my consulting business..." I trail off, not wanting to get into too many details, and knowing that I have Suzy's offer.

"You two would figure it out. People in much worse situations have children. I can't imagine Eric not being on board."

She just had heart surgery; do I want to break her heart again? Especially on our last family dinner for a while?

I just say, "Well, he might not be ready. And if he's not, then I have some serious thinking to do."

My mom eyes me critically. "What do you want?"

I look at her. She knows.

"Darling, not to be sappy, but you and your brother are my greatest pride and joy. And these last few years, I've watched you go after your dreams and achieve so much.

Relationships are compromises, but don't compromise your dreams." She shakes her finger at me.

"I know how long you've wanted to be a mother for, and so I nudge. If this is something you really want, and for whatever reason Eric doesn't want it...do what you think is right," she says, holding my gaze. She then shrugs. "And, anyway, men can be persuaded. Just start dropping hints."

The timer on my phone goes off, and I jump up to check the pasta. "Okay, thank you. But don't be weird around Eric tonight," I say, though I may have just guaranteed that. "And remember, don't mention this to anyone."

"My lips are sealed," she calls out, and I can hear the smile on her face.

There is noise at the front door, and my dad comes in with Jake behind him. "Look who I found loitering on the street," he says.

"Hey, guys!" I catch a glimpse of them as I pop my head out of the kitchen.

"Hi, Al, Mom," Jake says.

"Hey," another familiar voice says, and that familiar face peeks into the kitchen.

"Jordan?" I blink. My eyes blurry from the steam of the pasta I'm draining. "What are you doing here?"

"Jordan!" my mom says.

"Yes, hi, Theresa." Jordan gives me a shrug and ducks into the living room. "How are you feeling?"

"I've been better. But this is a delight! What brings you to visit us?"

"I was in the neighborhood, reviewing some client notes at The Cauldron, and thought of stopping by, and then I, uh, ran into Jake on the way here."

"Yeah, I spotted them when I was walking out of the

park," my dad says. "So I joined them and invited Jordan to come up and say, Hi."

I frown. The Cauldron and the park are in opposite directions. And what was my brother doing in Lincoln Park? But I'm too busy finishing up the pasta to join the conversation.

"Allison is making us a pasta dish tonight. Can you stay for dinner? It's my last night here before we go home," my mom says.

Jordan knows a "can you stay" from my mom isn't so much an invitation but a demand. "Uh, sure, if there's food to spare. Is that okay, Allison?"

I can tell by the way she asks, the subtext is, "please, say there's not enough food." But I can't hide the extra, so I'm forced to say, "Of course!" (And then make a mental note to mouth, "I'm sorry," to Jordan when no one's looking.)

I quickly text Eric, hoping I haven't missed him.

Dinner is almost ready. Jordan is joining us. If you're still at work, any chance you can bring an extra dessert for her?

Eric responds with a thumbs up and, *Just about to leave. 6 Vegan Gluten-free brownies?*

Eric tries to stock the case with healthier baked goods, and so he can usually be counted on to bring something that's heart healthy for my mom.

Perfect, I text, with a thumbs up.

Since my mom is enjoying talking to Jordan and having new company, Jake helps me set an extra place at the table.

"What were you doing in the park?" I ask him. "I thought you always worked right up to dinner."

"Just stretching my legs, getting some fresh air," he says. "Would you like me to fill up everyone's water glass?"

"Um, sure." And Jake is already heading to the kitchen.

Five minutes later, there's a knock at the door, and Jake says, "I'll get it."

It's Eric, bearing a dessert box. "I heard we needed extra dessert."

"Thank you, babe." I take it from him and give him a kiss. "I'm going to put this in the kitchen, and I think we're all ready to eat."

When we gather around the table, my mom directs everyone where to sit. Even though it's my home, she takes the head of the table, though, to be fair, it's closest to her chair. But she then directs my dad to sit at the other end, with me and Eric beside each other and Jordan and Jake together.

I feel unsettled after what I just told my mom, and I hope she doesn't bring up anything regarding babies and Eric. Jordan also seems off. While she was talking to my mom, Jordan was her cheerful self, but now she's a little quiet, looking down at her napkin, rather than making eye contact or conversation with anyone. Maybe she had someplace else to be, but thought she had to stay because my mom asked.

As we all dig into the asparagus soup I made to start, I ask Jordan, "Any plans with Sean later tonight?" Maybe I can at least give her an excuse for a hasty exit after dinner.

But she shakes her head quickly.

"Who is Sean?" my mother asks.

"Another student friend," Jordan says. "We studied together and dated for a little bit. But it's already fizzled out now that we've both been busy."

Not wanting my mom to nose into Jordan's love life, I jump in. "Jordan's already seeing patients."

"Well, yes, but under supervision. I have to get three thousand supervised hours in before I'm allowed to have my own practice. But, still, after all those classes, it's been really great to finally talk to patients."

I turn to Eric. "I hope you let Jordan get on with her work today."

Eric looks at me, then at Jordan, and cocks his head in a question. "Jordan was studying at The Cauldron today," I explain. I look back at Jordan and her eyes are wide.

"Oh, no, I said I was getting coffee while studying. I was at the Starbucks. Sorry, Eric." She makes a face. "I peeked into The Cauldron and didn't spot any empty seats, so I moved on."

"It happens," Eric says. "Just don't let it happen again." He shakes his spoon at her, and then grins.

We all laugh. Then my dad asks Eric how business is going, and Jake and Eric start talking about CrossFit and plan to go to Eric's box in the morning before Jake's flight.

Jordan is quiet for most of the dinner, and I wonder if maybe she and Sean have officially broken up. She doesn't linger afterwards, and so I'm not able to ask.

Before Eric and I head back to his place, I text her, *Sorry if dinner was too much. Everything okay?*

She doesn't respond.

* * *

WHEN WE GET INTO BED, Eric says, "So, what's up with Jordan?"

"What do you mean?"

"I don't know how long she was at Starbucks, but at no point this afternoon were all our tables full. And you know I always save yours in the back and would have given it to her."

"Huh. I don't know. She did seem a little off tonight. Maybe she didn't want to stay for dinner, but felt guilted into it. First by my dad, then my mom."

"Maybe."

"Or maybe things with Sean are officially over, but she hasn't had a chance to tell me yet?" I check my phone charging on the nightstand. Still no text from her. *Huh?* "Hey, thanks again for bringing the brownies. They were delicious."

"That's my job."

"Bringing brownies?"

"Making you happy." He smiles.

"Awww...aren't you the best?" I roll over and on top of him, holding his face in my hands, before I lean down and kiss him.

I initiate sex, probably both consciously and subconsciously to impress upon him how fun baby-making will be. While I've been distracted in other areas of our relationship, lately I've stepped up my A-game in the bedroom department, considering...Maybe if Eric thinks there will be a lot more of this, we won't have to thaw my eggs but can do this the old-fashioned way. That is...if he's changed his mind. I put it out of my mind to focus on the task at hand—getting enough of my gorgeous boyfriend.

After all, my mom said men can be persuaded. *Oh, god, am I really thinking like her?* I shake the thought out of my head and the bedroom.

7

───────

The next morning, Jordan replies to my text with, *Everything's fine. Last night was fine. Thank you for dinner.*

Hmm...Two "fines," and I still don't quite believe her. I type back, *Okay. You're welcome.*

When she doesn't respond, I decide not to press. She'll let me know in her own time; and at the moment, the baby discussion with Eric is weighing heavily on my mind.

* * *

Now that my parents have returned to the suburbs, I spent last night alone in my condo to clean and set everything back in its place. But being in bed by myself felt too quiet, and too lonely. When I told Eric that I wanted to spend the night at my place, he said, "I understand. But tomorrow, we're getting dressed up and I'm taking you out to dinner. We haven't been on a proper date in a long time. Our reservation is at seven."

When I asked where, he said it was a surprise. I put on a dress and heels and took extra time with my hair and makeup, none of which I've done in a while.

And when the Uber drops us off at our destination, I'm glad I took extra care. Eric is taking me to Boka, where we had our first official date.

Once we're inside the restaurant, the familiar eclectic interior, with its moody hues and whimsical animal portraits, instantly transports me back. I hadn't seen Eric dressed up before, and I remember the frisson of nerves and excitement I felt back then. Looking at him tonight, I still think he's the kindest, most wonderful, and attractive man I've ever been with; and I decide to forget about the big talk for now, and just enjoy our dinner together.

We're seated at the same table as our first date, and Eric gives me a knowing smile. As soon as the server arrives, Eric orders two glasses of champagne.

"Oh?" I say.

"Yes." He grins. "We're celebrating."

I set down my menu and lean toward him. "What are we celebrating?"

"Let's wait for the champagne, and then I'll tell you."

Luckily, it arrives quickly, and Eric makes a toast. "To the future."

I'm not sure what he means, so I just repeat, "To the future." And we clink glasses.

After we take our first sips, he says, "I'm reopening The Cauldron in Lincoln Park."

"That's amazing! Congratulations!" I clink my glass with his again. "When did this happen?"

"The space has been sitting there empty for years. And so a couple of weeks ago, the new building owner contacted me, wondering if I'd be interested in leasing the space again. Plus, he's giving it to me at its original rate."

"Wow! I'm so happy for you!"

"Thank you. Yeah, well, as you know, business has picked up in the Gold Coast. I think by putting all my focus on the one location, I've been able to figure out ways to streamline our processes and get new customers. And after setting up online ordering, we've really increased our revenue. So it was perfect timing. Plus, I know the layout of that space and it shouldn't take much to get it up and running again." He leans forward and smiles. "Also, I have a lead on a new apartment building going up in Wicker Park, and they're renting retail space below. So I'm looking into securing one of those spaces too. Captive customers!"

I laugh. "That's fantastic! I'm so proud of you." I knew things would turn around for him.

During dinner, he tells me more about what's been happening at The Cauldron, and I fill him in on some of my consulting work. Even though I spend my nights at his place, we haven't had a real catch-up in a long time, and it feels so good to see a happy, relaxed Eric.

Before our dessert arrives, he takes my hands in his on the table.

"I know you just got your place back, and I get wanting to stay there last night," he says. "But I was lonely. My place only feels like home when we're together."

"Aww...I felt the same way."

"And why are we paying two mortgages, assessment fees, *and* taxes?"

I shake my head and swallow. I sense where this is going...

"So, why don't we make it official? Move in with me."

I swallow again. Eric's question is forcing my bigger question, and though all I've thought about for the last month is the baby discussion, I don't want to do it at this moment. It suddenly feels too soon.

"I hear you. It's something to think about," I say.

He gives me an amused look.

"What?" I ask.

He laughs. "I mean, we've practically been living together for years now. We've spent more time together at my place than apart."

"I know." I try to laugh too, though it comes out as a squeak. "But you just sprang it on me, and I like to think about things, that's all."

"Hey." Eric looks at me, his eyes softening. "It's a big step, I know. We've both had our own places for so long. And we don't have to move into mine. We could get a brand-new one that's ours."

"Yeah. Well, like you said, owning property together is a big step, and I don't want to jump into things..." I hedge, looking down. I'm not fooling him, though. The way things have been going, there's no reason we shouldn't get a place together, except...

"Or maybe we should make things more official? Is that what you're thinking?" He lowers his head to meet mine, looking up at me, forcing me to look at him again.

I reluctantly look into his eyes. *Oh, Eric, it's so* not *what I'm thinking. Please don't make us have this conversation right now.*

"You know, during your mom's surgery, when I couldn't join you in the ICU to wait with you and your dad because I wasn't 'family', it killed me not being there for you. You *are* my family. And I didn't want to bring this up until we knew your mom was in the clear..." He pauses before continuing. "But I've also been thinking that maybe...maybe we get married?"

Is this a proposal?

Eric looks so hopeful, yet unsure.

"I...I've been thinking about things too, and Eric, we need to talk. But I'd rather not do that here."

He freezes for a second. His eyes flicker from confusion, to worry, then to devastation. He starts to pull his hands away from mine, but I grab tighter.

"No, no," I try to reassure him. "It's not like that. I love you, and I would totally marry you. I want to be with you forever...but can we talk about this at your place after dinner?"

"Sure," he says, but his voice is flat.

Since Eric and I started dating, I've never hidden anything from him. Our entire relationship we've always been open with each other, and I can't possibly make it through the rest of the meal looking at his upset face. And since I've already talked about this with everyone else, hopefully, it will be a relief to finally say it aloud to him—or so I steel myself.

"My mom's heart attack made me realize that life is fragile, and time waits for no one." I take a deep breath. "And, so, recently, I've been thinking that I'm ready to be a mother."

He stares at me.

"I want a baby, Eric." I stare back.

"When did this happen?"

Okay...not exactly the response I hoped for, but not a "no."

"I've always wanted one. I mean, we broke up before because I wanted one. And then I froze my eggs."

"But that was three years ago. I had no idea you still

wanted this." As he speaks, his face pales and he slowly lets go of my hands. This time, I let him.

"Yes, the last time we talked about it was over three years ago, and a lot has happened since then, and the timing wasn't right. But now we're in a completely different place in our relationship, and we're talking about moving in together, maybe getting married..." I trail off, feeling more scared with each word because I can see I'm losing him. "I never changed my mind; it just didn't come up."

He leans back in his chair and drags his hands down his face. "Oh, Allison. I...I..." He stops, unable to finish his thought. His eyes are sorrowful, and a sharp pain goes through me as he says, "We didn't talk about it again, so I assumed you accepted this about me."

"You haven't changed your mind either?" My voice is calm, but it's only because I've left my body.

He shakes his head.

I don't know what to say. He's right. I kept quiet for too long.

But is this a game of chicken? Who loves who more? Does he really not love me enough to have a child with me? Do I really want to be a mother more than I want to be with him? If only we could make the people we love want the same as us.

"Maybe I should stay at my place again tonight," I say.

Eric looks defeated and nods. "That's probably a good idea." He sighs. "I'm sorry, Allison. I need to think about some things, too."

We ask for the check without touching our desserts.

8

———————

When I get home that night, I quickly take off my dress and makeup and crawl into bed alone. Huddled under my blankets, I tell myself—*Eric didn't say no. He simply said he had to think about things.* While I'm trying to be respectful of his feelings, it's still hard not to fall into a pit of despair. He was willing to propose, but hesitated at the idea of having a family with me. I can't help but wonder if this is my situation with Neil all over again. While they might say, "You'll be an amazing mother, blah, blah, blah," neither could envision having children with me. Actions speak louder than words. It's hard not to think I have some gigantic flaw others feel shouldn't be passed down into the human gene pool.

It's only nine p.m., so I text Jordan.

What's wrong with me?

A few minutes go by. She responds, *You text vague questions. What's up?*

I told Eric I was ready to have a baby. He hasn't changed his mind.

My phone rings two seconds later.

"Oh, sweetie," Jordan says. "I'm sorry. What happened?"

Once I recount my conversation with Eric to her, she says, "I totally understand why you're upset, but he didn't give you a hard no. *And* he pretty much proposed, which is huge!"

"I suppose," I mumble.

She continues in a soothing voice she must use on patients. "He was just caught off guard. All you can do is give him some space."

"Yeah, I don't really have a choice. I mean, I'm back at my place." I groan. "But, first Neil, and now Eric. So many of our friends have families, that it's hard not to wonder why no one wants a family with me?"

"Okay. I'm not letting you go down this path again," she says, her voice stern. "It's not you, it's never been you. Neil was terrible, and you dodged a bullet. I never liked or grew to like him. And as for Eric, he said from the beginning he didn't want kids, and he has some real hang-ups about being a father. So it's okay to be disappointed, but there's no reason to pity party tonight. You're amazing, and you know it."

I don't believe her, but she's right about the self-pity part. All along, I knew Eric's reaction tonight was a possibility, so I need to suck it up for now.

"Okay, thanks for listening and the pep talk," I say. "It's out of my control tonight anyway, and in some ways, after an entire month of worrying about *the talk*, it's almost a relief to have ripped off the band-aid." I change the subject. "What are you up to?"

"Ugh. Studying. The license exam is coming up this month, and things are getting real."

"You got this. *You know why?* Cause you're amazing too."

She laughs.

"And if there's anything I can do to help you, let me know," I add.

"Thanks. I just need to finish up my assignment tonight so I can go to bed."

"In that case, I won't keep you. Good luck, and thanks again for listening."

When we hang up, I pull the covers up to my chin and roll over onto my side, away from the empty side of the bed. How quickly sleeping alone has shifted from feeling like a comforting change of pace to a bad omen.

I WAKE EARLY and head out for a run by the lake, even though it's drizzling and chilly. I keep my head down and listen to my feet hit the wet pavement, each step making a satisfied *splat*. Last night I was sad, but this morning frustration bubbles inside me. Why would Eric assume, *I thought you accepted this about me*? I could have assumed the same thing—that by continuing our relationship, it meant he was okay with us having kids. And, sure, I didn't bring it up again when we got back together. But, *one*, we thought the world was ending. And then, *two*, when it didn't, our personal world and businesses weren't in a great place, and so there was no point discussing it. Or maybe that was the lie I told myself in order not to disturb the status quo. Eric's shocked face last night made me feel a little guilty, as if I'd been keeping a secret. Still, I can't help but be angry at his assumption. Why would he think I'd give up something so important to me?

With a swell of anger, my mind rushes to plan C. And to

quash the tiny voice in me that says I won't be enough, I start making a list in my head of how prepared I am to have a child: I own my home, a condo with two bedrooms. So I have one room for me and one for a nursery. I own my business, and I have a backup plan with Suzy's job offer. Whatever happens, I'll be able to support us financially. I have parents nearby who would be doting grandparents, and I can count on them to help with childcare if needed. Though Jordan professes not to like children, I know she would be an amazing godmother. Finally, even though Jake lives in New York, he showed up for our mom this last month. I'm sure he'd be a supportive uncle.

While it's scary to think that I might struggle financially, might be overwhelmed balancing work and childcare, and might have a hard time being the only parent in the middle of the night with a sick child counting on me, I can figure it out. Over the last few years, I've grown so much that I believe I can handle any storm. I am enough.

The drizzle turns to full-on rain, and instead of depressing me, it makes me more determined to finish my three-miler and face my future.

When I get home after my run, I don't let myself wallow. I still want to cry or scream, perhaps both, but I suppress the urge. Instead, I decide to take fate into my own hands and focus on my higher purpose—my soon-to-be child who will eventually need to be clothed, fed, educated, and given braces. So I eat a quick breakfast, shower, and dive straight into work.

If I don't keep busy, my anxiety will creep up on me. The good news is I have a lot of work on my plate. The other week, I finished putting together a presentation and proposal for Abbott. Kate and Suzy reviewed it, and then

Suzy asked if I would join them on a Zoom meeting with the client. While I've done a thousand presentations before and I'm always detail-oriented in my work, all stakes seem higher right now since I might have to take Suzy up on that in-house offer.

Already, I'm envisioning what it would be like to go back to corporate life and trying to psych myself up for that. Working in an office again could be invigorating. Sometimes I miss the immediate exchange of ideas, being able to physically turn to someone and brainstorm in real time. However, while my consulting business was almost thrust upon me when I lost my job, I've realized how much I enjoy the autonomy, being able to work in yoga pants, and saving the money I used to spend on commuting, buying lunch every day, and maintaining a more professional wardrobe. If I start working for Suzy, I'll have to commute again and either start brewing my coffee at home or going back to my old Starbucks before the El ride. This makes me think of Eric, but I swallow it down.

I'm tied to my laptop all morning and afternoon until dinnertime. While I thought I had a lot of work, I finish everything. It's a Saturday, and being on my own at home seems like a dangerous idea.

I text Jordan, *What are you doing tonight?*

Studying, she replies.

Oh. I don't want to be the needy friend, but my fingertips hover over my phone, debating what to write. Another message from her appears. *I'm planning to order a pizza if you want to come over for dinner tonight.*

Yes, please. Thank you.

* * *

Around seven o'clock, I show up at Jordan's place with a bottle of wine. When she opens the door, we're in matching outfits of joggers and sweatshirts, and our hair in scrunchies.

I laugh. "Glad to see we're twinning tonight."

She laughs and takes the wine from me. "A Zin', nice. Thanks. I already ordered the pizza cause I'm starving."

"Sounds good."

I hang my jacket and purse on her coat stand. We walk into her kitchen, and holding up the bottle, she says, "Let's open this now. I really need a break."

"How's it going?" I ask, while taking two wine glasses out of a cabinet.

"The material is more interesting than studying for the bar was, but it's still just as anxiety-producing," she says, pulling a wine opener out of a drawer and going to work on the bottle. "Without a license, I can't practice on my own, you know."

"Yeah. But you got this. You were a straight-A student."

She groans. "It gets harder when you're older. I'm not so much into burning the midnight oil to study anymore. Also, I'm balancing this with getting my clinical hours in." She opens the bottle with a pop and pours the wine into our two waiting glasses. "Anyway, I could use a change of topic. What did you do today?"

"Went for a run. Worked. And basically tried not to think about things with Eric." I grimace.

"Have you heard from him?"

"No. But it's been less than twenty-four hours since our talk, and I promised myself to give him seventy-two hours before I officially panic."

She nods. "Good for you."

I take a big gulp of wine. "Well, to keep my mind off Eric,

I also came to the decision that I'm ready to do this whole motherhood thing with or without him."

"Oh?" Her eyes widen. "That's huge."

"It is, but I also feel like the timing and my support system couldn't be better." I tell her about the list I made in my head during my run. "Of course I want to do this with Eric. But I know I can do it by myself too."

"Good for you!" she says, again, raising her glass to me. "I know you can, too. And, like you just said, you're not alone. But just don't make me change a diaper or anything in that realm."

There's a knock at the door. I laugh and say, "Saved by the bell."

While she grabs the pizza, I grab some plates and napkins, and we settle in at her kitchen table.

"So, hey," I say, after our first bites of pizza, "we haven't had a real talk about what happened with Sean."

Jordan's mouth is full. She holds up a finger, and I swear I see a faint blush on her cheeks. When she finishes chewing, she says, "There's not much to talk about. We hadn't been spending a lot of time together lately. So, rather than just drift out of each other's lives, I met him for coffee to talk. And we simply decided that we're too busy to continue our relationship."

"Huh. Still, that's sad in its own way."

She shrugs, and I detect a small smile that makes me wonder. "Is there someone else?"

She shakes her head. "No. I don't have the time to date right now. I'm just focused on getting through this next month and passing the exam."

"That makes sense." I nod. "And lucky for you, I'm

focused on *not* focusing on my problems, so if I can help in any way?"

"In that case..." She trails off and grins. "How do you feel about flash cards?"

After dinner, we sit on her couch while I read out the flash cards to her. It's a great distraction and reminds me of our college days when we were roommates.

As I read off the various disorders on the cards and she recites back to me what to look for, I say, "Wow, I feel like I have five out of eight of these attributes. How do I know if I have Narcissistic Personality Disorder?"

"If you're wondering if you're a narcissist, then you're not. Next question."

A few times during our breaks, I notice Jordan checking her phone and giving it a little smile. I'm not so sure I believe that she's not dating anyone, but I let her keep her secret for now. I'll grill her on her love life after this test.

Around ten o'clock, we're yawning.

"Would you mind if I slept on your couch tonight?" I ask. Even though my back will hate me in the morning, I fear all my worries will come rushing back once I'm alone in my bed again.

"I'll get you a blanket and pillow," she answers.

* * *

IN THE MORNING, we drink coffee on her sofa. After our second cups, she says, "Love ya, but I need to take a practice test this morning," and kicks me out so she can get back to studying.

The sun is out and there's a hint of spring in the air, and so I walk home to my place—passing by the Water Tower, then up Michigan Avenue, and turning down Oak Street to the Gold Coast. Trees are flowering, and tulip buds are beginning to poke up in the sidewalk gardens. A combination of tourists and shoppers fill the streets, and I take my time window shopping and enjoying the mild weather. Then, as I near home, I tack on a few extra blocks to avoid passing The Cauldron.

Once I'm home, I realize it's a bad idea to sit around. So I throw on my workout clothes and force myself to attend a yoga class at my gym. Afterward, I go grocery shopping, stocking up for the next few days. Home again, I start a load of laundry and take a shower. But after that, I'm not sure what to do with myself. Trying to read a book or watch television will cause my mind to wander. It's been close to forty-eight hours since I talked to Eric, which is the longest we've gone without talking since we got back together in March 2020, and I can't help but feel that this is a bad sign. All I know is that to stay sane, I have to stay in motion.

My condo has two bedrooms, and I use the smaller one as an office and as my general overflow room. I decide to do some spring cleaning, and as I toss out old papers and files that have collected on the desk, I consider the room. It's west facing and nothing blocks the view from the window, so the late-afternoon sun streams in. If or when I have a baby, this room would make a nice nursery. I can easily move my desk and bookshelf to the other rooms. I try to picture it: a crib along one wall, a changing table and dresser on the other wall, a chair in the corner where I will probably spend some long nights. After I finish tidying up the space, I know where I can go.

I walk over to Restoration Hardware and head straight to the nursery and children's floor. I stroll through the rooms:

there's one fit for a princess with a draped canopy over a white crib, another has darling little tables set up for tea, and then there is a safari-themed room with drawings of baby animals. While these displays are over the top and not exactly what I imagine for my baby's nursery, they're still fun to look at. And I must have a smile on my face because I notice other customers looking my way, smiling or nodding back at me.

My phone buzzes with a text. I carefully sit down on a pink pouf in the teenaged girl's themed room to read it.

It's from Eric.

Hey. Can we talk tomorrow night?

My heart hammers in my chest as I text back shakily, *Yes.*

I'll come over to your place after The Cauldron closes. He ends with, *I love you.*

I write back: *I love you too.*

By tomorrow night, I'll have my answer. I was trying to give it seventy-two hours before I panicked, but I now have a major case of the Sunday scaries.

9

Luckily for me, Mondays are always a busy administrative day, and I spend the morning responding to emails and messages. My go-it-alone determination from Saturday is gone, and my emotions are all over the place. Anxiety makes my mind spin. *If he was ready to talk, why didn't he want to come over last night rather than making me wait the entire day?* And, *Couldn't he have given me a hint about his decision in his text?* I also can't help over-analyzing his "I love you." *Was it an "I love you" to say everything will be fine, or to soften the blow?* As the hours tick down, I console myself with the knowledge that at least I'll be out of my misery soon.

When the doorman tells me Eric is on his way, my thoughts and heart race—*Are we breaking up or committing to each other forever?* I'm dressed casually, but in what I know is Eric's favorite sweater on me and my softest but most flattering jeans. I may have spent an inordinate amount of time blowing out my hair and perfecting my no-makeup makeup look. I may have also lit some candles in the room, both for ambiance and to soothe my nerves. I even have a bottle of wine at the ready—either for celebrating together or for crying alone. The few minutes of waiting are agony.

The elevator dings on my floor and my heart thuds against my chest. Before he knocks, I open the door. Eric stands there; his cotton T-shirt looks a little rumpled from a long day, a five o'clock shadow lines his jaw, and his blue eyes appear both tired and contrite. An invisible band around my chest stretches tighter.

"Hey," he says, in a manner where I can't read either his expression or tone. But he's also holding a bouquet of my favorite flowers—peonies—despite them being out of season.

"Hey," I say, my neutral tone matching his.

For a second, he looks unsure of whether he should come in, so I open the door wider and step aside.

"How are you?" I sound weirdly formal, but feel the need to fill the silence.

"Allison," Eric says gently. Then, as if remembering, he holds out the flowers. "These are for you. I didn't get a vase because I know you have vases and hate the extra clutter."

"I do. Thanks." I take them from him, wondering if these are I'm-sorry-flowers because he changed his mind, or because he's going to break my heart.

"If you find me a vase, I'll put them in water," he says.

I'm grateful to have a task, to delay for a few more minutes. While I retrieve a vase from the hall closet, Eric has already trimmed the bottoms of the stems in the kitchen. Taking the vase from me, he fills it with water and then sets the flowers inside, fanning them out. "There," he says.

I can't help but comment, "I didn't realize you knew how to arrange flowers."

"One of my many talents," he quips. Then he says more seriously, "Come here." And I do, stepping into his arms as he wraps them around me, rubbing my back. "I missed you. Let's sit down and talk. Okay?"

With my cheek against his chest, I nod and then pull away. He holds my hand as we head to the couch and sit down. This doesn't feel like a breakup, but it could still go either way, depending on what he says next.

"Thank you for giving me some space this weekend to think," he says. "I'm sorry about Friday night. I was so shocked, though maybe I shouldn't have been." His voice is soft at this last part. "I needed a day or two to get my head around this, and to make sure I say the right thing."

"Of course," I say, but want to get to the heart of the matter. "Just so you know, I haven't changed my mind about wanting to have a baby."

He nods. "I figured. But I'm here to say that I have changed my mind." He swallows. "Or more like, I'm more open to the idea of kids than I was before."

"Yeah?" I stay very still and hold my breath, awaiting his next words.

"Yeah. On Saturday I went to the 'burbs and talked to my mom."

I give him an encouraging smile. Eric would only worry his mother about something serious, and I think it's sweet that he talks about his life with her.

"What did you say?" I ask. "And what did she say?"

"I told her you wanted kids, and how you've always wanted a family; but that I was scared, you know, after what happened with Dad. She seemed pretty surprised, and said that didn't sound like me, that I've always been someone who has taken risks. But when I told her it was because I worried that maybe I would die early too, and that I couldn't do that to my kids, she started to cry."

"Oh no!"

"I know! I felt terrible. I explained it wasn't so much that it was hard for me, though obviously it was, or that I regret anything by having to step up in the family. And then she stopped me and said that wasn't what made her cry. She was crying because my dad wouldn't have wanted his death to prevent me from having kids. She said my sister and I were the highlight of his life, and he would be brokenhearted to know that his legacy was my being scared to have kids."

"Oh, Eric." I scooch up and put my arms around him, wishing I could erase his pain and grief. He pulls me into him. We are quiet for a few seconds, until Eric pulls back and rubs his eyes.

"Yeah, she said nobody knows what will happen, and I could live to a hundred for all we know. Then she called me a dummy for possibly missing out on something wonderful because I'm scared." Eric gives me a small smile. "And then she called me a dummy again for possibly losing you. Her exact words were, 'And if you died, you'd leave Allison all alone!' So, if you didn't already know, she's Team Allison on this one."

I give a small laugh. "Even so, I don't want you to feel pressured or like this is an ultimatum." Though if I'm honest, it has the same result. But I want Eric to *want* to have children, not just to appease me.

"Well, then my sister came over with the boys, and I told her what was going on."

I swallow at this because though Elaine tolerates me, I've

never gotten the feeling she's been Team Allison. "She, too, called me a dummy and stated the obvious: anyone who didn't want kids wouldn't be so invested in their nephews like I am or volunteering for a youth program."

Babysitting and being an actual parent are two different things, but I keep this thought to myself while quietly thinking, *Thank you, Elaine!*

"And, you know, they're right. It's not that I don't *want* kids; I'm just worried about the future." He rubs his jawline. "I don't know...I think I convinced myself you had changed your mind on the subject...but really, I just didn't want to bring it up."

Even though initially I was upset with him, I thought the same, so I stop him. "We're both guilty of that. I could've also brought it up earlier as something I still wanted."

"Thanks for that." He kisses my forehead. "But deep down I knew. I just avoided talking about it."

I sigh. "So," I gently prod, "where are we?" I think I know where we are, but I need to hear it from him.

"I think we're going to have a family," he says.

I exhale, suddenly feeling light-headed. "Really? You're sure?"

"Oh, I'm freaked out." He laughs cautiously. "But I'm sure I want to have a family with you."

He tells me about the rest of the visit with his family. How they looked at old photos of themselves as kids, and with their dad; and their mom told them stories they hadn't heard before.

"Even though I didn't get to spend my entire childhood with my dad, I'm so grateful for the memories and times we did have together," he says, and I imagine myself taking photos of Eric with our children and preserving all our future memories.

"So, there was something else I wanted to talk to you about," Eric says.

"Oh?" I say, snuggled up beside him while he strokes my hair.

"I'd like to continue our conversation from Friday, when I, um, brought up marriage."

Oh?

"We didn't finish talking about it," he says, uncertainty in his voice, "because of the other issue."

I gulp. Now it's time to face my fears. I want to be with Eric forever, but...I sit up.

"We don't have to get married. I don't want you to feel like this is something we should do because we're planning on having a family."

"Well, that's it. I *do* want to make it official. It was something I already wanted."

I want it to be official too, but..."If you're scared of having kids, honestly, I'm afraid of planning another wedding and having everything go south. It's happened before."

"Aw, c'mere." He slides off the sofa onto one knee on the floor and holds my hands. "We can do whatever you want. Elope, city hall, keep it a secret." This last one makes me laugh.

He then reaches his hand into the front pocket of his jeans and pulls out a ring. My hands tremble.

"My mom gave me her engagement ring. It made her happy for all those years, and she would like it to be a happy memory again." He searches my eyes, and I'm sure pure love beams back at him.

He smiles. "Allison James, will you marry me?"

"Yes!" I say, and feel the prickle of happy tears beginning to form in my eyes and my cheeks stretched tight from the huge smile on my face.

He slides the ring on my finger, and we kiss. The ring is a simple band with filigree on the sides and two smaller diamonds flanking a larger central one. I remember the Tiffany ring, with its wide platinum band and enormous center diamond, that I had picked out for Neil to propose with, and it suddenly seems so impersonal and ostentatious compared to the one I'm wearing now.

Almost as if he knows I'm comparing the two, Eric says, "If you don't like this ring, that's fine. We'll get you another."

"It's perfect. I love it," I say. "And you." We kiss again.

"Should we call anyone?" he asks.

I shake my head. "Can we just keep it between us for now? We'll tell people in the morning."

And for the first time in a long while, I don't take my pill that night.

IN THE MORNING, I'm bursting to tell everyone, "Eric and I are getting married!" But I also have a Zoom meeting scheduled with Suzy, Kate, and the head of Abbott's Human Resources and their PR coordinator to tackle first. I walk them through the presentation, showing them the different types of volunteer opportunities, such as Zoom tutoring, packing boxes at the Greater Chicago Food Depository, or some of the youth sports activities programs that might interest their employees. I also show them how to set up an internal page on their website for employees to select, sign up for, and track their volunteer hours. The Abbott representatives seem impressed and want to move forward with the program.

After the call, Kate FaceTimes me. It's not unusual for us to follow up right after a client pitch; but when I answer, both her and Suzy's faces fill the screen.

"Um, excuse me, but what was that on your hand during our call?" Kate says.

"Oh, this?" I say faux innocently, waving my ring finger.

"Yes, girl. Do tell!" Suzy says.

I laugh. "Eric proposed last night."

"*What?*" Kate says while Suzy simultaneously asks, "Oh my god, how did he do it?"

"It was a surprise for sure. On Saturday, he had been talking to his mom about us, and she gave him her ring. And last night we were sitting on my couch discussing kids and the future of our relationship, and he proposed, and I said, yes." I shrug, grinning and wiggling my ring finger in the screen again.

"Congratulations!" they both say over each other.

"This calls for a celebration," Suzy says. "Are you having an engagement party?"

"Well, you two are the first people to know...other than Eric's mom, of course. I don't know about a party. I still need to tell my parents." Which I will have to do right after this call.

"I want to talk more about this," Suzy says, and Kate follows up with a, "Me too," and so we decide to meet up later in the week for a celebratory drink.

After getting off the phone with them, I text Eric. *Our secret is out. Suzy and Kate noticed my ring on our Zoom call.*

Good. Then can I tell Brian?

Sure, I type. *And I should really tell my parents before the news spreads. I'll call them now.*

Wait. Maybe we do dinner with them tonight? Surprise them.

This makes me love him more, which I thought was impossible. *Should we invite your mom too?*

No. Let's keep it simple.

I smile to myself. Though they're always cordial, I know Eric's mom finds mine to be a lot.

Got it. I'll ask my parents now.

I call my mom.

"Hello, darling. I'm glad you called. Did I leave my robe at your place? I've been looking for it everywhere."

"Hi, Mom. Yes, you did. I'll bring it to you. In fact, I'm actually calling to see if you and Dad are free for dinner tonight."

"Oh? Well, that's quite short notice, but yes, we're around," she says, sounding a little suspicious.

"Okay, how about Eric and I drive out to your house? We can go to that French place you like."

"Eric is coming too?" Her suspicion turns to delight. I roll my eyes as I imagine her clapping with glee that Eric is joining us. Then she says, "You're pregnant!"

"Calm down," I say jokingly. "I'm not pregnant. But, hey, I gotta go. We'll see you around six tonight."

I feel kind of bad cutting her off, but I knew her next statement was going to be "you're getting married," and I want to surprise her with my dad there.

Next on my list is Jordan.

I have news! I text her. *Can I call you?*

My phone rings.

"What's the news?" she asks. "Is it Eric?"

"Yes! We're getting married!" I allow myself to do a full-on girly "*Eeeee*" that Jordan blissfully returns.

"I knew he'd come around!" she shrieks back at me. "That's great, Allie! I'm so happy for you guys."

"Yes, he proposed last night. I wasn't expecting it, but he had his mother's ring—"

Jordan stops me. "I want to hear all the details, but I'm on my way to see my advisor, and I just arrived. Let me call you back tonight."

"Of course. Oh, wait, Eric and I are having dinner with my parents, so it will be on the later side," I say. "Or, actually, Suzy and Kate were talking about grabbing a drink this week. Would you like to join us?"

"Uh, sure. Just text me the details. Okay, I gotta go or I'll be late. Love you," she says.

"Will do! Love you too!"

I should call Jake, but I decide to wait until after we tell my parents. And since I can only talk in exclamation points and sitting down to work feels impossible, I lace up my gym shoes to go for a late morning run.

As I jog along the lakefront, I smile at every mother, grandmother, nanny, and caretaker with a stroller or little one. I even start eyeing some of the running strollers, thinking happily to myself—*soon that will be me!*

* * *

Eric and I make sure to arrive at the restaurant early so that we're seated first. I keep my hands hidden under the table while the host brings my parents over. Eric stands up to greet them, kissing my mom's cheek and shaking my dad's hand.

When they sit down, my mom is practically vibrating with excitement.

"So?" she asks.

"So..." I raise my hand to show them the ring. "We're getting married!"

My dad catches Eric's eye and winks, and it makes me think they've already had a conversation about this. So it's really just my mom who is surprised by our news.

She clasps her hands together and says, "Oh, that's wonderful! Congratulations, you two!"

My dad motions to the server to ask for a bottle of champagne.

Of course, only moments later, my mom asks, "When is the wedding?"

"Er, we haven't exactly gotten that far," I say. "We just got engaged last night."

"Oh, well, don't worry. I can see if we can get a date at our club."

I look at Eric for help. "That's a generous offer," he says diplomatically. "But Allison and I haven't discussed yet what we want to do."

My dad jumps in too. "Let the kids figure it out, Theresa," he says, patting my mom's hand.

But I already know, the last place I'd want to have our wedding is at my parents' country club. I'd prefer something less traditional and more intimate.

"Honestly, Mom. I think I'd simply like to do city hall or maybe a destination wedding with just our closest family members and friends," I say, inwardly bracing myself for her response.

Her face falls. "I understand," she says, her voice dropping from her initial excitement. "You just got engaged. There's plenty of time to think about it."

I feel a little bad about dashing her hopes for a big wedding; but not so bad that I want the headache of planning a two-hundred-guests-extravaganza for an entire year again.

After dinner, we briefly stop by my parents' house to video call Jake, who says, "It's about time!"

We all laugh since the words are especially funny coming from my brother, the confirmed bachelor.

* * *

ON FRIDAY, I meet Suzy, Kate, and Jordan at Pops for Champagne, our go-to bar for celebrating.

After ordering and a celebratory toast, Suzy asks the same question as my mother: when and where Eric and I are planning to get married.

"I don't know yet, but I know I don't want a big to-do. It's not our style," I say. "A church wedding feels silly, since neither of us is particularly religious; but city hall feels too impersonal. And while I love to travel, there's not a destination that's meaningful to both of us where we'd want to get married."

"So basically you want the wedding fairy to wave her wand and just declare you two married?" Kate says.

I laugh. "Something like that."

"Hmmm...so you want a small wedding with no brouhaha?" Suzy taps her nails on the table. "Ooh! I know a place. It's a flower shop, but it has an event space and a small outdoor area. It's not fussy, it's all black steel and glass, industrial but cozy..."

As Suzy talks, an idea takes shape in my mind. I, too, know a place that's industrial, rustic, and cozy and has a lot of meaning for both me and Eric.

"If you'd like, I can give you their manager's number," Suzy says.

"Thanks, I'll talk to Eric and let you know," I say.

The server comes by and tops off our glasses. Holding up the now empty bottle, he asks, "Do we need another one, ladies?"

"I think so," Suzy answers.

The only glass the server didn't top off was Jordan's, who has been barely sipping her first, which is still full.

"You gotta catch up, Jordan," Kate says. "I know you're not a lightweight like I am, and these two will make me finish the bottle with them." She gestures to Suzy and me, and I playfully clink my glass against Kate's on the table.

Jordan laughs. "Yeah, usually, I'm all for champagne, but I'm not feeling that great today. My stomach's been off."

"Are you sick?" Suzy asks.

Jordan shakes her head. "No. It comes and goes, and I don't have a fever or anything. I think it's nerves about this exam. It's only a couple of weeks away now."

"You got this," Kate says in a rare note of positivity.

Jordan shrugs. "I hope so. The next one isn't until October, and you can only fail three times and then you can't take it again. It's different from the bar, as I'm older now. Back then, I thought I'd die if I failed, but honestly, the stakes were lower. Now I've quit a lucrative career and paid for school all over again—I can't afford to mess this up."

I knew Jordan was anxious, but I didn't know she was *this* worried. I put my arm around her shoulders, giving her a little side hug. "It's stressful, sure, but you've done harder things. And you could recite everything on those flash cards the other night. I believe in you. We all do," I say, looking around the table.

Everyone nods, and Suzy raises her glass. "To Jordan! Who will give us the opportunity to meet back here and toast her passing her licensing exam!"

Jordan laughs, and we all raise our glasses and clink again. "Hear, hear!"

After we take our sips, Kate turns to me. "So, if you're getting married, I'm assuming Eric got over his hang-ups about having kids," she says.

"He's still nervous, but it's more of a healthy fear now. And even though this is something I want, I'm a little scared, too."

"It's normal," Suzy says, reaching over to pat my hand. "Your world changes, and you two are going into parenthood knowing that. If you weren't at all nervous, then I'd worry."

"True. I guess he just had to change his perspective." I fill them in on the discussion Eric and I had before he proposed. "It wasn't that he didn't want kids; he was worried about the possibility of not being there for them. But as someone who has taken risks in all the other areas of his life, he finally decided that he can't worry about what-ifs."

"Smart man," Jordan says. "Because the worst 'what-if' would be letting you go."

"Aww, thanks, lady," I say, and touch my glass to hers.

The rest of the night the four us of catch up. Throughout the evening, I notice Jordan continues to micro-sip her first glass, letting the bubbles go flat. And Kate only has one other glass from the second bottle, so it really is just Suzy and me who polish it off.

* * *

THAT NIGHT I come home to Eric's a little buzzed. Even though he's asleep, I tackle him awake.

"Oh, what's going on here?" he says.

"Hello." I giggle. "So, hey, I have an idea about where we can get married."

"Is that so?" His voice is thick with sleep.

I straddle his hips and bend to kiss him, playfully holding down his arms. Then he's suddenly fully awake, and grabs me and rolls me over. My wedding venue news can wait.

10

______

The wedding space fits about fifty of our guests, which I knew it would. Because most of our family members live nearby, the wedding was easy to organize, and it all came together in a month. Now Eric and I are surrounded by my parents, Jake, Eric's mother, sister and nephews, and a handful of our closest family and friends. We made a rule of only close family and five friends each, including their spouses, which perfectly left me with Jordan, Suzy, Kate, and Darren from my old job—the people who have stuck with me through my hardest times. For the ceremony, I'm wearing a simple white slip dress that I bought off the rack at Nordstrom. It mimics the simplicity of my first wedding gown, which still sits at the back of my closet. Jordan asked if I was going to wear it, but I thought better of it.

The Cauldron is closed this Saturday night. Fairy lights line the walls and drape across the ceiling, and candles in glass votives sit on all the tables, creating a magical glow. Little vases with flowers are dotted all around the space thanks to Suzy's hook-up at her flower shop. When she had mentioned an alternative space rather than a church or hotel, I immediately thought of The Cauldron. It's where I met Eric when I thought my life was at its worst; little did I know that day was the start of everything good to come. When I presented the idea to Eric, he loved it. I knew on some level he wanted a wedding, even if I didn't, and this was the perfect compromise. I thought my parents might be disappointed, so I was shocked when they were thrilled. "Though I still would like to throw you another party," my mom said, and I figured I would just let that one go.

Brian got ordained online so he could officiate, and that, too, seemed fitting. Eric is handsome in a dark navy suit, and his youngest nephew is our ring bearer. Once the ceremony is over, we hired a caterer to provide small bites that are set out, and two of Eric's baristas are helping out as servers to make sure everyone's plates and glasses are full.

The only slight hiccup is that Jordan, my maid of honor, seems distracted. I know she took her exam and is waiting to hear her scores, so she's been on edge lately. Similarly, Eric's best man, my brother Jake, is acting as if his mind is elsewhere. Although he makes polite conversation with everyone, he listens more than he speaks, and his smile doesn't reach his eyes. Also, Jake and Jordan aren't being as friendly as they normally are when we all hang out. In fact, they always seem to be on opposite sides of the room, which is strange. We have music, a playlist Eric and I put together, and some people are dancing. Feeling like I need to loosen up both my best friend and brother, I go up to Jake and say, "Hey, Jordan's been stressing about her test results."

My brother's eyes widen. "Her test results?" he says, slowly, tilting his head.

"Yes, she took her licensing exam a couple weeks ago and

is waiting for her results. Anyway, she seems a little out of it, and I want her to have fun tonight. Go ask her to dance."

"Maybe she doesn't want to dance?" he says.

I give him a look and a small push. "You won't know unless you ask...so go. For me."

He nods and heads over to Jordan, who looks wary to see him. But he takes her hand, and they go over to the small makeshift dance floor and stay for one song. Then, for the rest of the party, they are inseparable and look like they're in intense conversation. At the end of the night, I notice they share an Uber, which makes me smile. Eric and I head out soon after.

* * *

WE DECIDED to hold off on a proper honeymoon until fall, after Eric's new coffeehouses are up and running. My parents offered to gift us a night at a luxury hotel of our choice, but it felt right going back to Eric's, *our* place. For now, I've moved in, and we're talking about putting my place on the market.

With the wedding, and also my birthday in early May, life has been a whirlwind of activity, and one day I realize that it's been over three months since I've had my period. I've been spotting, but haven't gotten my period back since going off the pill. However, I also stopped taking the pill mid-cycle and have been waiting for my hormones to regulate, which I read online could take three months. So after several days of spotting with no period, and thinking it's coming, I'm ready to call my doctor. But before I pick up my phone, I half wonder, *Could I be pregnant?*

I buy a test at Walgreens and take it as soon as I get

home. I don't even have to wait the full three minutes for the result—*It's positive!*

With shaking hands, I put down the test and find my phone to take a photo, almost as evidence. I don't want it to disappear. I'm tempted to text the photo to Eric, but I'll wait until tonight to break the news. For now, I have to do something to make this feel more real. So I call my doctor and make an appointment. She can get me in later this week.

Next, I text Eric, *What time are you coming home tonight?*

I would call, but I don't want him to hear the excitement in my voice; I'd rather tell him in person.

He texts back: *Probably around 7.*

I respond: *Great! I'll make us dinner.*

I'll be there.

I put my phone in my purse and head out to the grocery store to buy ingredients for tonight.

As I shop, I can't believe how easy everything has been the last few months. All that agonizing, my mom's heart attack, wondering if Eric and I were through, and now I'm married and pregnant, about to surprise my husband with happy news and his favorite meal.

* * *

By the time Eric gets home, it's already eight o'clock, and I'm in the kitchen putting the finishing touches on our dinner.

When he walks in the front door, he says, "I'm so sorry I'm late..." then pauses. He appears in the kitchen and sniffs the air. "Is that beef stroganoff?"

"It is!" I chirp. His mother gave me the recipe for her beef stroganoff that Eric loved growing up. "Why don't you wash your hands while I plate this up." I'm keeping my head down over the stove, so as not to betray my big news with a big smile.

He goes to the kitchen sink.

"Oh no. Not here." I wave him away. "Go to the bathroom. I need the sink."

He pauses and gives me a strange look since I'm standing at the stove. So I say, "I, uh, need to rinse the herbs."

There is already a bowl of chopped parsley sitting out. He glances at it, and then at me. "*Okaaay*," he says really slowly, and heads out of the kitchen.

I hear him open the door to the bathroom and then his footsteps rushing back to me. I'm about to burst.

His eyes are wide and shining as he says, "Is that what I think it is on the counter?"

I nod. "Yep! We're pregnant!"

"Oh my god!" He stands frozen in place for a second as it sinks in. "We're having a baby?"

"Yes! We're having a baby!"

Eric swoops me up, spinning us around in a circle. "We're having a baby!" he repeats. And I laugh, "We're going to be parents!"

He sets me down, still laughing. "Now I *really* need to go wash my hands, since I picked up that stick."

* * *

AT MY DOCTOR'S office that week, I take a urine test that confirms I'm pregnant, as well as a blood test. Then she has me lie down so she can take a sonogram.

As Dr. Kahn moves the wand over my stomach, she comments, "It's still early, so it might be hard to see anything.

We're just looking for the sac." She continues listening and watching the screen. "Hmmm..." she says. "You might be one of the more difficult ones."

My stomach sinks.

"Could it be a false positive?" I ask.

She shakes her head. "False negatives, yes, but not false positives. And your uterus lining is thick, which indicates it's preparing for pregnancy. Since you just went off the pill mid-cycle and it's still very early, let's make another appointment for next week."

This wasn't exactly the joyful news I was hoping for, and I can't help but feel a little wary as I make my next appointment with the receptionist.

11

———————

"So, what did the doctor say?" Eric asks me the second he gets home.

It's a little after six o'clock and I'm on my laptop at the kitchen table, trying to get some work done. Eric's question stirs the anxiety in my belly, and I can't tear my eyes from the screen to look at him. I didn't text him after my appointment because I wasn't sure what to say. The doctor's answer wasn't the definitive yes I hoped for, and her comment that I might be one of the more difficult ones has been playing in my head all day.

"Uh, well," I start, while keeping my eyes on my computer and not Eric. "She said that if my pregnancy test was positive, then I'm pregnant."

"Oh, wow," Eric says. He comes over to me, putting his hand under my chin, gently lifting my face up to him. "You're pregnant? This is really happening?"

I finally look at him. His blue eyes are shining, and he gives me a big grin as he waits for me to say more.

I swallow and smile tightly. I'm not sure I can mirror his excitement.

The brightness in his eyes changes to confusion. "Aren't you excited? What's wrong?"

"I am, I think. But she did an ultrasound, and she couldn't see anything."

"Is that normal? Is there anything to even see at this stage?"

"I'm not sure. She said my uterus looked like it was preparing for pregnancy, but she didn't see a sac." I shrug.

"Okay," Eric says again. He pulls out the kitchen chair next to me and sits down. "And is *that* normal?"

"This is the first time I'm pregnant, so I don't know." I shrug again. "She did say it could be too soon to see anything. Also, she took a blood test to confirm that I'm pregnant, and will call me with the results."

"I'm sure it's all fine," he says.

I nod. "Yeah, I guess I just wanted more of a confirmation or something."

"We'll have more information soon enough." From Eric's tone, I can tell he's reassuring himself as much as me.

"Right. Anyway, until then..." I trail off and close my laptop, thinking we both need distracting. It's too early in the process to worry. "How was work? Did you get to meet up with the new landlord for Lincoln Park?"

While we prepare dinner, Eric catches me up on the new properties.

* * *

THE NEXT MORNING, my phone rings with my doctor's office number. I'm at home and I answer immediately.

"Hello," I say.

"Hi, Allison. It's Doctor Kahn. How are you?"

"I think that depends on what your next words are."

She laughs. "Good news. The blood test confirmed that you're pregnant. Congratulations."

I punch my fist up into the air, mouthing, "*Yes!*"

"That's great news! Thank you," I say. "But, you know, I'm still spotting. It's nothing major, but should I be concerned?"

"Spotting can be common early on. It might be implantation bleeding. Keep track of it."

"Okay." My free hand immediately goes to my belly, and I give it a little rub, as if saying *good job* to my embryo for implanting.

"But the blood test also showed that your progesterone is low. So I'm prescribing you progesterone capsule supplements, which you should start today. And, then tomorrow, I'd like you to take another blood test. You can come to the lab here or I can send you a list if you'd prefer to go somewhere more convenient."

"Sounds good. Thank you."

After we end the call, I get up and do a little jig around the kitchen table. *This is the feeling I wanted all day yesterday!* I'm also way too excited to wait until tonight to tell Eric, so I pack up my laptop to spend the rest of the afternoon working at The Cauldron and pick up my prescription on the way.

When I get to The Cauldron, I immediately spot Eric at the register. There are two people in line, and I wait behind them while smiling like a maniac the whole time. When Eric sees me, he grins and shakes his head in a "What's up with you?" manner.

When I finally reach him, he says, "Well, hello, wife. This is a nice surprise."

As I lean over the register to give Eric a kiss, in my peripheral vision, I see Brian cringe. While Eric and I still get a kick out of calling each other husband and wife, it appears not everyone is a fan of our new terms of endearment.

"Yes, well, I have some good news. But first I'll have a mint tea and my regular table." Then I lean across the register again and say quietly, "My doctor called."

Eric's eyes go wide. "And?"

I nod a vigorous yes.

He comes around the counter and gives me a big hug, whispering in my ear, "I told you it would all be fine."

"You were right," I whisper back.

Another customer comes up and Eric lets go of me, and I head to my table. I have work to catch up on from yesterday; but now I'm distracted for an entirely new reason, and I find myself looking at baby names websites. It's not my most productive afternoon, but it's a happy one.

* * *

THE NEXT DAY, I dutifully take my progesterone capsule in the morning. As I swallow it down with water, I feel like I'm on the first step to officially becoming a responsible mother. And that afternoon, I head to the lab for another blood test.

The day after, my doctor calls me again.

I answer cheerfully, "Hello."

"Hi, Allison, it's Dr. Kahn." Her tone is businesslike. "I'm calling because we received your blood test results, and it looks like your HCG levels went down." She asks if I'm still spotting, and I say yes.

She continues, "I'm concerned because, normally, this number should be going up. I'm going to need you to take another blood test tomorrow."

"Okay..." I say. "But what does it mean that my HCG number is going down?"

"I'm not sure yet. Let's see what the next test shows, okay?"

"Okay," I mumble. As I feel my stomach drop, my hand unconsciously goes to my belly again, this time resting over it protectively. When we hang up, I slump back into the kitchen chair, my thoughts churning.

Eric and I agreed not to tell anyone about the pregnancy, but right now I wish we had made an exception for Jordan. I know Eric should be my person, and normally he is, but he's just come around to the idea of having a baby, and what should have been a simple "We're pregnant" moment is getting more confusing each day.

I've been resisting the siren call of Google, but I need answers. So I turn to my laptop. I search for "HCG levels go down," and I don't like what I see. The first results show that a possible cause could be miscarriage.

No.

I close my computer.

And that is exactly why I don't research medical stuff online. I take a deep breath. My doctor prescribed me progesterone. Maybe she already suspects that I'm having a miscarriage but doesn't want to say anything yet? Or she's trying to prevent one? Panic grips me.

I want to go for a run to shake off these worries, but I'm also concerned about moving around too much, jostling anything inside me that might be trying to hold on to my uterus. I put my hand briefly on my belly, and say aloud, "Hang in there," speaking to both myself and, I hope, my future child.

On some level, I knew it had been too easy—going off the pill and getting pregnant right away. I head to the sofa and lie down. Several times I'm tempted to call Jordan, but I resist. I would call my mom, but that's like calling the wind to a forest fire. I need to keep this contained. Before I can sink too much into worry, I pull up a meditation app on my phone. Listening to the calming woman's voice telling me to focus on my breath gives me a feeling of some control. I won't know anything until tomorrow, so I just need to get through the rest of this day.

Hours and many meditations later, I'm still lying on the sofa when Eric gets home after nine.

"What's going on?" he says, looming over me. "Are you okay?"

Ever since my doctor's call, I debated whether to tell him anything, and decided not to. He was so happy yesterday; why should I make both of us miserable with the unknown? So until I know anything conclusive, which hopefully will be tomorrow, I'm staying mum.

"Just tired," I say.

Eric looks at me with concern. "Are you sure? You're not sick or anything?"

I shake my head. "I'm sure." Swinging my feet over the edge of the sofa, I sit up. "How was your day?"

"It was fine," Eric says, slowly, and I can tell he's wondering whether to press me with more questions.

"That's good." I stand and give him a light kiss. "So, hey,

I'm going to head to bed now." *And wait for better news tomorrow.*

"Okay," Eric says, his voice still tinged with concern. "I'll be in soon too."

* * *

TWO DAYS LATER, my doctor calls again. "Allison, I need you to stop taking the progesterone, and I would like you to get blood tests for the next three days."

"Is everything okay?" I ask. "Am I...am I miscarrying?"

She sighs. "I don't want to jump to any conclusions yet. The blood tests will give us more information."

I do as I'm told and head to the lab. Each test has me more nervous than the last. The nurse thinks I'm afraid of needles, and I just nod mutely, not saying what I'm really afraid of. I go about my normal daily routine, minus any exercise, but something doesn't feel right. I'm still spotting, though what were small brown dots are now bright red. Yet my sense of smell has suddenly heightened, and my breasts are tender, making me feel like I'm still pregnant.

* * *

ON MONDAY, my doctor calls me and says, "I just want to make sure. Did you stop taking the progesterone?"

"Yes, I only took the one pill and stopped when you told me to."

"Okay, hon. So here's what's happening. Your HCG levels should either be rising steadily in case of pregnancy, or going down in the case of a miscarriage. But instead yours are going up and down. So I need you to come in for another ultrasound so we can get a better look at what's going on."

After we schedule an appointment for the next day, I end the call with a shaky hand and feel sick. I've been avoiding alcohol and coffee since my positive test, so I attribute some of my nausea to that. But right now I could really use a glass of wine.

Also, for someone who has wanted to have a baby for what feels like forever, I'm realizing how little I know about pregnancy. So far, I've resisted doing another Google search, since my earlier one didn't tell me anything conclusive or consoling, and I know how quickly I can spiral. But I can't hide my fears anymore. I need to let Eric know what's happening.

When he gets home that night, I give him the recap of my doctor's call. He seems as confused as I am.

"So, should we be worried? Are you having a miscarriage?"

I give him a sad smile. "I hope not, but maybe? I guess I'll find out tomorrow."

"What time is your appointment? I'd like to come with you."

"It's at one fifteen."

His face falls. "One fifteen? Shoot, I have a meeting with the bank at one for a loan for Wicker Park." He rubs his chin and then pulls out his phone. "Here, let me see if I can move it earlier."

"Don't do that." I put my hand on his phone. "Keep your meeting with the bank. That's important."

He looks up at me. "But your appointment is important. I'd like to come."

"I know, babe. But please don't reschedule your meeting

for this. You've been so excited about the Wicker Park location, and I don't want you to lose out on it."

He presses his lips together, and his eyes search mine. "But...but I want to be there."

I want him there too, but I know how hard he's worked to get his paperwork and business plan together to apply for the loan.

"It's okay. We're just doing another ultrasound to get a look, and she'll either confirm that I'm pregnant or having an early miscarriage." I reach out and squeeze his hand. "And if it's good news, I'd rather you come to the later appointments," I explain in what I hope is a positive tone.

Eric studies me for a second. "Are you sure?"

I nod. "Yes. You already have a lot going on, and this is just going to be a quick visit."

He searches my eyes, and then rubs the back of his head. A sign that he's resigned to my answer. "Okay."

I give him a kiss and a hug to reassure him.

* * *

AT THE DOCTOR'S OFFICE, I change into a gown, my fingers fumbling while trying to close the ties. When Dr. Kahn enters the room, she gets right down to business, saying, "Okay, let's see what we can see this time," in lieu of a greeting.

I lie down and she rubs the gel on my stomach. Then we look at the monitor together as she moves the wand around my belly. I can't make out anything definite on the screen, but I'm not sure if I would be able to, anyway.

"Hmm..." she says. "I'm still not able to see anything in

your uterus. Looks like we'll need the transvaginal ultrasound to get a better view."

She explains what to expect and what the difference is between the two, and that the second ultrasound will get a more detailed picture of all the organs around my uterus. I'm grateful for her chatter, but I'm only half-listening. Right now I just want to hear, "Aha! There it is."

I try to read her expression during the exam, but she is calm and focused. Even though she's not giving anything away, I can't stop thinking about how she's already labeled my condition as one of the difficult ones.

Suddenly she goes still while looking at the screen. She clicks on some images and then finishes the procedure.

Turning to me, she says, "I'm sorry to tell you, Allison, but it looks like what you are experiencing is an ectopic pregnancy."

I shake my head. "I've heard of that, but...but I don't totally know what it is?"

"It's when the pregnancy happens outside the uterus."

"Outside the uterus..." I repeat, confused.

"In your case, it appears the egg was fertilized in your right fallopian tube." She taps on an image on the screen, but it clarifies nothing for me.

"So what happens? Does it move into my uterus?" I ask.

"No, it doesn't move." She shakes her head, and I see the sympathy in her eyes. "It's unsustainable. A fetus can't develop there. And the more it grows, the higher the risk that you'll rupture your tube. It's a good thing you came in and tested early, otherwise this could have been a more serious issue." She pauses and takes a deep breath. "We have to stop the cells from dividing, so I want to give you a shot of methotrexate. It's a cancer drug, but it's been found to stop ectopic pregnancies before they can grow."

My head is spinning. "But how did it implant in my fallopian tube?...Are you sure?"

"This is it right there." She points to the screen again. "As for how it happened, that's a question for another day. There could have been a blockage in your tube. We'll test for that after we see what the shot does."

"Do I have to do the shot?" I ask, my voice high-pitched and panicky. "Can't we wait and see?"

"We can't wait. There is no way this pregnancy will survive. It's not viable, and it's dangerous for you. There's a high risk of your fallopian tube bursting and needing surgery."

Everything feels like a mistake. Should I be getting a second opinion? But the more I resist her advice, the more adamant she becomes.

"This isn't something we should wait on," she says. "It's not viable," she repeats, her eyes serious as she looks into mine.

I've been with her long enough to trust her expertise and her obvious concern for me and the situation. I look at the dot on the screen, and a lump begins to form in my throat as I realize I'm saying goodbye. Oh, how I wish I had let Eric come with me. Why did I turn down his offer? I feel incapable of making any decisions. Though it sounds like this is not a decision. There is only one choice.

I walked in pregnant, and soon I won't be.

After Dr. Kahn delivers the shot, she tells me to stay home and take it easy the rest of the day. I will have to come in for blood tests the next few days to make sure my HCG levels are going down. Then we will schedule a follow-up appointment to check my fallopian tubes for any damage or blockages.

When I walk out of her exam room, I see women in the waiting room with their round, full pregnant bellies and feel my own insides ripped apart.

I take an Uber back home, trying not to cry until I'm alone. Once home, I move cautiously around the loft, scared that my tube could burst. Maybe it's unlikely, but this is all news to me. I don't hang out with enough women who are pregnant or trying to conceive, and so I only hear the good news that people share. Dr. Kahn warned me I might be nauseous from the medicine, and so I make myself a preventive mint tea.

Eric texts: *What did the doctor say?*

I promised to text him after the appointment, and it's been an hour already. I want to call and tell him to come home, but I also don't want to worry him. There will be time enough tonight, and so I put off responding right away. But, in the meantime, someone should know what's happening. I feel like a ticking time bomb. I text Jordan: *Just got back from a doctor's appointment. Really need to talk. Are you free?*

When fifteen minutes go by and there's no response, despite my better judgment, I Google ectopic pregnancy and confirm everything the doctor told me. I've also learned that it isn't a given that the medicine will work, and there's the possibility that my tube could still rupture. I'm also not supposed to have alcohol for three months, as it could affect my liver, which makes me suddenly crave a glass of wine, but I take a sad sip of my tea instead. And the final kicker—I need to go back on birth control for six months because the drug causes birth defects.

In a panic, I call the one person who has to answer.

"Hello, darling. I was just thinking of you. Your father and I are going to a fiftieth wedding anniversary party downtown this weekend, and we were wondering if we could stay in your condo?"

"Hi, Mom. Sure, that's fine."

"Have you thought about what you're going to do with it? Now that you're married, it's just sitting there empty."

"I know. We haven't gotten around to anything on it. I was waiting until after the wedding, but I can't think about that now."

"Well, it's spring. It's prime time for the market—"

I cut her off. "So, Mom, I have some news. I just got back from the doctor."

"Oh?"

"Yes." I have her attention now, but I better tell her everything quickly, so she doesn't interrupt. "I had taken a pregnancy test, and it was positive, but I just learned today that it's an ectopic pregnancy. The egg was fertilized in one of my tubes. So they gave me a shot to keep the cells from dividing, and then we'll follow up with blood tests..."

At this point, I lose it and start to cry.

"Honey, I'm so sorry." She doesn't try to placate me, and I appreciate it.

"Thank you," I sniffle.

"Is Eric there?"

"No, I haven't told him yet. He had a meeting with the bank and then at his new location. And, I don't know, I just learned about all of this today and everything happened so fast. I need to get over the shock before telling him."

"Would you like me to come downtown? Just to sit with you?"

It's already getting toward dinnertime, and Eric is due to

be home around six or seven tonight. I'm not sure I want anyone else here when I tell him.

"That's okay."

"Then how about I call you in another hour to check in with you? See how you're doing?"

"That...that would be great," I snuffle. Another consequence of sitting here alone: I'm worried about side effects from the shot. "Thank you."

"Of course, darling."

After hanging up, I finally text Eric to ask if he can come home a little earlier tonight.

Is everything okay? he replies.

I'm not sure how to respond to that. Nothing feels okay right now, and I hate to deliver bad news via text.

Want to tell you about my doctor's appointment today. I'm sure he can read between the lines here. *Also, please could you pick up dinner on the way home?* Though I'm not sure either of us will have much of an appetite.

Then I cry myself to sleep on the sofa.

12

When Eric gets home, I fill him in on everything that happened at the doctor's office.

We sit on the sofa, our dinner getting cold on the kitchen table.

Eric just listens as I talk. He runs his hand down his face, his expression shattered. While Eric is usually pretty Zen, he can get a little stoic and quiet when stressed, and I can see him working through it all in his brain. He has always been my rock, but right now I need to be his. I'm glad I cried it out earlier because I'm able to keep it together while delivering the blow.

"I should've gone with you. I'm so sorry," he finally says.

"No, it's okay. I'm the one who said not to reschedule your meeting." I rub his arm. "I didn't know. We didn't know."

He sighs and puts his hand on top of mine that's on his arm. "How are you feeling?"

"I guess I'm doing as well as can be expected. I'm not in

pain, just sad and worried. And I won't know anything until my next blood tests."

"So, an ectopic pregnancy...Is this common?" he asks.

I shake my head. "Only two percent of pregnancies. And it was caught really early, so it was lucky I took a pregnancy test."

"C'mere." He opens his arms, and I fall into them, my head against his heart, and he rubs my back. We hold each other on the sofa for a couple of minutes while Eric processes the news, and then we reluctantly get up to eat our now-cold takeout.

After half-eating our dinners, we settle back into the sofa and watch a baking show, or I'm watching it while Eric is on his phone. I'm not sure if he's looking at work stuff or Googling everything about ectopic pregnancies, like I did earlier, but he is unusually quiet the rest of the night.

*　*　*

WHEN I WAKE in the morning, I smell fresh coffee, which is weird. It's already after eight, and I slept in because of yesterday's news and probably the medicine. I shuffle into the kitchen to find Eric examining the contents of the pantry cabinet.

"Hey, you," I say. "Aren't you supposed to be at work?"

Eric jumps a little at my voice, and I notice he has air pods in his ears.

He quickly pulls them out and says, "You're up? You should stay in bed. I can get you whatever you need."

"It's okay," I say. "What are you doing here?"

"I figured I should stay home in case you needed me."

"Awww, that's sweet." I wrap my arms around him. "But who is opening the Gold Coast?"

"Brian's got it, and Meg is going to come in today, too, to help cover."

"You didn't have to do that." I squeeze him a little more tightly, feeling my muscles relax, knowing I won't be alone with my thoughts today. Yet, I worry I'm being selfish. "But don't you have a lot going on with getting the new properties up and running?"

"Don't worry about that," he says, and kisses the top of my head. "I wasn't there for you yesterday when I should've been. And, also, you should be taking it easy."

"I am." I let go of him to get a glass of water. "Other than going out for my blood test, I'm just going to work from here today."

"When is that? I can drive you."

I can tell he's trying to take back some control and is still feeling like he let me down somehow, even though he didn't. While I'm a wallower, Eric is a doer, so I say, "That would be great. I was going to do it after lunch."

Even though Eric insists that I stay in bed, I set up shop on the sofa for the morning, while he takes over the kitchen. He says he was inspired by the show last night and wants to test out some new baking ideas. I hadn't realized he'd been paying attention.

"I haven't made anything new in a while, and I've had some cool menu ideas, but no time to test them out. And I really liked some of the flavor pairings last night, like lemon and thyme, and orange and ginger, to update our scone selection. And maybe we do a dessert, like strawberries and cream but with a coconut cream. Though I would need to keep that light..."

And my husband is off. In the same way that I need running to clear my mind, Eric is a stress baker. Considering his big plans for the day, I ask if I can help.

"No, you stay put," he says. "But you can be my taste tester."

* * *

ALL MORNING WHILE WORKING, I keep having intrusive thoughts. It's hard not to feel like something was my fault. Like maybe I did a yoga move I shouldn't have. Maybe my jeans were too tight the day my egg tried to make its way down. I can't shake the feeling that I failed my baby in some way.

During the drive to the lab and back, Eric and I don't talk at all about the pregnancy. It's like neither of us wants to remind the other. Instead, he talks about what he's baking, and I tell him about issues I'm having with coordinating an event. Neither of us mentions the elephant in the car. And while I thought I'd be relieved not to be alone and think, avoiding talking about it is even worse.

In the afternoon, after the blood test, my mom calls to check in on me. Funny how not too long ago it was me calling my mom every day to check in on her once they went back to suburbs. She also reminds me that she and my dad will be in town tomorrow, and if I like, she can come by earlier and visit with me. I say yes.

Between my husband's manic baking and trying to hide my own grief and anxiety, I want him out of the loft. I've never felt this way before, and it scares me a little. And when I tell Eric that he should go to work tomorrow because my mom is coming over, his shoulders visibly relax and the lines on his forehead smooth like he just got a Botox shot. Is he relieved that I won't be alone or that he, too, won't have to pretend in front of me?

* * *

During the last few weeks, my mind laced with worry and now sadness, my focus has been scattered. I forget to follow up on things with my business, and Kate has had to ping me more times than necessary to ask how projects are going. Finally, I call her.

She answers on the first ring. "Hey, what's up, Allison?"

"Hi, Kate. First, I want to apologize that I haven't moved faster on the Donnelly project. I just sent them another email to find out when they could best use new volunteers for their Dream Academy."

"Okay, thanks. The client asked me about it again today. So I'll let them know we'll get back to them soon."

"Great. And, hey, I'm also calling because I won't be able to attend the Food Depository event with Kirkland. I'm having some health issues. Is there any chance you can go in my place?" I squeeze my eyes shut while I say this. Kate hates being in charge of these events.

"Sure," she says, "but what type of health issues are you having? Is everything okay?" Worry tinges her voice.

"Oh, thank you," I say, and then hesitate, stalling my news, not really wanting to hear it aloud. "So, well, it's kinda serious and hopefully everything will be okay, whatever that means."

"Whoa, you're scaring me now."

I take a deep breath. "Last week, I was diagnosed with an

ectopic pregnancy in one of my fallopian tubes. So I'm not supposed to be doing any exercise or exerting myself."

"I'm sorry to hear that," she says. "My sister had one. I guess they're really common. Anyway, she went on to have two kids, so you'll be fine."

Even though I know she's trying to be supportive, I'm a raw nerve these days, and so her casual remarks feel like tiny dismissive daggers poking at my pain.

I constantly feel an ache on my right side, but I don't know if it's real or imagined. I didn't feel it until I was diagnosed, so I suspect it's in my head. I keep my phone on me at all times because every day I live in fear of my fallopian tube possibly rupturing and internally bleeding to death while I work at home alone. But I'm also grateful to be alone. I've been sleeping in later and going to bed before Eric gets home, sleeping from eight to eight. The few times he crawled into bed when I was still awake, I pretended to be asleep. I don't want to share my fears with him until this is over. And to top things off, we can't even start trying again for another six months and I'm already thirty-nine.

I want to tell her all this, but, instead, I say, "Yes, hopefully everything will be okay. I'll know more next week. Anyway, thank you again for standing in for me at the Food Depository. Since I wouldn't be able to help with the food boxes, I don't want to have to explain why or make something up, you know?"

"Of course. And, hey, before you go. Since you mentioned Dream Academy, I've been wanting to talk to you more about programs with kids outside of tutoring."

Oh, that's right. I dropped the ball on that research with everything else going on. "What about Girls Run It? Their training season starts soon," I suggest.

"Yeah, we already have clients who do that, so I'd like something different. Something still physical maybe, but where volunteers can do it year-round. Not everyone's meant to be tutoring kids," she adds, chuckling.

"Okay, yeah, I hear that. I'll come up with something this week or next and get back to you."

* * *

AFTER TALKING TO KATE, I realize how much I've let slide in my business these past weeks, and I buckle down. I go through each of my projects and review their status, making a task list. One of those tasks is The Cauldron. With two new locations opening, I should ask Eric whether he wants to do a soft launch or any special opening day promotions. I make a note to discuss it with him.

Once I start tackling the list, the momentum keeps me going, and worrying about work is a good respite from everything else. When Eric gets home around nine thirty, I'm still at the kitchen table on my laptop.

"You're up!" Eric says when he walks through the door.

I smile at the surprise in his voice.

"Yeah, I've been catching up on work. I talked to Kate today, and I realized how much I've been ignoring my business." I twist my neck from side to side to get out the kinks from hunching over my laptop for the last several hours. "How was your day?"

Eric drops his keys on the hallway console and then pulls out a chair at the table.

"Same old at the Gold Coast. But it looks like I might be able to move up my opening date at Lincoln Park."

"That's great!" I say.

"Yeah, it is. And I just learned that I can apply to set up a parklet there, which will be perfect with summer coming up." He smiles.

"Even better!" I reach out and grab his hand, hoping my enthusiasm will mask the tightness in my throat about the fact that I've been avoiding him in order to deal with my fears.

"Yeah. So I need to start thinking about hiring a staff and getting them trained."

"Also," I say, "we should talk about your opening day. Do you want to do a soft launch or a big event? Any advertising, press releases, etcetera."

"Good call. Let me think about it." Eric's grin widens. "So, I take it you had a good day?"

I force a smile and nod. These last weeks, no day feels like a good day, but I can at least acknowledge this one was productive.

"That's wonderful, baby." Eric squeezes my hand. "Are you heading to bed soon?"

"Soon. I've been trying to think of kids' organizations, outside of tutoring, that could use volunteers year-round. I suggested some of the community garden programs and Girls Run It, but Kate wants something that volunteers can do regardless of the season."

"What about my CrossFit box?"

"What about it?"

"We could use more volunteers for the at-risk youth program. Right now it's just me and Jonah, and I know I'm going to be busier these days."

"But don't you have to be a certified coach?"

"Yes, but it's a weekend program for Level 1, and I bet the owner, Kelly, would do it in exchange for a certain number of volunteer hours. Maybe free certificate training in exchange for a six-month, once-a-week commitment?"

"Oh, wow! That's a great idea. Would you mind feeling her out for me first, and then doing an introduction?"

"Sure. Next time I see her, I'll ask."

"Thanks. And since you just did my job for me, I think I'll turn in."

In bed, I snuggle up to Eric to make up for the past couple of weeks. We're a team and I'm lucky to have him. And with that thought, I drift off.

13

A week later, my doctor calls to let me know that the bloodwork confirms that I'm no longer pregnant. She gives me a number to call to schedule a hysterosalpingography (HSG) test which will tell us if there are any blockages or damage in my fallopian tubes. I call the number right away to make an appointment for the following week.

The whole ordeal has lasted only three weeks, but it's felt like the longest three weeks of my life.

After my doctor's call, I have complicated feelings. All the fear of a possible rupture and internal bleeding is gone, which is a relief. But I'm sad because even though the pregnancy wasn't viable and wasn't, in a technical sense, a baby, I still feel it was my baby. And I don't know what to do with these conflicting emotions.

On Saturday morning, instead of heading out for my usual run, I had asked Jordan if she'd like to take a walk. Even though I have the all-clear, physically I still feel a little fragile. Other than my doctor, the only people who know what's been going on with me are Eric, my mom, and Kate.

Normally, I tell Jordan everything, but lately we've been missing each other, and when she finally replied to my first "can you talk" text, I no longer wanted to talk about it. I just needed to get through it.

A little after eight, I meet Jordan at her place in Streeterville, and we decide to walk to Navy Pier and then along the lakefront, but south toward the Loop instead of north toward the more residential Lincoln Park. We wanted to beat the heat and the crowds, and so this area of the trail, that's normally filled with tourists during the day, is mostly people out exercising, walking their dogs, or claiming prime beach space.

A woman around our age runs by with a stroller, and my stomach clenches. But as she passes, I notice a toy dachshund in the seat with its tongue hanging out and ears flapping in the breeze, obviously living its best life. I audibly let out the breath I was holding, and Jordan looks at me strangely.

"I don't think I can handle seeing families and baby strollers at the moment," I explain to her.

"Oh? Why's that?"

I fill her in on the last few weeks.

"Oh my god, Allie, I'm so sorry. How are you feeling now? And you know, I mean physically and emotionally. And I'm so sorry I wasn't there. I've been so wrapped up in my own stuff."

"I'm okay, I guess. And don't be sorry. I wanted to tell you, but it got to a point where it was so hard that I couldn't even talk about it. Not even with Eric."

"How's he been?"

"I guess he's okay now. It was a shock for him too, and I hated telling him. He offered to go to the doctor's appointment with me, but I said it wasn't necessary. Then he felt horrible he hadn't been there too, so he started hovering around the loft, which...I know he was trying to be there for me, but..." I trail off.

"But what?"

"I don't know. After I told him, we didn't really talk about it. And so his presence was actually more oppressive than when I was alone with my grief. Is that weird?"

"Not weird. He might just be processing the loss in his own way," Jordan says.

"True. But it's just that he's usually so up front with his feelings. I don't want him to have to feel strong for me. This is something we're doing together."

I tell her about Eric's manic baking, trying to lighten the mood. "But to be honest, when my mom offered to come over, I immediately took her up on it, so he'd feel better about leaving me alone at home."

Jordan stops. "Hold up. You were *happy* to have Theresa's company over Eric's?"

I grimace and nod.

"Huh," she muses.

While I feel a little guilty, the entire time my mom was over she was in top Theresa mode, criticizing the organization of my medicine cabinet (what she was doing in there is still a mystery) to the placement of our living room furniture, and generally offering advice that I didn't ask for.

Jordan continues. "Are you sure he's trying to be strong for you? Because it sounds like you're trying to be strong for him. He might just be following your cues. You guys need to talk. You're both grieving. I couldn't imagine if anything like that happened to me."

I give her a sideways look. Jordan doesn't want kids, so

this wouldn't happen to her. But I let it go as her trying to sympathize with my situation.

"He was just so happy when I told him I was pregnant. His face was like..." I put on a huge smile and hover my hands by the side of my cheeks, miming an even bigger smile. "And so I feel almost cruel now. Like, I talked him into starting a family with me, and now I put him in a place to mourn. The guilt is killing me, and I can't let him see how depressed I am."

"Oh, Allie, no—"

But I continue talking over her. Now that the floodgates have opened, things I didn't even know I was feeling start to come out. "Also, this is just one bump in the road. So many other women have had it worse with years of infertility and miscarriages, so I also feel guilty being depressed, when I should be grateful that I was even able to get pregnant the second I went off the pill."

"Hey, none of that 'hashtag grateful' toxic positivity shit. This is sad. It's a death. And you need to mourn."

I stop walking. Jordan turns toward me, and I give her a hug.

"Thank you," I say, as tears well in my eyes. Her words are what I've been feeling, but I needed someone else to say them aloud to me.

"And you should talk to Eric about it. He probably needs to talk about it, too. You promise?"

"I promise."

She pats me on the back, and we detangle ourselves and continue our walk.

"So what happens next?" she asks.

I tell her about my upcoming HSG test, and then say, "And on top of this, because the drug they gave me can cause birth defects, I can't try to conceive again for another three to six months. Six to be on the safe side."

"Oh, wow."

"Yeah. Plus, because it messes with my liver too, I can't drink for three months."

Her eyes go wide, and she shakes her head in horror.

"Right?!" I say. "After all this, I can't even have a drink!" I look up at the sky and shake my fist.

Jordan laughs. "Well, I'm right there with you for those three months."

"What do you mean?"

"So I have some depressing news of my own," she says. "Though not on the same level, it's still pretty upsetting for me."

"Oh no, Jor, what happened?" I've been so lost in my own bubble of despair that I also wasn't there for my friend. No wonder we'd been missing each other.

She takes a deep breath and dramatically exhales. "I failed my licensing exam."

Whoa! Jordan never fails at anything, so I know this is an enormous blow for her, and I'm shocked she didn't say anything to me earlier. I didn't think to ask because when she took the bar, I remember it took about four months for her to learn if she passed.

"I'm sorry to hear that," I say, putting my hand on her shoulder and giving it a little squeeze.

"Yeah, it's a bummer. I knew forty to forty-five percent of people fail the test, but—not to be conceited—I didn't think I'd be one of them."

"Ouch. That's a pretty steep curve, though. So what happens now? Do you take it again?"

"Yeah, I have to wait until October before taking it

again," she says. "But I'm also trying to get as many clinical hours in as possible, so it's going to be a challenge to squeeze in my studying."

"Oh, wow. But, hey, you got this. And if I can do anything to help you, let me know."

"Thanks." She takes a deep breath and then jabs me lightly in the ribs. "Anyway, guess we'll be having a pretty sober summer."

* * *

BEING that it's Saturday night and wanting to take Jordan's advice, I decide to surprise Eric by making him dinner. When he gets home, I have the table set, candles lit, and our wedding playlist on quietly in the background.

"Wow! When you said you were making us dinner tonight, I didn't expect all this," he says, gesturing to the table. "Why, thank you, wife."

"You're welcome, husband," I joke back to him, and give him a kiss when he joins me at the stove and looks over my shoulder to see what's cooking. "I went pretty decadent tonight—spaghetti carbonara. I got a bottle of red too, but it's all for you."

"You don't mind?" he asks, tilting his head toward the wine bottle.

"No, I got it for you. Go for it."

Eric opens the bottle and pours himself a glass. I put the finishing touches on the salad and then serve us each a plate of pasta.

When we sit down, I raise my water glass and say, "To us."

Eric clinks his glass against mine. "To us."

We each take a sip, and he says, "Good toast."

"Thank you." I laugh.

Then we spend the rest of the meal catching each other up on our days.

After we finish our dinner, and the dishes are in the dishwasher, I join Eric on the sofa.

"So, hey," I say, taking one of his hands. "I wanted to talk to you about the last few weeks."

"Yeah?" Eric looks a little nervous.

"Yeah. I guess I wanted to check in to see how you're feeling with everything. I know we didn't talk about it much, and that's on me."

"Oh, no, come here." He opens his arms and invites me over. I lean against him and put my head on his shoulder. "Nothing was on you. I didn't know what to say, and so I was trying to follow your lead. I thought maybe you didn't want to talk, so I didn't."

Okay, that makes sense and was also what Jordan speculated; but, he still hasn't said how he's feeling.

"So?" I press a little. "Are you sad?"

"I'm sad for you because I know you were depressed. But really, I was more scared than anything. I had been so wrapped up in my fears about my dad that I hadn't thought past that. Then when you told me that your tube could rupture, it made me realize, oh my god, something could happen to *you*. And that really freaked me out."

I'm quiet, hoping he will say he's sad about losing our baby.

"I just don't want to lose you," he says instead, and he holds me closer to him.

Maybe Jordan was wrong. Eric isn't grieving. And even

though his words are loving, I feel a little alone in my sorrow.

"What a way to celebrate the first month of marriage, huh?" I say.

"Yeah." Eric gives a rueful laugh.

We sit for a few seconds in silence. Then Eric says, "Do you want to watch anything?"

"Um, sure. It's too early to go to sleep. What do we have?"

We watch a couple of episodes of *Succession*, but I'm not totally sure either of us are enjoying it.

ERIC DRIVES me to the doctor for my HSG test and stays in the waiting room. After our discussion on Saturday night, we haven't really talked more about the pregnancy or what will happen during the test today. Eric's mind has been on his new coffeehouses, so most of our conversations have revolved around that. In the car, he asked whether I was nervous, and I said, "A little." But mostly I'm hoping for answers.

In the exam room, the nurse and lab technician explain everything to me about the test beforehand. And then during the test, the doctor talks me through each step. "I'm injecting the dye now. It might sting a little."

The procedure itself isn't as scary or painful as I was expecting, and I can see my tubes on the monitor.

"Good news. I don't see any blockages," the doctor says. "No polyps or fibroids."

"That's good," I say. "But then, why did this happen?"

"There might have been something there, or your tubes

were inflamed. The risk goes up after age thirty-five. But sometimes there's no obvious reason."

I know I should accept the good news that my tube is fine, and I won't need surgery. But deep down, I want a reason so I can prevent this from happening again.

THE NEXT MORNING, I decide to head outside for my first run in over a month. I drive over to Lincoln Park. I miss living and running by the water—this lakefront path is an old friend. Today, the turquoise waves slap lightly against the concrete barrier and the sun warms my shoulders. As I run, I think, *I'm fine. I'm healthy. Eric and I will try again in six months. Everything is fine.* I repeat this as a mantra as I run next to the lake, making my way toward Oak Street Beach. Another runner with a stroller passes me, and I briefly glance inside. A little boy who looks around a year old smiles at me as they pass. And suddenly my heart clenches. I stop running and burst into tears.

Nothing is fine after all—and I'm not sure it ever will be.

14

——————

Back at home, I throw my keys on the hallway table and shudder. Bursting into tears in public at the sight of a stroller? What was that? Even though Jordan verbalized the permission I needed to hear to grieve, I still can't help but feel my emotions are out of proportion to what happened. I was pregnant for such a short time, and it wasn't a traditional miscarriage, so how can I be so devastated?

This morning, before Eric left for work, he asked, "How are you feeling today?" Lately, I answer with a shrug or an "okay." Today it was a little of both. He then usually just gives me a hug; we haven't talked more about it since our one big talk. While Jordan said she thinks he, too, is grieving, I think he's already moved on and his focus is solely on work. When I ask him how he's doing, he'll say, "I'm meeting with the landlord in Wicker Park this morning," or "I'm interviewing new baristas today." So I feel like I can't be depressed in front of him because he has a lot going on, and I'm relieved most days when he's out the door before me or comes home while I'm already in bed.

Maybe it's the medicine. Maybe it's hormones. Maybe it was the worry during those weeks of not knowing what was happening inside me. But I'm definitely going through a different grieving process than Eric, and I don't want to keep avoiding him so as not to burden him with my sadness.

Instead of lessening my grief, each passing day has me feeling stuck and unable to move forward. Every morning, I make a to-do list, which is usually a carryover from the day before. I'll tackle only my most urgent work tasks and let the rest pile up until I receive a gentle client reminder, like the one from Kate asking, "Where are we on the Donnelly project?" Just keeping up with these commitments uses all my energy and leaves me with none left over to do any truly creative, stellar work.

Part of me wishes I could go into an office, because being alone with my thoughts is too distracting. I'm uncomfortable working at The Cauldron these days, so the other day I tried working out of a Starbucks nearby our loft (even though it made me feel like I was "cheating" on Eric). As soon as I settled in with a latte and opened my laptop, a group of mothers clad in designer athleisure wear and pushing the latest in stroller technology walked in. Once they had their coffees and took over a table, they began a conversation of one-upmanship in who was the most sleep deprived.

"At least your Asher is sleep trained. This guy kept me up all night," said one.

I glanced over at the mother who was speaking and saw her hint of a smile. She rubbed her baby's downy head and looked at him with such love and tenderness in her eyes, I could feel my own threatening to spill with tears. I quickly packed up my things, almost tripping on one of the stroller's wheels in my rush out the door.

Recalling this embarrassing memory, I shudder again as I pour a large glass of water, and then sit at the kitchen table and open my laptop. I tentatively type "how long does grief last after an ectopic pregnancy" in the Google search bar. Some general articles come up describing the five stages of grief, which I'm already aware of and don't seem that helpful. *I need a timeline, people*, and so I keep on scrolling. One article says that if you're still feeling this way four to six weeks after the loss, you should talk to a medical professional. Since I'm past the four-week mark and nearing on the sixth, this doesn't give me any consolation; rather, it seems to confirm that I'm an aberration. That leads me to seek out other women's stories, many of which are much more intense than my own—stories of infertility, multiple ectopic pregnancies, emergency surgeries. Soon I've moved on from personal essays to the wild west of the baby boards, each story getting worse, and each woman's grief raw and palpable through my screen.

My phone buzzes with a text, causing me to jump, snapping me out of my scrolling stupor. I pick it up and see that it's Eric.

Just a reminder that I'm going to my CrossFit box this afternoon and hope to talk to Kelly. But then I'm headed back to work. Will be home late. Have dinner without me.

Eric's text wakes me up to my situation. I work with kids too—I can't be tearing up at the mere sight of them. I quickly click out of the baby board website, as if all the bad outcomes I've read on there are contagious, and close my laptop.

I've been here before, though—different circumstances, but same headspace. Deep down, I know the only way to move forward is one step at a time. And I know exactly where the answers lie and where I should go to take that first step. I grab my car keys and head to Wicker Park and the closest bookstore.

* * *

THE LAST TIME I felt hopeless, a few years ago when I had lost both my fiancé and job, I made my way through it to the other side thanks to the self-help aisle at my local Barnes & Noble. Now that I've moved to a different neighborhood, it's time to make new friends with a new place.

The indie bookstore I walk into is bright and welcoming with blond wood bookshelves and macrame-covered pots filled with leafy green plants hanging from the ceiling. It's small but looks well-stocked. It also has a café that serves wine and literary-themed cocktails alongside its coffee offerings, and I sigh audibly, remembering I can't drink alcohol for the next few months.

I make my way through the bookcases, searching for a "Self-Help" sign. After a quick perusal through those shelves, I find books on grief, but most are too general. So I head to the Health & Pregnancy section. Seeing all the books on having a healthy baby discourages me, making me feel worse, like I failed. I try to remind myself that there will be a time to read these, but that time is not now. Today, I need to let go of this constant heaviness pressing me down.

There are some books on miscarriage, with images of empty cradles and broken hearts on the covers, and I almost can't bear to read their pages. Again, that's not exactly my situation, and I'm starting to fear I'm going to walk out of here empty-handed. Then I see a slim book with a blue pastel cover and flower illustrations and the title

Expectations. Reading the back cover, I learn that the author also suffered an ectopic pregnancy and couldn't find any books on the subject, so she wrote her own. Holding her book in my hand feels like hope. Also, flipping through it, I see some active steps to take to help recover from grief along with journal prompts at the end, so I pick up a new Moleskine notebook before I head to the cash register.

Though the café looks tempting, this is a book I should sit at home and read alone. I need to feel broken without any witnesses. After telling Kate, I don't want to go through another well-meaning friend's comments. I need someone who knows what I've been through.

And I can't burden Jordan with this. Though she's now a therapist, she can empathize with me, but she can't fully understand. She would do anything to avoid getting pregnant, and this is one of those times when I know she supports my choices but also doesn't relate to them. Plus, she was already there for the big breakdown, and she has her own stuff going on. As her friend, I need to give her space to focus on retaking her licensing exam.

ONCE HOME with my purchases and knowing Eric won't be home till late, I light a candle, make some tea, and sit on the sofa with a throw blanket over me despite the warm weather. I then proceed to blow off the rest of my day to read this book.

The book has me alternately weeping and nodding along. When the second line appeared on that pregnancy stick, my baby was real to me. And, worse, I had no choice but to say goodbye. Kate's comment "You'll be fine" and her assurance that I'll get pregnant again weren't what I needed to hear. I still missed out on *this* child, and the perfectionist in me can't help but feel I failed *this* child. When I looked at that dot on the ultrasound screen, I was saying goodbye to all the future memories I would have with this baby. While I understood that the doctor kept saying the pregnancy wasn't viable, it didn't make me feel any less pregnant.

Because the author experienced her own ectopic pregnancy, I listen to her. Physically, her story is more horrific because, after years of infertility, she didn't know she was pregnant and her fallopian tube burst. She ended up in the emergency room and with only one functioning tube after surgery. She assures me that I will not feel this way forever and says to focus on things that give me joy. The only healer is time.

After all the tears and reading, I'm too worn out to do the journal prompts, but one catches my attention: write a letter to my baby and do a release ceremony. It feels too final right now, and since I can't try for another few months, I'm going to hold on to my grief for a little longer. I decide to save the idea for a later date. Also, I just spent the afternoon reading and need to get back to the real world. Knowing I can't sit on this couch forever until the feelings pass, I check my phone to see what I've missed.

While I was reading, Eric texted me:

Just talked to Kelly about the volunteer program and she loves it. I'm coaching tomorrow and she'd like you to come and observe.

I text back: *That's great! What time? Can I bring Kate?*

4 p.m. And of course on Kate.

I email Kate at work.

Tomorrow I'm going to observe one of the CrossFit kids'

coaching programs for the volunteer program. Want to join me? We can get coffee and catch up?

I haven't seen her in person for almost a month. Even though she doesn't know I've been avoiding her a little, this email is my peace offering.

She writes back, *Sure. What time?*

I send her the time and the address, and she responds, *See you there.*

I put the book along with my journal into my nightstand drawer, to return to at a later date.

15

When I arrive at Eric's CrossFit gym, or box, as he calls it, I immediately spot Kate sitting in the reception area, looking down at her phone. My muscles tense slightly, since this is the first time I've seen her in person since my ectopic; but I'm also excited about hanging out with her. Her wry humor is the distraction I need from my intense emotional mood swings these days. I just remind myself to avoid any baby-related topics.

As I approach her, I say, "Hi, Kate."

She looks up and smiles. "Hey, you. Good to see you." She puts her phone in her bag and stands.

"Same here." I'm about to say it's been a while, but stop myself, not wanting to bring up the reason it's been a while, i.e. my pregnancy.

"So, what is this place? Are you sure it's safe for kids?" Kate gestures at all the weights and equipment, which look like torture devices.

I laugh and say, "Eric loves it. And since he's been volunteering here for years, I have to assume the kids love it as well."

She shakes her head. "Have you ever tried this workout?"

"Yeah, but let's just say, I don't love it as much as Eric does."

When Eric and I were first dating, I joined him for a few workouts at his gym. Though I appreciate the cathartic release of the exercise called the Wall Ball, where you repeatedly slam a ball against the wall while doing squats, the Olympic-style weightlifting wasn't my thing. I prefer my workouts to be more meditative, like running or yoga. So while Eric and I occasionally enjoy running together, we go our separate ways after that.

I spot him in a far corner of the gym, and he waves at us, grinning and looking in his element. I wave back, and Kate chuckles. Between Eric's grin and Kate's company, a smile spreads across my face, and already this afternoon feels like the perfect antidote to spending all of yesterday alone on the sofa.

"Let's head over there," I say, and I point to where Eric is standing, watching over the kids as they start to gather and sit in a circle.

During some of those early morning workouts with Eric back in the day, death metal played on the speakers, and the combination of that and the crashing sounds of shirtless, bulked-up dudes dropping heavy weights made for an intimidating atmosphere. This afternoon, no music is playing and there are more kids than adults in the gym. The loudest sounds are the children's laughter and Eric's direction. Kate and I settle in at a little distance on some foam plyo boxes, so as not to interfere.

"What type of animal do you want to be today?" Eric asks

the kids, who are all now standing in a circle after their warmup.

"Snake!" "Lion!" "Guinea Pig!" Ranging in age from five to twelve, some of them shout over each other, while the older ones tend to be quieter.

"Okay, okay." He puts his hands out. "Who here wants to be a bear today?"

Several of the kids growl and some giggle. Soon Eric has them crawling on the ground between two cones, while Kate and I watch. A lot of the kids are super agile, climbing ropes, doing pull-ups, and running in between various exercises such as planks and squats.

Kate says to me, "Eric is really great with them."

"Yeah," I agree. "He's wonderful with his nephews, too."

At the moment, Eric is coaxing a little boy who looks to be around seven to climb the rope. The boy has been quiet this whole time; I can tell he's not sure about the rope and keeps looking up to where it's attached to the ceiling. With Eric's encouragement, he takes his first tentative step. With each knot he ascends, he looks down at Eric, who says, "Don't look at me. Just focus on the next knot. You're doing great."

This is my husband in a nutshell—always encouraging others. I can't believe someone like him was ever worried about being a father. The boy's big brown eyes light up as he heaves himself up to the next knot, his little sneakers rising to rest on the last one. I have to restrain myself from cheering him on, even though the other kids are already clapping. When he reaches five knots and finishes his climb, Eric says, "Everyone give James a high five!" The others gather around him, slapping their hands against his. Their positive energy is infectious, and it takes all my strength to tuck my hands under my legs and merely observe rather than rush over to join them.

After the hour-long session, I say a quick goodbye to Eric before talking to Kelly.

"I'll see you tonight," he says and gives me a kiss, and then turns to Kate. "So good to see you, Kate. Thanks for doing this, you two."

Through Kelly's office windows, I see her on the phone, so Kate and I wait outside until she hangs up and then waves us in with a bright smile. Kelly is a petite picture of health with clear blue eyes, sun-kissed blond waves, and tanned biceps that rival some of the men's. Eric told me she runs the box with her husband but that the youth program is her passion.

"Please sit down," she says. "It's so great to meet you both!" Her smile and eyes shine with enthusiasm.

"Same here," I say. "Eric has told me so many nice things about you."

"Oh, Eric. He's the best. I don't know how he does it all."

"I could say the same about you. Business owner, mom, and volunteer, and you can probably lift twice your body weight."

She laughs and waves away my compliment. "Okay, let's get this love fest over and get down to business."

I introduce Kate and explain how we're looking to expand her PR clients' volunteer options. "Allison is great at matching volunteer programs with corporate sponsors," Kate says. "So I'd love to learn more about your youth programs and what type of volunteer opportunities you have."

"Of course!" Kelly says.

Kelly gives us the background on the program. Some

CrossFit members who were teachers turned her on to the idea. They first tested the program with older, more rebellious kids at school, the ones who seemed to need an outlet. "CrossFit teaches the power of hard work and applying oneself, and the kids started seeing results and getting validation in a supportive environment, something they might not otherwise get from the best sources," Kelly tells us. Her teacher friends reported that the kids' time at the box was helping them focus and get better grades in school, too.

"We teach our regular CrossFit Kids to three groups, kids, pre-teen, and teens," she counts on her fingers, "and those are with our staff coaches. For the free programs, we have the kids split into two groups, ages five to twelve and thirteen to seventeen, and we're able to do only one class a week for each group since we don't have enough regular or volunteer coaches. But as you can see, the kids really enjoy it, and if we had more volunteer coaches, we could expand both the size and scheduling."

"Kate and I will see what we can do," I say.

Kelly beams. "You two are angels!"

Before we leave, Kelly and I agree to meet up in a couple days to hammer out more details, so I can put a presentation together for Kate to give her clients.

* * *

"I LOVE THIS IDEA," Kate says, once we've ordered at a nearby coffee shop and sat down to discuss next steps. "And as long as I don't have to work out, it suits me. I can already think of other clients that this would be a good fit for." She pauses and then rolls her eyes. "If only because the free coaching certificate gives them bragging rights."

"Ha! That's great." Then I shake my head. "All this time Eric has been volunteering, why didn't he tell me any of the stuff Kelly just shared? This is a perfect match for what I'm doing with my business."

Kate laughs. "Eric Caulder, man of mystery."

I laugh too. "Right?"

We're briefly interrupted by a server bringing us our coffees.

"So what's up with Jordan these days?" Kate asks after taking a sip. "I haven't seen her in a while."

"You know, I haven't seen much of her either. She's been swamped studying for the exam."

Kate tilts her head. "I thought she already took that. Did she fail it?"

Oops. Me and my big mouth. I'm sure Jordan doesn't want me blabbing about her problems. I don't say anything more, but give Kate a look, followed by a grimace.

"Oh, wow. I'm shocked," she says. "That's not like her."

"I know. She was shocked too. But I guess there's a steep grading curve, so a large group of test takers are set to fail. And, you know, as you get older, these things are harder."

"Still. That sucks."

"Yeah. She's already signed up to take the next one in the fall and is buckling down the next few months."

"Good luck to her. But what a bummer to have to spend a Chicago summer studying."

"Jor will get through it. After law school and practicing corporate law, she's no stranger to pressure." I carefully change the subject. "Speaking of people we haven't seen lately, how's Suzy?"

Kate gives me the latest office gossip, and as we chat, in

the back of my mind, I'm already working out how I plan to attack Kelly's volunteer program.

* * *

THAT NIGHT I wait up for Eric. I thought I'd be sad being around kids this afternoon, but instead I'm feeling energized and purposeful again.

As soon as he's through the front door, Eric asks, "How was the meeting with Kelly?"

"Great! She's amazing!" I gush, recounting some of the details of our meeting and plans. "But you know who else is amazing? *You.*" I give him a playful poke in the chest. "You were so wonderful out there with those kids. Especially with that little boy, James."

"Ah, yes. James is great. He's quieter than the other kids and not as naturally athletic, but he also works harder at it than them. And that's what it's about, the effort." Eric smiles. "I love that little dude."

I think of James's eyes when he was looking at Eric, and smile too. "I think the feeling is mutual," I say, as Eric pulls me in for a hug.

16

———————

After meeting with Kelly, I was so excited that I spent that evening and the next day putting together a rough presentation for Kate and her clients. On this late Friday morning, I meet with Kelly again at her office to fill in holes in the presentation, such as more details on the certificate program, volunteer hours, and time commitments to make it all work.

Once we've exhausted our business discussion, I bring up something that has been on my mind.

"That little boy with the curls and big brown eyes in the program..." I start to ask her.

"James?" Her eyes soften at his name.

"Yes. If it's not confidential, I was wondering what his story is?"

Her face takes on a somber look, and she presses her lips slightly before speaking. "He's a foster kid, and he's been in the program now for six months. It's really sad. He lost both his parents in a car crash."

"Oh no! That's terrible," I say. Though I recognize that all these kids are in the program because of something terrible. "But what about the rest of his family, like aunts or uncles? Grandparents?"

She shakes her head. "Both his parents were only children, and unfortunately no grandparents, or close enough family who could take him in." She sighs. "I think the foster family sends him here hoping the physical activity will help him make new friends. He's so quiet that I wonder what goes on in his mind. He's only started talking a little more a couple months ago, and that's due to Eric. He's figured out how to get James out of his shell some."

"That's encouraging to hear."

With every word Kelly says about James, a hot feeling expands in my chest and my eyes burn with the prickle of holding in tears. *I'm going to do everything I can to help these kids*, I promise myself.

* * *

When I get home that afternoon, I'm greeted by a barreling ball of yellow fur on four legs jumping on me.

"What the?" I exclaim, putting my hands up.

"Thank god you're home. I was just about to call you," Eric says, rushing toward me. "Down, Finlay!" And he gently grabs the dog's collar to nudge him off of me.

Once I recombobulate, I say jokingly, "So is he friendly?"

Eric laughs. "To a fault."

Finlay pulls away from Eric to lick my hand, and I bend down and give him a rigorous petting on his head. "Well, hello, Finlay. And where did you come from?"

Eric tells me how his sister sprung the dog on him today. "Elaine adopted Finlay for the boys as a surprise, and it turns out the surprise is that Liam is allergic to dogs. The boys wanted to keep him, but Liam's wheezing is too bad. So she tried to get my mom to take him, but my mom can't handle Finlay's energy."

"So she just brought him to The Cauldron? With no warning?"

"Yep." Eric shakes his head. "What was I going to do? He was tied up outside because we can't have pets inside, so I had to bring him home. She doesn't want to take him back to the shelter because, thanks to the internet, she worries the boys would find out and she'd be mean mom of the year. So now I'm tasked with finding him a home. But I can't take care of a dog right now." Eric starts pacing in the living room.

As he is talking, Finlay has gone from licking my hand to licking my face and I've fallen in love. "It's fine. I can take care of him until we find him new owners."

Eric stops and looks at me. "You're sure you're okay with this?"

"Yes, don't worry about it. I haven't had a dog since I was a kid, and that was Barry, our old Basset Hound. It'll be fun." And then I say to Finlay in my for-dogs-only voice. "Yes, it will. Yes, it will." When Finlay jumps up, putting his front paws on my shoulders and licking my face again, I can't help but think he agrees.

"Oh, boy, it looks like I have competition," Eric says, laughing. "Thank you. I really appreciate this."

* * *

"YOU GOT A DOG?" Jordan says, as she approaches me and Finlay outside The Cauldron. Her eyes are wide looking at the pair of us.

I grin. When I invited her out for a walk this Sunday morning, I didn't tell her about the dog because I was looking forward to seeing her surprised face. "Not really. This is Finlay."

I spent Friday and Saturday trying to keep the rambunctious seventy-pound Finlay entertained. The shelter guessed he's only two years old, so he has a lot of energy. And since neither Jordan nor I are drinking this summer, I thought I'd ask if she'd want to do a big catch-up walk this morning. I'm hoping Finlay will appreciate the long walk and then take an even longer nap this afternoon.

"Hey, Finlay." She puts her hand out so he can sniff it, and then she gives him a good rub behind the ears. "So, whose dog are you?"

"He's Eric's nephews' dog, but it turns out Liam is allergic. So he's staying with us until we find him a good home."

Jordan looks at me. "Judging by your smile, I think he's already found his *fur*-ever home."

"Ha, ha." I smile even more and reach down to pet Finlay. "Though I'm afraid you might be right. We'll see. I'm not sure Eric is up for caring for a dog since he's so busy with the new places...but I'm totally smitten."

Eric comes outside. "Speak of the devil," Jordan says. "Hey, Eric. How are you?"

"Hey, Jor," he says. "Good, good. You?"

"I'm okay. And, hey, congratulations on your new dog." She grins.

"So I see you met Finlay." Eric laughs. "Hopefully you two will get some of his energy out on your walk. Speaking of which, can I get you a coffee for the road?"

Jordan shakes her head. "Thanks, but no thanks. I

already caffeinated at home, and I don't want to have to pee during our walk."

"Gotcha."

"A little too much information there, Jor," I laugh. "A simple 'no, thank you' would've sufficed."

She puts up her hands and shrugs. "Well, I could use the bathroom right now before we leave."

"Come with me. I'll give you the key," Eric says, shooting me an amused look.

It's around ten when Jordan and I finally start walking. We head north toward Lincoln Park so we can walk in the park first and then make our way back along the lakefront.

Even though it's still technically spring, the early June sun is shining, and it's already creeping to 80 degrees out. As we walk, I notice Jordan's face is puffy, and she looks a little tired. She's wearing an oversized sweatshirt with shorts. I'm in a T-shirt and my running leggings, and I'm already warm.

"Aren't you dying in that?" I ask her, pointing to her sweatshirt.

She shakes her head. "Nope. I'm fine."

"Okay," I say. Though the bead of sweat at her hairline begs to differ.

"So, how's the study prep going?" I ask.

She takes a loud, deep breath and exhales. "It's fine. Just trying to fit it in with my clinical hours. I might finish most of my hours by the end of this year. So I could be ready to either start or join another practice next year."

"Wow! That's great!"

"It is," she says, turning to me and smiling. "And then I can finally say goodbye to my current advisor. Seriously, if anyone needs therapy, it's her. Under all the beaded necklaces and peasant blouses, there lurks some serious OCD and control issues."

"Oh yeah?" I laugh. "What's the latest?"

She fills me in on her advisor's annoying micromanaging behavior, which, funnily enough, sounds like some of the partners she used to complain about at her old firm.

"And what about you?" she asks. "How are you doing?"

"Same old, but I'm okay. Just keeping busy, you know. And now, this fur ball helps."

She nods. "Just keeping busy, huh? And that's working?"

"Well, I may have also read a book about grieving a miscarriage…"

"Oh?" Jordan's ears perk up. "Go on."

I give her a quick summary of the book and how it helped to learn about someone else's emotions and experience, and reassured me that everything I've been feeling was normal.

"And because I know this is something up your alley," I say. "At the end, it recommends writing a letter to the baby and doing a release ceremony."

"Did you do that?"

I let out a breath. "Not yet. I just read the book last week. And so I'm sort of focusing on the other stuff, the stuff that makes me feel good, like connecting with friends, exercise, nature, etcetera." As I say this, I sweep my arm toward us and then to the large trees lining the path. "And while it's not a constant ache right now, every day the sadness still hits me without warning. I think I need a little more time before I'm ready…" I trail off, thinking, *to really say goodbye.*

"Would you have Eric do it with you?"

"Nah." I shake my head. "After our one conversation, we haven't talked about it since. I feel like he's already moved on. But for me, maybe because it was something that happened to me, and it's something I wanted for so long, I'm taking it harder, you know?"

She nods. "Also, your body went through something. As women, what we have to deal with when it comes to hormones and pregnancy is no joke."

"Right?" And because I'm trying not to dwell on it too much, I change the subject. "Anyway, I have a new project with Eric's CrossFit box and that's what's been keeping me busy and out of my head this week."

I tell her about the new volunteer ideas for Kate's clients, and how Kate and I observed one of the volunteer sessions at Eric's box. "It was fun to see Eric in action. And he was so good with this one little boy." I fill her in on James and his backstory. "I was kind of worried working with kids would amplify my grief, but it's been the opposite. It's been giving me a renewed sense of purpose."

"That's great! Do you think you'll volunteer there too?"

I shake my head. "I still have my Girls Run It commitment, and so I think I'll stick with running. Also, my services are best used trying to get them volunteers so they can expand their programs." Finlay lunges for a squirrel, and I almost fall over before I can pull him back. "Plus, I have this guy to take care of now. It's better that Eric and I keep our separate schedules."

I update her on how his other coffeehouse openings are going, and then our conversation turns to television shows. She tells me the latest on *The Bachelor*, *Real Housewives*, and *Below Deck*.

Much as I enjoy Jordan's recaps, I ask, "How do you have time to watch all this? I thought you said you're swamped studying."

She pauses and is quiet for a second, and when I look at her, her face has turned red and I feel a little bad, like maybe I shouldn't have reminded her.

"Well, you know," she falters, as if caught out, "it's more about reviewing the same information rather than memorizing new stuff. So I can do it while the TV is on in the background." Now she changes the subject. "So what are you thinking about Finlay? Are you keeping him?"

I grin at her in response.

She laughs. "That's what I thought." She bends down to pet him. "Mr. Finlay Caulder, welcome to the family." He licks her hand in response.

17

In less than a month, the CrossFit kids' program is a go. When Kate presented it to her client, several of their employees immediately signed up for volunteer training. I also pitched it to some of my smaller clients in the form of donations and scholarships. And even though it's not necessary, I've been finding time to visit and observe the kids' CrossFit when Eric is coaching. It's been under the guise of learning more about the program, so that I'm comfortable pitching it to clients for donations, but really I love watching Eric with the kids and can't help imagining what he'll be like with our own.

It's also been almost six months since my mom's heart attack, and she's back to full health. My parents have had dinner downtown with us a few times and met Finlay, our newest addition. My mom complains when he jumps on her and sternly says, "Manners, Finlay," but I can see the affection in her eyes. I'm pretty sure my parents would be up for pet-sitting anytime. My mom even bought him a ridiculous collar and called him her grand-dog. Thankfully since my ectopic, she simply asks how I'm doing and doesn't ask if or when we're going to try again.

Eric and I decided to play it safe and wait the full six months so as not to risk birth defects, but I still feel a sense of urgency—not to replace anything, but because I've waited so long that I'm now thirty-nine, which means that even if I get pregnant right away, I won't be a mother until I'm forty. Much as my mother's constant nudging about freezing my eggs used to annoy me, I now thank god I did it when I was thirty-five.

Life has a rhythm to it right now. And with summer, Girls Run It training, all of our activities, and my business going well, I'm out of the loft more and engaging with others. Plus, Finlay gets me outside and out of my head on a regular basis. And though I'm still sad, I've made it through the constant fog of grief. I'm glad not many people knew. Kate told Suzy, and she sent me a beautiful card. I wouldn't say I'm feeling back to normal, but I think this is just going to be normal for a while. Overall, I'm ready to write that letter to my baby.

So one afternoon, while Eric is at work, and I don't have any pressing work commitments, I sit at the kitchen table and light a candle. I had planned to write this in my journal, but instead decided to buy a beautiful piece of stationery. Though Eric and I hadn't officially discussed baby names, I had some secret favorites. But instead I go with what my mother always calls me and write:

MY DARLING,

I know you're gone, and I have missed you every day since. I want you to know I will remember your life. When I saw that positive pregnancy test, you were real, and you were my child. I wanted you so badly, and you will always be my first baby. Thank you for visiting me for a short time. I'm sorry I will not get to know you in this life, but you will be in my heart, always. I wish your future brothers and sisters could have met you. If it is anything I did, I am sorry.

This is not a release letter. This is to remember you and honor your life.

This isn't a goodbye. This is a thank you.

I will carry you with every breath I take.

I will love you always.

Yours, Mom

I PUT down my pen and take a deep breath. Tears stream down my face and one drops onto the page. I lean back, not wanting more to ruin the paper. Though I was raised Catholic, I'm not a particularly religious person; but I say a prayer to God to keep my baby safe. And once the tears stop, I fold the letter in half and blow out the candle. Finlay comes over and scratches at my leg. His signal that he needs to go outside.

"Now? Really?"

I find a tissue and wipe my eyes, glad I'm not wearing makeup today. Finlay is already at the front door, doing his dance, so I quickly grab the leash and my keys.

* * *

WHEN FINLAY and I return home, Eric is sitting at the kitchen table holding the letter in his hands. In all the years we've been together, I realize I've never seen Eric cry before. And now here he is, tears rolling down his cheeks, and I don't know what to say, and so, surprised, I blurt, "What are you doing home?"

I unleash Finlay, who runs over to Eric, his favorite, even though I'm the primary caregiver. Finlay seems to have better instincts than me and he jumps up and tries to lick Eric's face. Eric looks up at me and says, "I didn't mean to read it. It was on the table, and I didn't know what it was, so I picked it up."

Now I rush to his side. "That's okay." I hug his shoulders, and he puts his arms around my waist. I had meant to put the letter in my nightstand, folded up and placed in the grief book for my eyes only. But in my haste to get Finlay outside, I figured I'd do it once I got back.

"Oh, Allison, I'm sorry." Eric's voice breaks.

"I'm sorry too. Maybe I should have written this letter with you."

He shakes his head and pulls back to look at me. "No, it's not that. I guess I didn't know how hard this has been for you. This..." he looks at the letter, "this just broke my heart."

I sit down next to him. "I've just been surprised at how sad I've been. And so I read this book about a woman who also had an ectopic pregnancy. And, anyway, she recommended writing a letter to your baby to help release some of the grief, and so I did."

"How are you feeling now?"

I take a deep breath. "I don't know. Instead of constant grief, I've been feeling a little better. I think time and being busier outside of the loft have helped." Finlay puts his head on my knee, and I pet him with one hand. "And, of course, this furry cutie has been helping...and so it felt like the right time to try this..." I wave my other hand at the letter.

Eric reaches out and grabs my hand. "I love you. A lot. You know that."

I give him a small smile. "I know. I love you too." Then I lean over and kiss him.

More tears threaten to arrive, but I'm feeling too cried out, and so I say, "So why are you home? It's only four."

Eric sets down the letter. "It's not important. I needed to cool off a little. The apartment building in Wicker Park wants to renege on the lease. Apparently, someone came in with a large cash offer and the leasing company wants to take it."

"Oh no! Can they do that?"

"Yes and no. They'd be breaking our contract, but my guess is the penalty is probably a small price to what they're being offered. I'm going to need to get my lawyer involved, and so I was going to call him from here once I got home."

I nod. "Is there anything I can do?"

Eric gives me a sad smile and shakes his head. "You worry about you."

"Okay, well, let's focus on the Lincoln Park reopening. I know we talked about a soft launch, but it's summer and you'll have parklets, so let's do a big event. Leave the details to me."

I take the letter from Eric, and put it in my nightstand where I wish I would have before. I stay in the bedroom to give Eric a few minutes to himself before he can call his lawyer.

Once he finishes his call and because he's already home, I suggest we grab an early dinner in the neighborhood before he heads back to the Gold Coast to close up. Over dinner, we talk about how things are going at his CrossFit box, and our favorite topic, James. And I catch him up on

Girls Run It, which is in full swing again. Then we simply catch up with each other. And I realize that Eric and I haven't had a real date in months. This is the most we've talked in I don't know how long. Granted, we've both been busy, but I still feel a little guilty for avoiding him while dealing with my grief. And so after we stroll back home after dinner and before Eric takes off for The Cauldron, I say, "I'll wait up for you." And he gives me the kind of deep, lingering kiss that he hasn't for a while and that I've sorely missed.

WITH THE NEW VOLUNTEER COACHES, Kelly has been able to increase the at-risk youth programs from one to three times a week. I continue to visit regularly to see how the program is coming along, and to watch Eric and the kids. Today when I go to the CrossFit gym, I'm still a little raw after the letter incident. I also notice that one of the regular kids—my favorite one—is missing. So when I see Kelly, I ask her, "Where is James today?"

"He had a visit with prospective adoptive parents today." She beams.

"Oh?" My heart flutters, but I'm not sure what the emotion is.

"Fingers crossed it works out for everyone. Even though he's still young, it's harder when they're past the baby and toddler stage."

"Right," I say, "fingers crossed." I know I should be filled with happiness and hope for the kid, but my grief makes an unwelcome appearance again. So I quickly say, "Good seeing you, and talk soon." And I make a hasty exit for the door.

In the safety of my car, I wait until my heart rate slows down. Then I text Eric, *Did you know James is being adopted?*

A couple minutes go by, and Eric doesn't respond. He might be in the shower. So I turn on the car and head home to walk Finlay, and wonder why good news suddenly has me feeling sad all over again.

18

After taking Finlay out for his walk, I set up my laptop on the kitchen table. Within five minutes, I've gotten up multiple times to get water, make tea, and sort through the mail, all while Finlay snores loudly from his dog bed. Deciding that I'm too antsy to spend the rest of the day working at home, I pack up my laptop to head over to The Cauldron. The Lincoln Park reopening is only a couple of weeks away, and now that we're going to do a bigger launch for it, I want to brainstorm some new ideas this afternoon and get feedback from Eric.

* * *

When I arrive, Brian is behind the register. "Hi, Allison. Good to see you."

"Hi, Brian. Good to see you too," I say, walking up to the counter. "Is Eric back yet?"

"Not yet, but he should be soon. In the meantime, what can I get you?"

I order my usual latte and head to my usual table to wait for my drink.

When Brian brings over my latte in a large cup, I stare at it for a second, and then look back at him.

"That's not my usual…" I start.

"It's not. Live a little. Try new things," he says, grinning.

"I'm not opposed to trying new things, but…" I pause, looking down at it again and then up at Brian. "It's green."

Now he smiles. "Yes. It's a matcha latte. If you don't like it, I'll make your regular latte."

"Oh, okay." I take a small sip, expecting a strong grassy flavor, but instead taste a sweet, earthy milkiness. "Wow, that's delicious! And I like the sweetness. What is that?"

"I put some honey in it. I have another version with coconut sugar."

"Ha! You sound like Eric." I grin.

"Hey, he's not the only creative around here." Brian looks mock offended, then continues, "I have a cousin who just started a business importing tea. So I'm talking Eric into expanding our tea selection to more interesting and higher quality products."

"Oh yeah?"

"For example, there's Butterfly Blue tea that brews into a blue color, and a jasmine flower tea that would bloom in a glass bowl," he says. "I'm also thinking of doing seasonal drinks, like a pumpkin-spice chai in the fall. We're going to add them slowly to the menu and see how it goes."

"How did I not know this? We should be updating the website with these and putting them out there on social media."

"You haven't been in that much lately." He gives me a sympathetic look.

I nod. Of course, Eric told him what's been going on.

"Still," I say. "Eric, should've mentioned something."

"Yeah, well, he's been pretty tied up with the Wicker Park nonsense." Brian grimaces.

I grimace back. "True."

I pull out my phone and take a photo of my only slightly disturbed tea, and then ask Brian for a short description of the matcha so I can post something.

The door opens and we both look up to see Eric. "Hey, you two," Eric says. "This is a surprise," he says to me.

"Yes, well I wanted to work on some more details for the Lincoln Park opening and figured it'd be easier to do it here, so I could ask you questions."

"That's great. Whatever you need." He leans over to give me a quick kiss on the cheek. Then it's all business.

For the next few hours, I work on the launch for The Cauldron, asking Eric questions as he passes by. I also update the website with Brian's latest menu offerings, and sketch together a social media plan to introduce the new teas.

When I finally check my phone, I see that Eric had responded to me earlier about James.

I heard. I hope they're good people. He deserves the best parents.

But neither of us mentions it again.

* * *

NOW THAT FINLAY is officially a member of the family, my mom gifts us some dog training lessons near our place. Luckily, Finlay hasn't shown any destructive tendencies, and I haven't found any chewed up shoes. Granted, I may have gone overboard in buying dog toys and bones to keep him occupied, so he hasn't had the chance to move on to our belongings. Also, I've been trying to teach him basic commands like sit and stay. So far, he seems to be a quick learner and gets it right more times than not. But taking him for a walk is as much an exercise in patience for me as it is physical exercise for him. The leash pulling is the most annoying thing; and once he's on a scent, it's hard to get him to listen. That and he likes to jump on every new person he meets. So, obedience school it is.

When Eric and I arrive at the first training session, we're greeted by a lot of barking and chaos. There are about ten other dogs of various sizes and breeds in the class, and there's a lot of "Down" and "Stop it" followed by each pet's name. The big and medium-sized dogs all want to greet each other, and are as rambunctious as Finlay; whereas the little ones stay close by their owners, while barking incessantly, trying to sound ferocious. Westminster Show it is not.

As we're waiting for class to start, another dog jumps on Eric. "Whoa, buddy," he says as the dog's owner simultaneously says, "Down, Henry!"

As Henry jumps back down and turns to Finlay and another dog, Henry's owner jokes, "You can see why we're at obedience school."

Eric laughs, then looks at the owner and the woman standing next to him. He's tall with brown hair and she's shorter with long, wavy brown hair with caramel highlights.

"Mark? Adeline?" Eric asks. He laughs again, this time in surprise. "What a small world. What are you doing here?"

"Eric? Hi!" Adeline says as Mark simultaneously says, "Good to see you again."

We all laugh at the coincidence. Adeline and I greet each other with a quick hug and hello.

A long, long time ago, before I met Eric, he briefly dated Adeline. But then she moved from Chicago to San Francisco, where she started dating Mark, another lawyer in her office. When she moved back to Chicago, Mark came with her. And since this is before Eric and I were dating, I may have jealously thought Eric and Adeline had a thing going until we ran into her and Mark at a restaurant. Mark and Eric used to be workout friends a few years back, but we haven't seen them lately.

"We miss you at CrossFit," Eric says to Mark.

"Yeah, well, life has gotten busy," he says.

"That, and a global pandemic," Adeline interjects. As she's talking, Henry jumps on me. "Down, Henry," she says, tugging on his leash. "Sorry. He's a jumper."

"We have the same issue." I laugh, reaching down to pet Henry. "What kind of breed is he?"

"We don't really know," says Adeline. "From his coloring, he's obviously a beagle mix, but with his large size we're not sure what the mixed part is."

A woman at the front of the room interrupts our chitchat, clapping her hands to get our attention.

"Welcome to the Basic Obedience and Manners class," she says, loudly, over the barking and conversations that quickly die down. "This class is for canines, though I'm sure we know many humans who could benefit from it as well." Several people around the room chuckle.

After she has everyone briefly introduce themselves and their dogs, we then work mostly on basic commands like "sit" and "stay," which Finlay does well, and "down" and "come," which leave room for improvement. The training all seems to be treat-based, and I can't help but feel my own stomach grumble near the end of the class.

When the class is over, Mark turns to us and says, "Addie and I were going to get some dinner a couple blocks away. They have outdoor seating and dogs are welcome. Would you like to join us?"

Eric and I look at each other, and I nod, smiling. "We'd love to," I say.

"Lead the way," Eric says.

* * *

OVER DINNER, with the dogs settled in under the table, the four of us talk about how we all became recent dog owners.

"We took in Henry to foster from PAWS," Adeline says, "but he quickly became a failed foster because we instantly fell in love with him and adopted him."

Eric and I laugh and share our similar story. Eric explains the incident with his nephew and sister that brought Finlay to us. "We were supposed to find Finlay a home, which ended up being ours," he says, rolling his eyes for comic effect.

"Henry was a little more premeditated," Adeline says, still laughing after hearing our story. "We're planning to have a family, and wanted to see how we'd do with taking care of another living creature."

"And in the meantime, he's enjoying being Addie's first baby," Mark says, reaching over and squeezing her shoulder. "What about you guys? Kids?"

I take a deep breath. "Not yet."

Eric grabs my hand under the table and saves me. "Allison and I just got married a few months ago," he says.

We talk briefly about the wedding and the conversation moves on, as we all discuss what we've been up to the last couple of years. Mark and Adeline are lawyers at a large firm in Chicago, but they're also both writers, and Adeline recently published her first novel.

"It was my pandemic project," she says. "Something I'd been working on for many, *many* years."

It also turns out they're at Jordan's old firm, and I make a mental note to mention this outing to her. Eric talks about his coffeehouses, and I talk about my startup, which is now a full-fledged business. And since Mark and Eric have the CrossFit connection, I tell them how I'm helping recruit volunteers for Eric's box to assist with the kids' programs.

"That's fascinating," Adeline says. "You know, I'm on the pro bono committee at Gilchrist. While we offer free legal services to those in need, our firm is also committed to community service, like volunteering with the Boys & Girls Club of Chicago. And so we're always looking for different volunteer projects, especially for our summer associates. We should talk."

"I would love that," I say.

* * *

ON THE WAY HOME, Eric jokes, "Who knew dog training would give you a new client?"

"Right?" I say. "You never know."

"So, hey," he says, swinging my hand that he's holding. "Were you okay with the talk about kids?"

I frown. "It was fine. But thank you for steering the conversation away."

He squeezes my hand.

"Overall, it was a nice evening, and it's been too long since we've socialized with a new couple," I say. "So, I'm looking forward to seeing them at the next training session."

"Same here," Eric says. "It made me realize I need something to get my mind off of work lately."

Of course as soon as he mentions work, he starts telling me about the latest troubles with his Wicker Park location. I can't stand hearing him sound so defeated, and I say, "Is there anything I can do to help?"

He shakes his head. "No, but just you asking is enough."

When he stops in the street and leans in to give me a kiss, I secretly make a pact with myself to be a better partner and do anything I can to lessen his work worries.

* * *

ADELINE MAKES good on her word and emails me the next day. We meet for lunch on Friday by her office.

Over our salads, she tells me about the different charities and programs her firm has worked with in the past.

"We already have our summer associate programs lined up for this summer, but I'm always open to new ideas. Since they're not licensed yet, they can't assist on many pro bono cases other than writing memos, so it's good to get them out of the office."

"That's perfect since there are a lot of seasonal programs that just run during the summer," I say. I tell her about Girls Run It and the community gardens. I also tell her more about the at-risk-youth CrossFit program.

"What are the kids like?" she asks. "What's their story?"

I explain how it started with some kids who were acting out in school and didn't have a great support system at home. I also mention how some kids are from foster programs. As I'm talking, I can see Adeline's eyes getting misty. She finally waves her hand in front of her face.

"Sorry about that. Discussions about kids can bum me out," she says. Then she sighs and admits to me that she and Mark have been actively trying to start a family. "We've done two rounds of IVF, and I don't want to do it again. I just turned forty and the statistics show that only eight percent of women over forty are successful. It's so hard on the body, and with work, and with those statistics, is it worth it?"

"I'm sorry," I say, swallowing down my own recent disappointment.

"Thanks." She takes a deep breath. "Anyway, so we decided we're going to adopt. We've applied to different organizations and just finished all the adoption classes. Now it's a waiting game."

"Oh, that's so amazing! Good for you." This makes me think of James, and I briefly wonder how life with his new family is going.

"Yes. Though it's a whole different type of stress. Now it feels even more out of our hands. We could be parents tomorrow, or have to wait a couple of years." She smiles weakly, and I nod in sympathy. "But that's why we adopted Henry. To distract ourselves. Though if our parenting skills are anything like our dog parent skills, we're in trouble."

I laugh. "I wouldn't know, but I think the two are different. What's the worst thing that can happen if you spoil a dog?"

"True." Now she laughs. "Sorry if I'm oversharing. It's just the topic of kids, you know?"

"I do." More than she knows.

"So, are you guys planning to have a family?" Adeline asks.

"Yep. That's the plan. But we're still enjoying our honeymoon period," I say, and leave it at that. Adeline's struggle puts things in perspective for me; she doesn't need to know I got pregnant on the first try or that I already froze my eggs as a backup plan.

After our lunch, I promise to put together some various volunteer and sponsorship options for her to review, and then we can set up another meeting when she's ready. "Until then, see you at dog training," I say.

In another few months, Eric and I can start trying again. That knowledge has been getting me through these last months. This is the longest stretch we've gone without sex, and while a relationship is built on more than physical closeness, I'm starting to miss him.

19

―――――――

Eric is the baker in our household, and I'm the chef. But during those bleak weeks, I wasn't motivated or inspired to do much cooking. Now that the weight of grief is slowly lifting and the farmers' market on Saturdays is bursting with fresh produce, I've found myself experimenting more in the kitchen. It's been hot these past couple of weeks, so I've been putting together salads with whatever vegetables and fruits I picked up that look good. And I've been packing lunches and sometimes dinners for Eric on the nights he gets home late, so he can just pull something out from the refrigerator.

This morning I took stock of the fridge, and with the tomatoes, corn, and peaches I bought over the weekend, I decide to make a Southwestern salad. So after my run, I stop at the grocery store to get the remaining ingredients. As I'm in the produce aisle inspecting an avocado, my phone rings. With my free hand, I pull it out of my pocket and see the name and number of the fertility clinic where I froze my eggs. I answer it.

"Hello?" I say.

"Hello. Is this Ms. Allison James?"

"Yes, this is she." It's Caulder now, but I don't correct her.

"Hello, Ms. James, I'm calling from the Reed Fertility Center with unfortunate news. Our refrigerator malfunctioned over the weekend, and we lost a portion of our clients' frozen eggs and embryos. I'm sorry to inform you that your eggs were part of the lot destroyed. You'll be receiving a letter in the mail, but we wanted to reach out..."

Her words sound garbled as my head throbs, and I squeeze the avocado in my hand as if it's a stress ball. It gives way and bursts, covering my hand in green goo. The woman across the produce aisle looks at me as if I'm unstable and hurries away with her cart.

"Ms. James, are you still there?" the voice on my phone says.

I awake from my stupor. "Yes, I'm here."

"We are waiving all storage fees to date, and will be offering free IVF and other discounted medical services, depending on your situation. The letter will detail your options, and we encourage you to call your physician to talk about your next steps."

"I don't understand. How did it malfunction? What happened?"

"The technical details will also be explained in the letter. But, in short, the alarm system failed and didn't alert us to the temperature change. We are talking to the manufacturer."

She sounds robotic, like she's reading from a script, which she most likely is, and I know I won't get any more details out of her.

As I end the call, I want to scream. A shelf stocker warily

hands me a paper towel and holds out a bag for me to drop the mashed avocado into.

"Sorry," I say, sheepishly, releasing it and taking the proffered paper towel.

He nods, his eyes wide. "It's okay. You don't need to pay for it."

"Thank you," I manage, and feeling like I'm about to hyperventilate, I quickly exit the store.

Standing outside on the sidewalk, the harsh sunlight hitting my eyes, my whole body starts shaking. My shock quickly turns into anger. *What the fuck, universe?*

I hurry back home to call my lawyer.

* * *

"My eggs are gone!" I shout into the phone to Jordan. "What do I do?"

"Hold up. What do you mean your *eggs* are gone?" she says, sounding confused. "Then, you buy some more?"

"No, not food eggs. *My* eggs." I quickly tell her about the phone call from the clinic.

"Oh my god! Holy shit!" she says, sounding as riled up as me now. "What you *do* is you call your lawyer."

"You're my lawyer," I cry.

"I *was* your lawyer friend. Now I'm your therapist friend," she clarifies. "But even when I was an attorney, this wasn't exactly my area of expertise." She takes a deep breath. "But my guess is there will be a class action lawsuit, so you might not have to hire a lawyer at all."

"But my eggs? All gone," I say, my voice a whimper now.

"I know, I know. I'm sorry," she says, sympathetically. "They should reimburse you for the procedure, too."

"They were my insurance policy."

"But that was before you and Eric started trying. You're still young, and so it's not like you can't try naturally. And you know you're not infertile."

"I don't totally know that. Cause it's not like that worked out." Also, thirty-nine isn't as young as thirty-five. And now the fear that I'll have another ectopic and have to wait another six months to try again is always at the back of my mind. But I can't say all this aloud because I'm scared I'll end up spiraling again, just when I was starting to feel better.

Jordan sighs. "This is a tragedy, yes. But it's not the end. Plenty of women get pregnant at our age. And if you're so worried, you can always freeze your eggs again."

I hear the tiniest hint of exasperation or something else in Jordan's voice.

She has her own problems right now, and I'm dragging her into mine.

"I'm sorry, Jor. I know you're supposed to be studying."

"No, I'm sorry. I feel for you. I really do. I'm just..." She pauses without finishing her sentence. "This exam has me worked up, and I'm not sleeping well."

She sounds exhausted, and I feel for her too.

"Is there anything I can do to help? Another flash card session? Bring you a home-cooked meal? Errands? You name it."

"Thank you, but there's no need. You're the best, Allison. Again, I'm sorry I'm not myself these days."

We end the call by reassuring each other that everything will work out for the best for both of us.

* * *

ONCE I'M off the phone with Jordan, my rage has died down, but only slightly. I pace around the loft; Finlay is alert and curiously watching me from his dog bed. Not wanting to scare the dog, I sit at the kitchen table. I don't want to bother Eric during the day. Kate isn't the best ear for this, and everyone else has their own life. How is it that I'm constantly surrounded by kids yet have so few close friends who are parents? With each child, my old friends' lives have faded away from mine, and they're too busy juggling careers, managing their kids' schedules, and keeping up their homes in the suburbs. The same life I thought I'd have with Neil. *Ugh.*

I take a deep breath and repeat Jordan's words to myself.

Other women who were counting on their frozen embryos or delaying motherhood, for them, yes, this is a tragedy. But Eric and I are going to try again. It will be fine.

"Everything is going to be fine," I say to Finlay. He cocks his head at me. I don't quite believe it either.

So much for perspective.

Still needing someone to be angry along with me, I call my mom and tell her what happened. She is suitably incensed.

"We'll sue!" she says, and even through the phone I can hear her hand slapping the marble countertop in her kitchen. "Your father is out, but when he comes home, we'll call our lawyer."

My mom's immediate response, guns a-blazing, finally tempers my anger a little. I tell her how the clinic said they would refund the storage fees and would offer new services at a discounted rate.

"Maybe we wait for the letter, see what they have to say, and then decide whether to call the lawyer."

After hanging up with my mom, I manage to get myself together for a scheduled Zoom call with the Girls Run It director. But immediately afterward, I Google how a fertility clinic could lose its eggs and find a bunch of news stories about similar incidents. I know it's the exception rather than the rule, but still, I had never heard of such a thing until today.

"They might want to put this in the pamphlets," I mutter to Finlay.

I go on a Google rampage, reading about other lawsuits, what my options are, and what the clinic should do. While I'm not feeling super keen on the idea at the moment, Jordan is right—I can always freeze my eggs again. I Google "freezing your eggs at 39." Just as I thought, there's a big jump between freezing your eggs at thirty-five versus thirty-nine. According to these websites, to have a decent chance of having a baby from frozen eggs, they will now have to retrieve three times the number of eggs. Which means three times the cost of the procedure, and three times the cost of storage. I'm not exactly in a place where my bank account can take this hit; but if I don't do it before I'm forty, the articles tell me my chances of having a successful live birth from frozen eggs go way down.

I'm deep into doomscrolling at the kitchen table when the front door opens.

"What a day," Eric says as he walks in.

"You can say that again," I answer, my voice heated. Instead of lessening my fury, the internet stories have fueled it, and I'm as worked up as if I just got the phone call a few minutes rather than several hours ago.

Eric regards me for a second and then slumps down in

the chair beside me. "So, it's official. I lost the Wicker Park spot."

"Oh no! I'm so sorry. Wasn't there anything your lawyer could do?"

Eric shakes his head. "Nope. He tried, but it's game over." He sighs. "They'll give me a payout for breaking the contract, but I just have to accept it wasn't meant to be."

"That *sucks*," I say, getting up from my spot to sit on his lap and envelop him in a hug. "But remember, we're going big on Lincoln Park. We'll do such an amazing party that people in Wicker Park will want to come in especially for your coffee."

"Thanks, Al." He kisses my forehead. "So, what's for dinner tonight?"

Now I feel even worse. Lost in my own ruminating, I forgot to make us dinner.

"I'm so sorry. I meant to make something, but time got away." I stand up. "Here, I'll put together a salad now."

I throw together a quick version of the salad I had planned, adding in extra beans to make up for the missing quinoa and avocado. While we eat, Eric looks so defeated that I don't want to dump on him. So I save my bad news to tell him tomorrow.

* * *

ERIC IS ALREADY GONE in the morning before I wake up. While I brew a pot of coffee, I open my computer and scroll through emails. The name of the fertility clinic pops out at me. I resist the urge to click on it until I pour my first cup.

Then I say, "Here we go," to Finlay and he gives a small

tail wag from his dog bed. I'm now officially one of those people who talk out loud to their pets.

I open the email and read. As promised, the letter describes what happened to the refrigeration unit in more detail. There was a mechanical failure, liquid nitrogen wasn't automatically administered and so the temperature increased, and then the alarm failed to sound, alerting them to the change. The letter says they're not asking me to release any claims, and they've initiated an investigation with the manufacturer. They promise to refund me for the full storage time. They write that, "our patients are our priority," and to make any appointments to determine what the next steps should be. It then ends with a hotline number to call for more information.

After this disaster, I don't plan to use them for medical services. And after yesterday's Googling, and at this stage in my life, I'm not sure about freezing my eggs again. I'm still enraged though, perhaps because I'm coming off the ectopic pregnancy. But it feels like a fresh punch to the gut, and so I just try to muddle through my day as best as I can.

TONIGHT, after dog training class and dinner again with Mark and Adeline, on the walk home, I finally say to Eric, "Sooo, I got some upsetting news yesterday." I recount the whole story to him, starting with the phone call from the clinic and ending with the letter this morning. I'm calmer than earlier today, but I still have an edge to my voice. Eric is quiet while I get the entire story out, along with my thoughts on the next steps.

"And they're offering discounted future services," I tell

him. "Well, I *certainly* won't be going back to them. The next time I see them, I hope it's in a courtroom." I huff. In the afternoon, I also received some emails from personal injury lawyers. Word must have leaked.

"Are you sure you want to be part of a lawsuit?" Eric says, wearily.

I whip my head toward him. *Where's the anger?* I wonder.

"Something should be done," I retort. "I mean, if not for me, think of the others."

I guess, as Jordan said, I hadn't really been injured. But again, it was the promise of things to come. I had no answers on what caused the ectopic, and so in a way it's cathartic to have an entity to lash out at.

When Eric doesn't respond, I continue, "Hopefully we'll be okay because we're going to try again. But even so, I'm pushing forty. Look at Adeline and Mark. What if we end up having issues and have to do IVF? I could've used those eggs." The statistics from yesterday's Google search are still fresh in my mind.

Eric puts his arm around me, and we walk the rest of the way home in silence. I tell myself he's been dealing with lawyers and the letdown of losing the Wicker Park lease, so I try to tone down my own frustrations and let him walk home in peace.

* * *

THE NEXT NIGHT, when Eric gets home, I've stayed up late to greet him with the latest fertility clinic debacle news. As he drops his keys on the entryway table and asks how my day was, I say, "A lawyer contacted me today, and there's going to be a class action suit. So I guess I won't need to hire a lawyer after all."

"About all this," Eric says, running his hand down his face. "I think we need to talk."

"Oh?"

He walks over and sits next to me on the sofa. I close my laptop and set it on the coffee table. I then fold my hands in my lap and wait for what he has to say.

Eric seems hesitant to begin. He takes both my hands. "I've been thinking about this a lot. And so I just want to share my thoughts and let you consider them. This isn't anything where we need to make a big decision right now, but I want you to know where my head is at."

"Okay." I gulp. "You're scaring me. This sounds serious."

He rubs his thumbs across the top of my hands as if to soothe me. "These last few months have been really hard," he starts. "Obviously, losing the Wicker Park location has been a headache, but things have been hard with us, too." He swallows before continuing. "When I decided that I wanted to have a family with you, I didn't consider everything."

Something in me sinks, and I must instinctively pull away because Eric's hands tighten on mine, not letting me go.

"Originally, I didn't want kids because I was worried about not being around for them, which I know now was an irrational fear. No one knows what will happen," he says. "But I didn't consider how hard this would be on you. The ectopic pregnancy really scared me because it made me realize something could happen to you. And, honestly, I'm just in this for you. And so watching you go through all that broke my heart. We're older, things are going to be more difficult. Are you prepared for that?"

His question shocks me, and I bristle. "Of course. I'm prepared to do anything."

"Okay. What if we have to do IVF? Or what if we have a miscarriage? You were devastated at the ectopic. So I worry about what something like that would do to you." He sighs, and his shoulders slump. "I thought I was prepared too, but I don't think I am anymore."

"What are you saying, exactly?"

"I guess, I'm saying kids would be a bonus, but it's not something I need to have to be happy. I just want you."

I take a deep breath to calm myself down, thinking, *We've been here before.* "You know I want a baby," I say.

"I know. But am I not enough?" he asks. "Could you be happy with just the two of us?"

I avoid his direct question and repeat, "You know I've always wanted a family." *And how many times are we going to have this conversation?* I'm trying really, really hard to empathize with him, but the disappointments are piling up.

"But we already do so much for kids, you with your business and Girls Run It, and me with volunteering at CrossFit. We make a difference in so many kids' lives. Do we need to have our own?"

"So you don't want kids now? You've changed your mind?" I say, finally losing my patience.

He doesn't say anything.

As my hopes of motherhood once again come crashing down around me, something unfurls in my chest, and I sputter, "I didn't want to get married, you know? I could've been happy in our relationship without a piece of paper, but I did it because I knew it would make you happy." I know I sound like I'm keeping score, but I don't care. And so I add, now sounding petulant, "And you agreed to have kids. That was the deal."

Eric's jaw visibly tightens a little. "Yes, I agreed to have kids. But we've only been married a few months, and I don't like what this is doing to you. Is it really worth it? With the ectopic, now the fertility clinic losing your eggs...It's hard not to feel like this isn't a sign."

"But it's always been my dream to have a family," I repeat for what feels like the millionth time. And I'm not sure if I'm saying it to Eric or to the Universe, because right now they're both testing me.

"You say this is your dream, but don't you think you would've had them by now? That you would've made different choices if that was the *one thing* you knew you wanted. I know you, Allison. And I see you go for what you want."

The truth is he didn't really know the old Allison, the people pleaser.

"Okay. Got it," I say flatly. "You *don't* want kids." It's no longer a question.

He swallows. "At the moment, to be honest, no, I don't. But this is just what I'm thinking *right now*. And I felt it was important to discuss it with you."

My hands tremble, and I yank them away from him. "I can't believe you," I hiss.

"Allison, this is just a discussion. Not a fight. I should be able to share what I'm feeling."

"What you're 'feeling' is breaking a promise. Having a family was the whole reason we got married!"

I rarely raise my voice, and Eric winces. He puts his

hands up in a "let's calm down" gesture and says, "I don't want to turn this into a fight."

But I'm too pissed to have a civil conversation. "What did you expect?"

"I've been tiptoeing around your feelings. But it's always about you, isn't it? How do you think I feel that I'm a second choice to you? That you would rather have some theoretical child you don't know yet compared to me. That I'm not enough."

There is so much hurt, and now rising anger, in his voice that a small part of me wants to apologize. But I will not feel guilty for what I want. Especially when he's known all along. This is Neil and all his broken promises all over again. My vision blurs, and my anger at Eric builds.

"That's not the case, and you know it. I want a family with you," I say, trying to keep my voice steady.

"And if I don't? Could you handle that? Could you see a future with just us?"

This is the second time he's asked me this question, and I don't trust myself to answer it in this moment.

I take a deep, steadying breath and stand. "I can't with this right now," I say. "I need some space." And I walk out of the living room to the bedroom to pack some things so I can get out of here.

20

I take Finlay with me to my condo, and Eric doesn't try to talk me out of it. With the wedding and then everything else these past few months, I haven't gotten around to putting it on the market yet, and tonight I'm thankful to have some place to be alone with my thoughts. As I drive, I grip the steering wheel, squeezing it while trying to stifle the urge to scream so as not to scare Finlay. But when the red light at Division Street takes too long and seems like one more thing working against me, I mutter some expletives.

This is our first ever big fight, complete with me leaving our place. But I knew I needed to cool off, because right now I'm simultaneously having a nervous breakdown and plotting murder against the male population. In my fury, I accidentally almost blow through a red light and slam on the brakes, receiving an angry honk from a car turning left at the intersection. Chagrined, I mouth "Sorry" and give a limp wave.

Waiting at the light, I take a deep breath to try to calm down...but seriously, *What the fuck is wrong with men?* Or at least the men I pick. That this is the second time this is happening in my adult life? *Why? Why?* I want to bang on the steering wheel. First Neil, who promised we'd have a family, and continued to promise for five years, only to impregnate my maid of honor right before our wedding. Next Eric, who I thought was emotionally stable, devoted to his family, and someone I could always count on. Now that he's my husband, I'm discovering he might be just as much of a bonehead as Neil...and it's even worse because I'm legally tied to him.

What's the saying? Fool me once, shame on you; fool me twice, shame on me. As I pull into my old parking garage, I'm feeling like a chump with a capital C.

ONCE I'M inside my place and have filled up Finlay's food and water bowls, I debate whether to call Jordan. I don't want to interrupt her if she's studying. But after five minutes of pacing back and forth and going over Eric's words, while Finlay anxiously follows me, I decide this is a DEFCON 1 situation. I finally text her, *Are you awake?*

She texts back, *Yup. What's up?*

Eric and I just had our first BIG fight. I left and am sleeping at my condo.

My phone rings, and I answer it.

"That doesn't sound good," Jordan says. "What happened?"

I give her the gist.

"Okay. It sounds like he's freaked out, but I don't think he was saying, 'No, I refuse to have kids ever.' He was just putting his thoughts out there, and feeling you out."

"I don't know. I just can't handle another curveball right now with this baby stuff. It was like one more thing, you know?"

Jordan stays silent.

I sigh. "Maybe it didn't have to turn into a fight. But I just feel so betrayed by everything lately. It reminded me of Neil stringing me along for years, only to leave me and have a baby with Stacey. Then my own body when I found out I was pregnant, but it was ectopic. And then the whole security of having my eggs frozen. *Poof!* No more eggs. No more backup plan!"

"I get it," Jordan says, her calm tone soothing my frayed nerves. "But now that you're alone, what are you thinking? You know I've always been your biggest supporter on having a kid. But what about what Eric is saying? *Could* you imagine a life of just the two of you?"

My head hurts. "Am I a jerk if I say no? It just seems so incredibly lonely."

"But you have other kids in your life. Like his nephews. And like he said, all the kids you volunteer with."

"It's not the same. I want more. I want to be a parent."

"Okay, I'm going to try an exercise and challenge you, so just hear me out." She pauses, and I keep quiet, bracing myself for her next words. "If this is what you truly want, wouldn't you have done something about it earlier? Wouldn't you have just met the first suitable guy in college, married, and started a family right away?" Her words sting even more than Eric's because she has known me longer.

"Well, it wasn't like any of the guys I dated in college were winners. You know, you were there. And then there was Neil."

"Ugh, Neil," she says. "But even then, I know Neil strung

you along, but you could've broken up with him earlier. And you knew Eric didn't want kids when you got back together with him. So you did choose him over a family."

"In my defense, we thought the world was ending. And I did initially break up with him over this issue and froze my eggs."

"Yet, in the end, you still chose him."

Whether or not it's her intention, everything she's saying makes me feel like not having a family already is my fault. And I'm too broken, tired, and confused right now to engage in this "reframing" exercise. (When she was a lawyer she called this playing devil's advocate; as a therapist she calls it "reframing.")

"What are you really saying, Jordan?" I ask, as I lie back on the bed, stare up at the ceiling, and await her verdict.

"I'm just saying, think about it. This is all probably a momentary freak-out on his part. Like you said, he just lost his lease on the Wicker Park place, and he's been under stress. Eric loves you more than anything and just wants you to be happy. You can still want a child, but he needs to feel heard; you know?"

Sitting on the sofa across from Eric, all I could hear was him saying he didn't want children; but now, going over his words again, he did say that his biggest fear was losing me.

I take a deep breath. "Yeah, you're right. I've been so riled up lately that it's possible I overreacted. Fair enough."

"So, *wow*, this is your first big fight," Jordan says, her tone changing from professional therapist to best friend. "Even when you guys broke up, you didn't fight about it."

"Oh, god. True. I guess we were overdue." I groan and then give a rueful laugh. "Maybe now that we're married, things feel bigger."

She chuckles. "They say the first year of marriage is the hardest, even if you lived together beforehand. And, also, you've been through a lot lately. Grief and anger are normal responses, so it's understandable."

I ask her how her studying is going, and she says same old.

"I have Finlay with me and was going to go for a run in the morning. I could swing by your place, and we could do a walk or coffee? It's been forever."

"I wish I could, but I have an appointment with a client early in the morning."

After a promise to take a raincheck, we say good night. As I get into bed, Finlay curls up beside me. I give him a good night pet on the head, and he licks my face. It's gross, but it's better than nothing.

* * *

IN THE MORNING, I take Finlay on a long run through Lincoln Park. He's already better with the leash and listening to me; we even make it past the pond with no duck-chasing incidents. While I run, I think about what Jordan said, that Eric was simply expressing his fears. I'm a little mollified and feel I should apologize. But I also want to be able to say how I feel, and I feel that he was breaking a promise.

Normally he texts me in the morning to say, I love you. But there is no text this morning.

So I decide to take the first step. After finishing my run, I bring Finlay to the condo, then head back out to The Cauldron for my coffee.

Eric is behind the register, and his expression is a combination of surprise and wariness when he spots me.

When I reach the counter to place my order, I say, "My usual. And I'm sorry. I love you." I swallow and then hold my breath, not sure of his response.

Eric's eyes brighten, and he smiles. "You got it. And nothing to apologize for. I love you, too."

I exhale and smile back. Since there's a line behind me, I step aside and wait for my coffee at the barista station.

When I have my latte and there's a break in customers, I return to the register.

"I just want you to know," I start, "I hear what you were saying last night. But it also surprised me, and I've been so upset with everything going on." I wave my hand in the air, and Eric nods in understanding. "So, I need a breather to think more about what you said before we talk about it again. Okay?"

"Of course, that's okay." Then he lowers his voice, so we can't be overheard. "Are you staying at your condo again tonight?"

I shake my head. "No. But remember, I have dinner with my parents tonight in the 'burbs, so I won't see you until probably after nine. Should I take Finlay with me?"

"You don't have to. If you walk him before you leave, I can walk him later tonight when I get home."

Then there's a customer behind me, and I give Eric a quick peck on the lips and leave. The fight might be over, but the discussion is not. For now, I need some time to breathe.

* * *

When my mom invited me to dinner at their house, she trilled on the phone, "I have a surprise for you."

"Can't you just tell me?" I asked.

"No. You will just have to see it for yourself."

Given all that's been going on, as I drive to the western suburbs, I'm not sure I even want to know what the surprise is. But my mom sounded so excited, and I don't want to let her down.

When I get to my parents' house, the front door opens, and I gasp when I see who answers it.

"Jake! What are you doing here?"

Our mother pops out from behind him. "Surprise!" she says, beaming and waving full-on jazz hands.

"Hello to you too, sis," Jake says as I step inside. He greets me with an air kiss, which never fails to amuse me.

"So is this my surprise?" I ask.

"That your brother is visiting, yes," my mother says. "But Jake also said that he has a surprise for us."

My mother is all smiles, but Jake's smile doesn't reach his eyes. "Yes, I wanted to tell you all in person."

A timer goes off in the kitchen. "I'll just get that," my mom says.

"Saved by the bell," I say to my brother.

With our mother out of earshot, I ask in a low voice, "You don't have to tell me what it is, but is it a good surprise or a bad surprise?" I can't handle any more bad news this week, and I gird myself, holding my breath.

"Good surprise." He pats my shoulder. "I hope."

I exhale.

My dad appears. "Hi, honey. Come on in. Can I get you something to drink?"

"Hi, Dad. Some water is fine, but I can get it myself."

When I walk into the kitchen, my mom says, "Your dad is grilling steaks for himself and Jake, if you'd like one. And I have stuffed peppers in the oven, and am marinating some vegetable kebabs for the grill. We also have a big vegetable salad."

"That all sounds good. I don't need any steak." I try to peek into the oven and then turn to my mom. "Stuffed peppers?" I ask her.

"Yes," she says proudly, straightening her shoulders. "They're from the cookbook you bought me."

"Your mother has been good about following the doctor's orders," my dad says, handing me a glass of water.

"Oh! Thanks, Dad." I take the glass from him.

"I only eat meat once a week," my mom continues. "And low-sodium everything."

"That's great to hear, Mom."

We chitchat for a couple minutes, and I ask if I can help with any food prep, but my mom says it's all under control.

When Jake goes outside to check on the grill, I follow him.

"No Eric tonight?" he asks.

I shake my head. "He's busy with work." Then I glance at the window, making sure my parents are still preoccupied in the kitchen. "Also, we just had our first big fight." It seems a little weird to confide my relationship woes to my commitment-phobe brother, but it's still on my mind and so I can't help myself.

"Really?" Jake says, turning over one of the steaks. "What about?"

"Don't tell Mom, but it was about kids. He's not sure about having them anymore."

Just then, my dad comes outside and joins us at the grill. "How are those steaks coming along?" he asks.

I give Jake a quick look to say, "keep quiet." He nods and

answers our dad. "Just a few more minutes, and they'll be ready."

At dinner, Mom says to Jake, "Did Allison tell you what happened to her? You'll never believe it."

He shoots me a look, and I widen my eyes at him, not sure what our mom is about to say. Interpreting this as a no, she launches into the fertility clinic fiasco. Though, as my mother tells the story, Jake doesn't seem as shocked as he should. Instead, he just keeps glancing my way with sympathy in his eyes, as his shoulders seem to lower with each word. While I joke that my brother is ever-stoic, I still expected more of a tempered angry response than an increasingly despondent one.

"We're looking at getting a lawyer," she says. "Maybe you know someone in the city?"

"This isn't my area of expertise, but I can ask around my firm. My guess, though, is that there will be a class action suit, and you'll probably get some money."

"That's what Jordan told me, and a lawyer has already contacted me about it," I say, and then turn to my mom. "So, no new lawyer is necessary. Anyway, I'm officially tapped out on anger about it now. It was just hard, especially after the ectopic." I give Jake another look to convey what I just told him about Eric. Without warning, my eyes prickle, and my face warms. *Oh god, I don't want to cry during dinner.*

"Oh, Allison, darling," my mother says. "Don't worry. It will be okay. You and Eric are going to try again."

"I know." The words come out in a croak. Though it's a lie, and I want to say, *I'm sorry, Mom, but it's looking like you'll never be a grandmother.* Needing a diversion, I say, "So, Jake, what's the big surprise you wanted to tell us?"

Our mom's head swings toward him. This is the big revelation she's been waiting for.

Jake clears his throat and says, "I'm thinking of transferring to my firm's office in Chicago."

My mom jumps up, clapping her hands. Her cheeks flushed and her eyes shining. "That's wonderful!" she says.

"For now, I'll be moving here part-time to see how it goes. And then if it works out, I might be moving here full-time."

"That's really great, Jake." My dad beams.

"Oh, wow," I chime in. "What's the job and the transfer?"

"It's still in the corporate department, so similar work, different office."

"If it's so similar then why move?" I ask.

"I could use a break from New York to be closer to family."

The look on my mother's face is pure delight, and I swear I can see cartoon hearts coming out of her eyes. "Oh, Jakey. You didn't have to move for me."

He smiles at her.

My brother, who rarely visits as it is, came all this way to tell us about this news in person? He could've just called.

"Have you already started the moving process?" I ask.

"Sort of. I'm here this week to figure out my housing situation and finalize things with my office."

"That's great," I say. "You know, you can stay at my place while you look for your own."

As his news sinks in, the draining emotions of the last few days dissipate, and I feel a new energy at the idea of reconnecting with my brother. We haven't lived in the same zip code since we were kids, and I start imagining us meeting up regularly for a drink after work or a run in the park on the weekends.

"Thanks, but that won't be necessary," he says. "The firm has already set me up in a corporate rental."

"Oh. Well, then in that case, when you find your own place, let me know if you need any help unpacking or anything," I offer.

My dad holds up his wine glass. "To Jake, welcome home."

We all clink glasses, saying, "To Jake!"

Finally, a good surprise.

21

———

At dog training tonight, Eric crouches down to get a closer look at Finlay's collar. "What's with the new collar?" he asks.

I glance down and say, "It's a Louis Paw-ton. A gift from my mother."

"That makes sense." He stands up and looks at me. "What was wrong with the bandana?"

When Eric first brought Finlay home, he was wearing a red bandana that had the shelter logo.

"It's her grand-dog. Let her have some fun," I say, and want to add, *After all, Finlay might be the only grandkid she gets.*

Even though Eric and I agreed to table The Talk until after his new coffeehouse reopening, the baby discussion is still simmering below the surface of our day-to-day interactions. The launch for the Lincoln Park location is next week, and I've been working my butt off on it. And it's not like we can try for a baby right now, anyway; so I just keep reminding myself to be patient.

"Is he really a Louis *Paw-ton* dog?" Eric asks, cocking an eyebrow, unaware of the emotion brewing in me.

"Is he really a bandana dog?" I counter.

I didn't have strong feelings about the bandana before, but suddenly I do. Jordan may be right that Eric is just experiencing momentary insanity, but I have to admit to some of my own unsavory behavior, like getting overly defensive about the latest in dog couture.

We're saved from this inane argument when Henry suddenly tackles Finlay and both dogs start tripping over each other in their usual greeting.

"Hey, guys," Mark says, while Adeline waves her hellos.

"Hey, you two," Eric says, and then pats Henry's neck. We all laugh as the two dogs roll over each other and ignore us humans.

"I guess as long as they're jumping on each other and not people, so far the training has paid off," I joke.

Mark and Adeline laugh heartily and have huge smiles on their faces. I know my joke wasn't that funny, so I ask, "How are you guys? You look happy."

"We are!" Adeline clasps and squeezes her hands in front of her. "We're going to be parents!" she squeals.

Oh! I feel an invisible fence come crashing down between us, creating a great divide—parents; not parents. While I'm truly thrilled for them, it's hard not to feel a little sorry for myself. Despite these jumbled emotions, I muster up the correct enthusiastic response.

"Wow! Congratulations!" I exclaim, and give her a big hug.

"That's amazing. Congratulations!" Eric says simultaneously, shaking Mark's hand and patting him on the back.

"Thank you," Adeline beams. "It happened suddenly; we

got a call from the adoption agency that a child was available. We met the mother, and we immediately loved her, and vice versa."

Adoption? That's right—I remember that this is the call they'd been waiting for.

I'm so in my head these days that my mind went directly to Adeline being pregnant, but there are so many other ways to have a family.

"Tell us everything!" I say, very sincerely.

"It's a baby girl. It's an open adoption. The mother is eighteen and has curls like Addie," Mark grins, touching his wife's hair.

"She does," Adeline says, her voice all dreamy, and she leans into him for a sideways hug. "Now things are moving quickly, and we have a house inspection later this week. And then hopefully, once the mother gives birth, the baby will immediately come to stay with us. We weren't quite expecting it."

Our conversation is cut short by class starting. During the lessons, I notice the way Mark and Adeline's eyes sparkle and how their expressions radiate pure joy. When Henry misses some of the new commands, Adeline and Mark don't bother correcting him. They may be physically here in class, but it's obvious their minds are back at home, focused on their new future. I can't help but smile when I look at their faces; however, every time I look at Eric, a small pang jolts my heart.

After class, Eric asks them, "Dinner?"

"We can't tonight. We need to head back to finish prepping the house for the home inspection visit this week," says Mark.

"We want to make sure everything is safety proofed and

perfect," says Adeline. She squeezes Mark's arm. We say our goodbyes, and they rush out before us.

Once we're outside, the warm summer air feels oppressive and sticky.

"So, I guess it's just us two for dinner," Eric says. "Do you still want to go to that café?"

Not really. While Mark and Adeline's happiness felt contagious during class, now that they're gone, any positive feelings have leached out of me as I'm reminded of our questionable future as parents. Sitting across from Eric over dinner, I fear I'll be too tempted to revisit our own baby discussion.

"I have some of that pasta salad from yesterday still in the fridge," I say.

"Oh, okay. Then would you mind if I get something more substantial on the way home, maybe at the burger place?"

"Sure. Sounds good."

On the walk home, I'm curious to get Eric's feelings on tonight's news. A seed has been planted in my mind, and I'm wondering if the same is true for him.

"Mark and Adeline seemed really excited," I say.

"Yeah. That's great for them," he says, stating it as a fact, without any emotion.

"Yeah, it is."

Eric doesn't respond. Reading the room, I realize I shouldn't try to pull more out of him on our friends' impending parenthood, so I subtly change the topic.

"Hey, have you heard anything about James's new family and how that's going?" I ask.

Eric shakes his head.

"Maybe no news is good news?" I offer.

"Yeah," he says, staring ahead.

Eric seems unusually taciturn and lost in thought. I decide not to press or ask what's up with him, and so we walk the rest of the way home in silence. Despite the warm night air, I feel a definite chill.

IN THE MORNING, I'm still thinking about Adeline's and Mark's good news. From what Adeline told me, they hadn't waited as long as they thought they would before getting The Call. Sitting at the kitchen table, I type in "how to adopt in Illinois" on my computer. Various adoption agencies populate my screen, and I click on a link that shows the requirements for prospective parents. Basically, one just needs to be a responsible resident of the state, apply to an agency, and go in for an interview. There would be detailed background checks—financial, health, family, criminal, etc. I know there's nothing in my history to worry about, and I can't imagine anything in Eric's. We'd have to complete courses, and the consensus seems to be thirty-nine hours, which we could easily manage, especially for something so important. Overall, it seems that the entire process could take anywhere from three to six months, less than the nine months of gestation.

I lean back from my laptop and take a sip of coffee. I would still like to be pregnant, and I've been imagining a child that's part me, part Eric for so long, but how important is that? Adeline's expression of pure joy last night mirrored my own when I saw the positive sign on the pregnancy test. If Eric's fears about starting a family stem from something happening to me, then what if we took that out of the equation? I tap my finger against my coffee cup. We're not there yet, but it's something to consider.

* * *

INTEREST in the CrossFit volunteer program is growing, and I'm meeting Kelly at the gym. It's unfortunate that it's at the same time Eric is doing his volunteering, as right now it's hard to watch him be so wonderful with the kids. Also unfortunate is that I had to pick up Finlay from the groomer earlier than expected. I hate leaving him alone in the car because he barks up a storm, so I asked Kelly if she would mind if I brought him to her office. Luckily, she loves dogs, but I still cross my fingers that he'll be on his best behavior.

When we get inside, I see kids assembling for Eric's class. One of them is James.

Eric notices me and sees that I spotted James. He gives me a nod and widens his eyes, and I don't know if it's because he's surprised to see him, too, or he has a story to tell me about it. Hopefully, I can catch him right after class to find out.

I make my way to Kelly's office, thoughts swarming, wondering if James's return is good or bad news.

During the meeting, while I update Kelly on my volunteer recruiting, I find myself looking out the window at Eric's class. Not able to wait until the class ends, once we finish talking business, I finally ask the question that's been on my mind since I walked inside.

"I see that James is back," I say. "How is he adapting with his new family?"

Kelly presses her lips together and shakes her head sadly. "Unfortunately, it didn't work out."

I feel a thud in my chest.

"Can they do that? It's only been a month, hasn't it? What happened?" The questions pour out of me, and I don't care if I sound like I'm being too nosy.

"Right after James went to live with them, the wife was diagnosed with cancer and it's terminal."

"Oh my god!" My hand flies to my chest. "That's tragic!"

"Yes. I guess they'd been wanting to adopt for a while, and then *this* when they finally became parents." She limply waves her hand and sighs. "James's old foster mom told me that he was shut down the entire time he was there, and between navigating the wife's care along with James's emotional issues, the husband was unprepared for being a single father. It was too much for everyone. And so now James is back with his old foster family."

My head reels with this news. *How much heartbreak can a little boy stand?* "That poor kid."

"I know. To lose both parents in a car crash, then to get adopted and learn the mother is dying...I hope he's getting some sort of counseling."

I nod, as I wonder what type of resources the state has for kids like James.

When I leave Kelly's office, I'm in a much more somber mood than when I arrived. Class has just ended, and so I approach Eric, wanting to talk to him. He's putting away some jump ropes and has his back to me. But before I reach him, I see James heading my way. Finlay pulls on the leash, and as James gets nearer Finlay jumps on him, almost knocking him down.

Horrified, I tug on his leash. "Finlay, down!" Thankfully, he listens and lies down.

"I'm so sorry, honey. This dog has bad manners," I say to James. "Are you okay?"

I thought James would be startled, but instead he's laughing and reaching over to pet Finlay, who is now sitting and thumping his tail in delight.

"I'm okay," he says, and puts his arms around Finlay in a hug. Finlay gives him a lick, and James strokes Finlay's neck. "Hi, Finlay."

Eric comes up to us. "James, I see you've made friends with Finlay."

James nods and rests his head on Finlay, and Finlay leans against him. "Is he your dog?" he asks Eric.

"Yes. And this is my wife, Allison. Allison meet James."

"Hi, James. It's nice to meet you," I say. Even though I feel like I know him, this is our first proper introduction.

"Hi," he says, looking up at me and not getting up from petting Finlay. "I've seen you here before."

"Yes, I work with the volunteer group. And I've seen you too. You're really good on the ropes."

James smiles. From what Kelly just told me, I would have expected to meet a withdrawn little boy, but James chats easily with us and asks questions about Finlay—how old he is, what his favorite food and toys are. Then a short, older woman with gray streaks in her brown hair approaches cautiously, her expression apologetic like she doesn't want to interrupt. "James, are you ready to go?" she asks.

He nods and reluctantly turns away from Finlay.

"Hi, I'm Sarah," the woman introduces herself. "James's guardian."

Eric and I say hi and briefly introduce ourselves.

"I hate to interrupt, but we're on a schedule," she says. "We've got two more stops."

Before they leave, James gives Finlay one last pat. He looks up at me. "Will you bring him next class?"

I wasn't planning to visit again so soon and definitely not with Finlay, but James's eyes look so hopeful, so I say, "I'd love to."

After they leave, Eric turns to me and asks, "Are you sure you're okay with this?"

I nod. "It's a small thing, and how could I say no."

Eric pulls me in for a hug, and I hug him back. He quickly kisses my head, then says, "Okay, then we better go clear this with Kelly."

He takes Finlay's leash from me and in his other hand he takes mine, as we head to Kelly's office.

"While it's not the best idea to have a dog around all the equipment, these are special circumstances," Kelly says. "We'll say he's a therapy dog or something."

So it's agreed that I can bring Finlay after class, but not before so as not to distract the kids. And she'll mention it to James's foster mom, to see if she can pick him up fifteen minutes later so he can spend some time with Finlay.

It looks like Kelly's CrossFit has a new weekly mascot.

22

The Lincoln Park Grand Reopening is hopping. It's August and despite the humidity, everyone is still taking full advantage of these Chicago summer days. Thanks to the parklets, many pedestrians have become curious and stopped by to enjoy the event. We have a table set up where Brian is hosting tea tastings. We have free dessert samples and iced drink "shots." We have a caricature artist who is creating a bit of a crowd. There's also a balloon artist to entertain the kids, while their parents caffeinate. I even invited some local press that I make sure to steer over in Eric's direction. It's turned into a full-blown block party. After all the heartbreak and disaster these last couple of months, at least this is something successful I can be happy with.

"This iced matcha latte is amazing," Kate says beside me.

"Isn't it?" I say. "Brian's taking the tea up a notch."

"Really putting the 'tea' in the coffeehouse," Kate jokes, as she looks over at Brian. He sees us and nods. Then Kate's attention is distracted past Brian. "Hey, isn't that your brother?"

I look over to where she's looking. "Yes, it is." I wave my arm in the air. "Hey, Jake! Over here."

Even though my brother has moved back to Chicago, I haven't seen him since dinner at our parents' house.

"Hey, sis. Hi, Kate," Jake says, reaching us.

He gives me a kiss on the cheek. He turns to Kate who rears back and holds her arm out. Reading her expression, he extends his hand for a polite handshake, skipping the air kiss.

Looking around, he says, "This is a great turnout."

"Yes, I'm thrilled with it. We wanted to do something big, and it's turned into a fun neighborhood party."

"Impressive." Jake nods. He spots Eric, and they wave.

"We have iced drink shots and some dessert bites circulating. And then there's a raffle for free coffee drinks for a month and a travel mug." I also point out the caricature artist and Brian's tea tasting setup.

"I highly recommend the iced matcha tea latte," Kate says, tapping the side of her cup with her finger.

Brian must overhear us because I notice him look our way and smile. Kate holds her drink up to him and smiles back.

Then she turns to Jake. "I hear you're moving to Chicago. How's that going?"

"I'm already here, and it's been good."

"Where are you living?"

"Downtown, you know," Jake says, and then takes one of the iced shots being passed around. "I have a corporate rental."

"Mmm..." she says, looking at him as she takes a long sip of her drink. "Didn't you offer your place?" Kate asks me.

"Yes, but he already had a place." I give her a curious look.

She nods. "So, where's Jordan today? Is she coming?"

"She's busy," I say. "I don't think we're going to see her until this exam business is over."

I haven't seen Jordan since our walk with Finlay, which was back in June. Since then I've invited her out for coffee, walking, or to help her study, but she's turned me down. I know she says she's busy, but even when she was working crazy hours as a lawyer, we still found time for a quick drink or coffee, so it's been disconcerting. I try to remind myself that when she took the bar exam after law school, I didn't see her for the full two months she was studying. Yet, a little voice in me can't help but wonder if she's ignoring me—if my baby fever has broken the friendship camel's back with one too many crises.

I've figured the best way to support her this summer is to respect her space. In the meantime, we've become those friends who send funny memes to each other to say, thinking of you, as if we're long-distance friends rather than one neighborhood over.

"Mmm..." Kate says again, and then shoots another look at Jake, holding his eyes for an uncomfortable few seconds, as if she's staring him down.

Jake's irises slightly dilate in response. He breaks eye contact and looks around again, turning his body away from us. "So, I'm going to find Eric to congratulate him," he says.

As he says this, I spot Suzy with one of her kids in tow and I wave to her. "Okay," I say to Jake. "I'll catch you later."

Suzy reaches Kate and me, and we chat for a couple

minutes, but then I have to leave them to check on the musicians inside. After that, my old work friend Darren and his husband stop by to say hi and congratulations, as well as some of Eric's CrossFit friends, and my Girls Run It acquaintances. Jake takes off after a quick goodbye.

It's two hours later when Kate reappears. "You're still here!" I say.

"Yes, I talked to Suzy for a while and caught up with Darren. Plus, I wanted to get another one of those matcha lattes."

Her expression turns serious. "So, hey, do you have a minute?"

"Sure."

"Let's go over there." She nods to a far table. "I need to talk to you privately."

I'm a little confused, but I follow her to the empty table. We sit down and I say, "What's up?"

She takes a deep breath. "You know how I asked you if you've seen Jordan lately?"

"Yeah…"

"Well, you need to see Jordan. I can't tell you why. But you need to talk to her in person."

"What do you mean? What's going on?" Now I'm really confused and a little concerned.

Kate sighs. "Here's the thing, I almost lost you as a friend the last time I kept a secret from you, when I suspected that Neil and Stacey were getting it on behind your back."

I wince, remembering that time well, and still wishing to forget it.

"And I promised myself I would never do that again."

"Okay? And what does this have to do with Jordan?"

"I'm telling you—you have to go see her."

I blink a couple times. Since the last secret was Neil and Stacey, my mind immediately flits to Eric and Jordan. Jordan avoiding me. Eric's sudden change of heart on kids. *No.* I physically shake these thoughts out of my head. *That's ridiculous.* Stacey was a snake who made clear her intentions on Neil with her over-the-top flirting. There's no way Jordan and Eric would get together. But then what kind of secret could Jordan be keeping?

* * *

EXHAUSTED from the reopening party when I got home yesterday, I decided to wait on contacting Jordan. But taking Kate's words to heart, I tossed and turned all night and am out of bed even before Eric. I head to the kitchen and set some coffee to brew, plagued with thoughts of what Jordan is hiding.

"You're up early," Eric comments when he wanders into the kitchen. I probably woke him up with my coffee-making. "Too much caffeine yesterday?"

"Guess so," I say absently, pouring myself a cup.

"Thanks for the incredible event," he says, coming up behind me. He gives me a hug and kisses my neck.

"Aw, you're welcome. It really *was* pretty incredible," I say.

And it was. We had a crowd all day and almost ran out of samples, and had to raid the Gold Coast location for more. Lots of people snapped photos, and I look forward to checking The Cauldron's social media this morning. Plus, there was some local media who wanted to do a piece on Eric that I should follow up on. While I want to revel in yesterday's success, I'm mentally counting down to when I can reasonably contact Jordan.

"Let me take you out to dinner tonight to celebrate," Eric says.

"Sure," I say, moving out of the way so he can pour himself some coffee.

"Okay, I gotta down this and get out of here," he says, and takes his coffee back to the bedroom to get ready for work.

* * *

I SPEND the first hours of the morning taking Finlay out, going to a yoga class, and updating The Cauldron's social media and website with photos from yesterday, but all with my eye on the time. When ten o'clock rolls around, I finally text Jordan. *Sorry you missed the party yesterday. Hope studying went well.*

Then I take a deep breath and type, *Would you be up for a coffee this week?*

She texts back immediately. *I wish, but I'm slammed. Back-to-back client hours and studying.*

I text back, *How about next week?*

Probably not. This is a busy time. She adds a frowny face.

I'm not sure how to respond.

She must read something in my silence. *Is everything okay? You can always call me. Want to talk tonight?*

Okay. She's willing to talk to me, so she's not *totally* avoiding me. And while Kate's ominous warning that Jordan is keeping a secret is still eating at me, I also want to keep my head in the sand a little longer. I can't stomach more bad news, especially a blow from Jordan, of all people.

So I text, *Everything's fine. I just miss you. Good luck.*

Dots appear and then disappear. Finally, I see the words, *Miss you too.*

* * *

Eric makes reservations at a popular Mediterranean place in the West Loop that's notoriously hard to get into. "I know some people," he joked when I asked how he secured us a table. Once we're seated with menus, and I admire the skylit dining room, taking in the greenery around the perimeter and the globe chandeliers above us, I have a passing thought that maybe we should add lighting to the parklets in Lincoln Park.

"Are you getting a cocktail?" Eric asks, interrupting my musings. "Or should we get a bottle of champagne to celebrate?"

"Oh. I don't know yet. Let me look," I say, turning to the menu.

There's an impressive cocktail selection, and after wondering about Jordan all day and now sitting across from another question I need to solve, I decide I need something stronger than bubbles. "Definitely a cocktail."

After our drinks arrive and we order some small plates to start, Eric raises his glass.

"To my beautiful and brilliant wife. Thank you for making the reopening of The Cauldron a success. I don't know what I'd do without you."

"You're welcome," I say, clinking my glass against his and then taking a big sip. "But, you know, that's my job."

"And you're excellent at it," Eric says smoothly, giving me a beatific smile complete with those eye crinkles I love so much. "Now what are you thinking for a main? Should we share something?"

We chat more about the menu and then place our entrée orders, along with a bottle of wine to share. Eric talks about both The Cauldron locations, and how busy Lincoln Park was. "We did better business today than back when it originally opened." He tells me how the new staff is working out, and that Brian seems ready to take over the Gold Coast location as its General Manager.

"I'd been really down about losing the Wicker Park space, and I let it dampen my feelings about reopening Lincoln Park," he says, almost looking a little embarrassed. "But yesterday made me realize I needed to let it go. It was a setback, but so what? Given the great turnout and today's traffic, I think that location is going to turn a profit quickly, and that will make it easier to sign a lease for a third one. Maybe a storefront in a building by us?"

"I'm glad," I say. "Good for you."

"Good for *us*," he says.

He reaches over and puts his hand on the table, palm up, in an invitation. I place my hand in his.

Now that the launch is officially behind us, it's time to revisit our earlier discussion. It's great that he's feeling hopeful that his dreams are coming true, but what about mine? If Eric thinks we're still a team, then he needs to get back on board with our baby plan. For all I know, this dinner might be his way of broaching the subject.

So I carefully say, "I've been looking into freezing my eggs again."

"Really?" He looks genuinely surprised. "After what happened with the clinic?"

I nod, and then pull my hand back to pick up my drink. I note he didn't ask, *Why?*

"It's going to be harder and more expensive this time around," I say. "But I feel like I need the insurance." *Since you changed your mind.*

This afternoon, feeling burned out after yesterday and trying to distract myself from thinking about what was up with Jordan, I spent the afternoon researching other facilities to freeze my eggs. I can't believe I'm here again, in so many ways. And Eric's right; I don't even know if I can trust this process. It seems I can't count on men or science. Also, when I looked at the prices, my heart dropped. I don't have that much of a savings cushion unless I sell my condo. And if I'm going to end up doing this alone, I probably want to keep my place.

Eric doesn't respond right away. He's completely still, and I can tell he's working out what to say. Finally, he starts, "I support whatever you want to do—"

"And your entrées," our server interrupts Eric's next words as he sets down our plates.

With our food in front of us, I hate to spoil a perfectly nice evening and let our food get cold, but the longer we don't talk about it, my anxiety grows.

After thanking the server, I say to Eric, "Thank you for this dinner tonight. I want you to know that I thought about what you said about no longer wanting to have kids. And I get what you're saying. I truly do." I put my hand on my heart. "But this is the *one* thing I want—to be a mother." I pause for emphasis. "You *know* that. And it's not some crazy pipe dream to want to be a parent. In life, sometimes we have to take risks in our relationships. I love you, but I can't live a small life of just you and me. I want more."

Eric nods solemnly. "I hear you."

"Okay..." I say, slowly. Does he just hear the words I'm saying? Does he agree? What does he mean? My heart is pounding so hard, I can hear the blood rushing in my ears.

"But can we talk about this at home?" he asks.

This doesn't bode well, and I swallow.

"It's just that we're both a few drinks in, and I'd rather talk about this when we're fully sober," he adds quickly, maybe registering the flush creeping across my face.

"That's fine," I say. If I'm honest, I'm a little buzzed, and I don't want to decide our future over a plate of falafel either.

We finish the bottle of wine. And like our last big date night out, we skip dessert and head home in silence.

23

———————

Over the past few days, Eric and I have both been too busy with work to finish the conversation we started at the restaurant. Also, Jordan continues to be monumentally unavailable; I've texted her a couple more times trying to meet up, but she's consistently blown me off. I'm not going to stay in limbo with both her and Eric. So, after my third failed attempt to see her, I decide I'm going to have to force the issue. I grab some brownies Eric made and head over to her place. It's nighttime; and if her texts are to be believed, then she's at home each night studying.

When I arrive at her building, her regular doorman is at the front desk.

"Hi, Allison. Good to see you. It's been a while."

"Hey, Frank. Good to see you too! Yeah, I've been busy."

I chitchat with him for a few minutes, asking about his family and his wife, who I know recently had knee surgery. After our little catch-up, I say, "So, I brought a sweet treat for Jordan." I hold up the box of brownies.

"That's nice of you. I'll call her and let her know you're here."

"Actually, I want to surprise her. Can you just tell her it's a special delivery, please? Would you mind?"

I open the box and show him the brownies. I know I'm asking him to break the rules, so I hold my breath.

He winks at me. "You got it."

He calls Jordan and tells her she has a perishable delivery at the front desk, and so he's sending it up. I offer Frank a brownie as a token of thanks and then head to the elevator and Jordan's floor.

When I get to Jordan's door, I take a deep breath, then knock.

The door swings open, and it's not Jordan standing there. It's my brother.

"Jake?" I gasp. My mind whirls.

"Al?" he says, equally surprised.

"What are you doing here?" we both say at the same time.

But after that, my normally articulate brother seems at a loss for words.

Is this the big secret Jordan's hiding? My brother?

Without meaning to, I start to laugh. "Oh my god!"

I'm so going to razz these two.

Once I catch my breath after laughing, I ask him teasingly, "So, why are you at my best friend's place?" Then I call out loudly, so Jordan can overhear. "Especially since she never has time to see me!"

I go to take a step inside, but instead of opening the door wider, he closes it slightly and blocks me with his body. I take a step back and cock my head. "What the heck? Let me in."

"It's not a good time," he says, his voice serious.

"What does that mean?" I narrow my eyes at him. "I brought Jordan brownies." I hold up the box.

"I can take those." He reaches out for them.

I pull the box away. "Jake, this is crazy. I get it. You guys are together. Right? That's what's going on here?"

"It's just not a good time," he repeats in an annoyingly calm but firm manner.

He raises his eyebrows and juts his chin toward the elevator, in code for "get out of here."

Oh, god, are they about to have sex and I'm interrupting? *Ew, ew, ew.* Now I'm freaking out, and I start to back away.

Then Jordan's voice calls out. "Jake, it's never going to be a good time. Just let her in."

I make a face at my brother and step inside. I look around. "Jordan?"

"I'm in the bedroom," she says. "Come back here. I can't get up."

Oh, boy, I was *definitely* interrupting something. With a gulp, I set the brownies on her kitchen countertop and head back to her bedroom, worried about what I'm going to see.

When I get to the doorway, at the sight of her in bed, I stop short. Once my brain finally registers what I'm seeing, I sputter, "You're...you're..."

She props herself on her elbows. "I'm pregnant," she says. "I'm sorry, Allie."

"I just...I can't believe..." I can't seem to say anything coherently. Then I turn around and look at Jake. I point at him, then to Jordan.

He presses his lips together and nods. I turn back to Jordan. She pats the bed and says, "Come sit down, Al."

I walk over slowly. *How could she not have told me? How*

could I not have noticed? How is it possible that my brother is the father of my best friend's baby?

Jordan must see all these questions on my face, because she takes both my hands in hers and gets right down to it. "Jake and I started seeing each other shortly after your mom's heart attack. It just sort of happened. There were drinks, a late night...and well, we thought it would be a one-night stand kinda thing."

I had noticed that their friendly banter was more on the flirtatious side, and Jordan had made several comments about how good Jake was looking, but I never suspected the extent of it.

"But then he came back a couple weekends, just to see if this was something more than a one-night stand. We didn't tell you because we weren't sure ourselves."

I nod. I understand that. I'm still a little repulsed by the knowledge that my best friend and brother have been getting it on. I guess I just have to put that visual out of my mind—though it's hard to do while I'm staring at Jordan's belly.

"But then, well..." She looks at her stomach. "It was a classic case of the condom breaking."

"Why? Why didn't you tell me?" *Cause you're a horrible, needy friend,* says a small voice inside me.

"Because when I first found out, I wasn't sure what I was going to do." She looks at me apologetically. "Motherhood has never been on my radar. It was scary to think about how I was starting this new career and having a child. And I know I always tell you, 'you can do it, be a single mom'...but being a mother is something you've always wanted, and so I know you'd figure it out. But, me...I wasn't so sure."

"Oh, Jor." I squeeze her hands. I'm about to say she can

always tell me anything, but she shakes her head, silencing me, wanting to get out her story.

"I first learned I was pregnant right before your wedding, and I had to tell Jake first. Then I had planned to tell you after the wedding, but there was never a good time to do it. I knew you wanted to get pregnant, so I wasn't going to discuss my options with you. Then when I decided to keep it, I was about to tell you, but you were going through the ectopic pregnancy, and so that felt like kicking you when you were already down. And more recently, the clinic losing your eggs, and Eric getting cold feet again and dropping the bomb on you that he didn't want kids..." She blows a curl of hair off her face. "Well, I didn't know how to tell you."

"I'm your best friend, Jor. You didn't have to protect me. You shouldn't have had to deal with this alone."

"But I'm not alone." She looks at Jake, who is sitting on the armchair across from us.

I then turn to Jake. "So this is why you moved to Chicago?"

"Yeah." He leans forward, his hands clasped in front of him. "And I'm sorry too, Al. I was going to tell you at Mom and Dad's house. That was my big news, and I thought I should do it in person. Jordan had told me about the clinic losing your eggs, but I still thought we should let you know. Then, seeing your face when you said Eric and you had a fight about having kids, I couldn't do it." He shakes his head.

I feel very small right now. "I understand you were both trying to be sensitive to me, but...I don't need to be protected."

"You're my little sister, of course I'm going to protect you."

Jordan squeezes my hands, and I turn back to her. "And I'm your best friend," she says. "It was just awkward. The timing was never working out. And now that I'm showing so much, I couldn't hide it anymore. So I just kept avoiding you and it sucked."

"But what about the exam?" I ask.

She snorts. "I didn't fail the exam."

"What?!"

"I totally aced it the first time." *Of course she did.* "And I'm a little insulted you bought that story so easily."

I never imagined Jordan could keep a secret from me, and so there's a part of me that feels betrayed. And I'm ashamed that she thought I couldn't handle her pregnancy news. I'm not really sure what to say next.

"Do you forgive me?" she asks, her voice hopeful.

"Oh my god," I say. "There's nothing to forgive." And I know exactly what to say next. "Congratulations! You're going to be a mother!"

"Oh, god, you're right. I am. I still can't believe it." She shakes her head. "And so while there was never a good time to tell you about the pregnancy, there was also never a good time to ask if you would be the baby's godmother."

"You want me to be the godmother?" My cheek muscles burn from the huge smile that breaks across my face. "Of course I will!"

I give her a hug, and Jake comes up behind me and squeezes my shoulder. I stand to hug and congratulate him. I had almost forgotten that he was in the room—for a minute, I kind of felt like Jordan and I were the ones having the baby together.

I sit back down on the bed and clap my hands. "Okay, then. Let's talk baby shower!"

Jordan rolls her eyes and laughs. "Can we not?"

"Oh, there's going to be a baby shower. Complete with ridiculous games and a diaper cake."

"Before you go planning my idea of hell, there's something else..." she starts.

What now? Then it hits me. "You're getting married!"

"Uhhh..." she stammers and looks at Jake. "That's not the something else." Her brow furrows. "I was diagnosed with placenta previa at my last exam, so now I have a more high-risk pregnancy."

"Oh no! What does that mean? Are you going to be okay? Is the baby okay?" My words rush out.

"Yes and yes. It just means the placenta is unusually low in my uterus, instead of at the top. And in my case, it's covering my cervix, so unless it moves, I won't be able to deliver naturally. But it could cause complications, like bleeding, or a worst-case scenario if I go into early labor, which is why I'm not supposed to be farther than ten minutes from the hospital." She waves her hand in the direction of Northwestern. Since she lives in Streeterville, her place is within a mile of it. She must register the stricken look on my face. "But first babies are typically born at forty or forty-one weeks, so I have a C-section scheduled at thirty-seven weeks to prevent that from happening. In the meantime, I'm supposed to take it easy, no strenuous housework or heavy lifting." She rolls her eyes and laughs. Even nonpregnant, Jordan's not a fan of either.

"Do you need help? What can I do? I can always stay, you know," I say, already mentally packing my overnight bag.

"Actually, that's why Jake moved in."

My brother is living with Jordan! I look between them. "And the news just keeps coming," I say. "Is there anything else? Twins?"

"Just a baby girl." She smiles.

"We're having a girl!" I squeal, again totally forgetting about my brother in the room.

"We are." Jordan grins and looks over to Jake.

I turn to him, a big smile on my face. "Just so you know, Mom already has a stockpile of adorable pink onesies coming your way."

* * *

As happy as I am for Jordan and Jake, as I walk home from Jordan's place, I feel like a monster. They were protecting me and trying to be sensitive; but the truth is they weren't wrong. Jordan never wanted to be a mother and yet accidentally got pregnant. My brother, whom even my own mother has given up on providing her any grandchildren, is finally going to become a father. It's hard not to feel a little like *And why not me?* But at the end of the day, those small feelings are all overshadowed by the news that I'm going to be an aunt *and* a godmother to their baby.

* * *

The third time I bring Finlay to CrossFit, I try to come closer to the end of the class so as not to distract the kids, per Kelly's suggestion. Today, James runs toward Finlay, holding his backpack in his hands. Finlay strains at the leash to get to him, and despite the dog training, jumps on James to give him a big slobber.

Eric comes up behind them and says to me, "James wants to show you something."

James sets down his backpack, which Finlay is now sniffing. "Down, Finlay," I say, and he lies down. James pulls out a folder from his bag, removes a sheet of paper from inside, and hands it to me. It's a drawing of a yellow dog.

"It's Finlay," he says proudly.

My chest expands as I say, "I can see that. Wow, this a great drawing, James. You're very talented." It's the truth. It's actually quite advanced and better than most adults, meaning me, could do. "How old are you again?"

"Eight," he says, and then he is engrossed in Finlay again.

Eric tells me what they did in class today, and James chimes in. We all chat comfortably about dogs, drawing, and what types of activities James likes to do in the CrossFit class. The fifteen minutes fly by, and soon his guardian, Sarah, is there to pick him up. I had asked Kelly about Sarah, and she told me that Sarah and her husband, who are both in their sixties, have been foster parents for many years. They're not trying to adopt, but rather to simply provide a safe haven for as many kids as possible.

When James gives Finlay a long hug goodbye, I have the urge to give James a big hug too. I clasp my arms behind me, physically restraining myself. As I watch him leave with Sarah, my throat thickens with emotion. I'm suddenly missing him and wishing his situation were different. Next week's visit can't come soon enough.

24

———

Ever since Jordan and Jake told me they're having a baby, I've been taking my best friend, aunt, and godmother duties seriously and hanging out at Jordan's place as much as possible. She's supposed to be on bed rest, so every day when my brother leaves for work in the morning, I show up with my laptop and Finlay. Jordan has been able to do her clinical hours via Zoom from the bedroom while I work in her living room, and then we take a break to eat lunch together.

This Monday morning, I brought us a summer chopped salad with chickpeas and a lemon vinaigrette that I prepped earlier at home.

As I'm in the kitchen, spooning our salads into bowls, with Finlay underfoot, patiently hoping I'll accidentally drop some food, Jordan comes around the corner.

"That looks good," she says.

"Hey, you're supposed to be in bed," I scold her. "Get back in there. I'll bring this to you."

She leans against the doorway, one hand protectively on

her bump, the other resting on her lower back. She's already in her third trimester, and I'm counting down the days until I'm an aunt.

"Taking it easy doesn't mean staying in bed twenty-four seven. I can move around at home. I can even go outside for a walk, you know," she adds, sarcastic but still good-natured.

"Preferably not. Why take any chances?" I joke back.

She rolls her eyes at me. "Sometimes I need a change of scenery. I'll go stir-crazy sitting around here," she huffs.

"I understand. But still...just go to the couch, please, and I'll bring our salads out."

She heads over to the sofa and groans as she lowers herself down. We have the same argument every day, with the same compromise.

I carry forks, napkins, and our salads into the living room. Jordan is on the sofa with her legs up, so I hand her a bowl and then take a seat in one of her armchairs.

"Mmm...I love the lemon smell," she says, bringing the bowl closer to her face.

"Glad to hear that. And sorry again about the last salad." I grimace.

On Friday, I made a roasted cauliflower and lentil salad, but the powerful smell of cauliflower made Jordan nauseous and sent her gagging.

She laughs. "It was the thought that counts. It's just my crazy nose these days. It's like my superpower, but I haven't yet figured out how to use it for good."

"Maybe it's little Haley making her preferences known?"

Jordan shakes her head and grins. I've been asking her and Jake if they've chosen a name yet, but they said they're still deciding. Though I secretly think they've picked one and aren't sharing, so I've been throwing out my guesses.

"Did I tell you Jake suggested your mother's name?" Jordan says.

"Really? What did you say?"

"I suggested my mother's name right back." She wiggles her eyebrows and then takes a forkful of salad.

"Actual name or nickname?" Jordan's mom was named Bluebell, but she goes by Belle. One is definitely better than the other.

"*Actual* name."

"Oh!" I laugh. "Yeah, well, it's probably best not to saddle the kid with a name that has any history attached. That could cause drama between our moms."

"Agreed. And you're not getting any other names out of me." She narrows her eyes and points her fork at me, then changes the subject. "So, tell me, what's the latest with you and Eric? Anything new over the weekend?"

"Same old, same old. Even though we agreed to revisit the baby issue after the Lincoln Park reopening party, we still haven't had another big discussion. He's been working a lot. But also, since we can't actively try, neither of us wants to go there and start a fight."

Ever since our dinner out where we tabled the discussion, we haven't directly brought it up again. I've tested the waters here and there, like when I told him about Jordan and Jake getting together.

Eric laughed and said, "No surprise there."

"Really?" I said, taken aback at his response. "What makes you say that?"

"They've always had a vibe. There was that night at RH wine bar. And remember that dinner with your parents when your dad bumped into them outside? Jordan said she'd been studying at Starbucks, but that

Starbucks doesn't even have chairs." He gives me a look and grins.

"Oh yeah. I totally forgot about that," I said, the obvious finally dawning on me. Back then, maybe my subconscious just didn't want to pick up on it. While I'm happy for them now, I'm sure I would have felt awkward about all this early on.

But then when I told him about their being pregnant, it was Eric's turn to be shocked. His eyes went wide, and he was silent for a second before saying, "But neither of them wants kids."

I wasn't sure if he was saying it to himself or to me, but I responded, "Well, they do now." My tone was light, but my insides churned, waiting for his reaction.

Eric simply nodded and said, "Good for them."

Then I told him how Jordan asked me to be a godmother, and he gave me a congratulatory hug. As he squeezed my shoulders, I felt like he was genuinely happy for me, but he was quiet. Likely wondering why two people who never wanted a child were soon going to be having one. It was late, and we were both tired, so we went to bed without any further discussion. He fell asleep right away while I tossed and turned, wondering about our future as parents.

"I see," Jordan says. "Any news on the fertility clinic? Do you think you'll freeze your eggs again?"

"Even though they're offering free services, I don't trust going there again. But then I've looked into it at other places." I tell her about my findings: more cost, more eggs, etc.—the same summary I gave Eric. "And maybe it's irrational, but in some ways it feels like if I freeze my eggs, then I've given up with Eric. And, you know, I'm pissed off that I'm here again."

"I get that. But it's not an either/or situation. Like I said before, I think Eric will come around. And when you try again, what if those eggs come in handy? Or maybe you get pregnant right away, have a kid, but then have trouble having a second?"

"Right," I say. What she says makes sense, but…"I'd just be happy with one at this point."

She sets down her bowl and napkin on the coffee table and gives me a serious look. "So what is it about wanting so badly to be a mother? Is it that you want to carry a child? Because I can tell you this part," she makes a sweeping motion toward her belly, "is no picnic."

"I've been thinking a lot about that, too." I set down my salad bowl next to hers. "If Eric's concerned about me, what if I take that out of the equation?"

She raises an eyebrow. "What do you mean?"

I take a deep breath. "I've been thinking about adoption."

Her eyes are wide, and she scoots up so that she's seated fully upright. "Since when?"

The tiny seed after talking to Mark and Adeline has grown, and I tell her all about their situation and recent adoption news.

"Ever since we saw Mark and Adeline at our last dog training session and how excited they were, I've been researching adoption agencies, and what the requirements would be, and I don't know…if Eric's new hang-up is about something happening to me, then it just seems like this might be another option."

"That's an amazing idea!"

I smile. Even though I've spent hours visiting the adoption agency websites, now that I've said this idea aloud to

Jordan, the possibility of it happening seems more real. "Thanks! I think so too. I just hope Eric agrees."

"Oh, he will," she says decisively. "We just need to get your arguments ready and prep you." She raises her fist in a victory motion.

I laugh while thinking, *once a lawyer always a lawyer*. But Jordan loves a project, plus I know she's bored sitting around her place, so I'm happy to have her help *and* help distract her.

* * *

AT FINLAY'S next dog training class, I'm surprised to spot Mark walking through the entrance with Henry. He gives us a small wave, and Eric and I wave back. As they approach, I note Mark looks tired. But while he has shadows under his eyes and exudes a general air of exhaustion, there's a lightness in his expression and a small smile on his face. He looks like a man at peace.

"Hi, you two," he says when he reaches us.

"Hi, Mark. I'm surprised to see you," I say.

Mark gives us a tired grin. "Since it's the last class, we thought one of us should take Henry. Didn't want him to be a dog-school dropout."

Eric and I laugh. Meanwhile, Henry tackles Finlay, and the two dogs roll around on the floor in front of us.

"So, how are things going? Are you all settling in?" Eric asks.

"It's going well, I think," he says. "Nights are a little hard, and one of us sleeps in the chair in her room. For someone so tiny, Lucy eats like a champ. And while she can't talk yet, she makes her opinions known." He laughs as he mimes plugging one ear.

"I'm sure," I say. "And what a sweet name, Lucy."

"It's short for Luciana. Her name means 'light.'" He beams.

"That's so beautiful," I say, while feeling like I'm about to cry.

The dogs start barking, pulling our attention toward them. I use the distraction to collect my emotions. "And how is Henry with her?" I ask.

"He's very protective and patient. I'm sure he thinks she's his baby." Mark chuckles. "We were a little concerned, but it's turned out okay. More than okay." He grins again.

I look at Eric, and he's looking at me, as if we're both wondering what the other is thinking—although I know what I'm thinking, which is, *See how happy this new father is! Why don't you want this?*

The instructor claps her hands to start the class, and we stop our conversation.

After class, Eric and I don't bother asking Mark if he'd like to join us for dinner, since it's clear he wants to rush home and be with his family.

"Don't be a stranger," Eric says as we all walk outside together.

"We won't. Once we've all settled into a comfortable routine, we'll have a party."

I tell him to give my regards to Adeline, and then he's off like a shot into the night.

"That's a happy man," I comment to Eric.

"Yes. I'm glad for them," Eric says, watching Mark dart away. Then he looks down, pets Finlay's head, and says, "Come on, Finlay, let's go home."

"Um, did you want to get dinner?" I ask Eric. "I didn't have time to prepare anything this morning other than lunch."

"Nah. That's okay. We can just pick something up on the way home."

Knowing he doesn't want to sit across from me over dinner, I feel a little deflated. He probably thinks I'll bring up the conversation we've been avoiding; even though, little does he know, I'm working on a new angle.

"Perfect," I say, trying to sound cheerful.

And except for a quick stop at our local market to pick up some ready-made meals, once again, we walk home silently.

* * *

FINLAY HAS QUITE the social calendar these days. After dog training, his next commitment this week is at CrossFit. As usual, I bring Finlay closer to the end of class, so as not to be a distraction. But as if James has a sixth sense, the moment we arrive, his head swings toward us. He keeps turning our way for the remaining ten minutes, and Finlay thumps his tail each time James looks over. Immediately after class, James makes a beeline for us.

"Hi, Finlay," he says, hugging him, while Finlay licks his face. "Hi, Allison. Thank you for bringing him."

"Of course. He's just as excited to see you as you are him."

While James's first interest is naturally Finlay, today he seems open to having a conversation with me. So, I tell him how Finlay just recently passed dog obedience school, and that I've been practicing with him.

"Want to see what he's learned?" I ask.

"Okay." James had been sitting on the floor with Finlay, but now he stands.

"Okay, here we go." I take out the bag of treats from my purse, and Finlay's attention shoots to me.

"Finlay, *sit*," I say. And as he does, his eyes are intensely focused on me and the treat he knows is coming his way.

"Good boy," I say, giving him a small dog cookie.

"Want to try?" I ask James.

He nods vigorously in response.

James goes through the basic commands of "sit," "down," and "give me a paw," which is his favorite. Then he asks if I can take a picture of him with Finlay. I take it with my phone and promise to print it out for him for our next visit.

When Sarah approaches, she says, "Hi, I hate to interrupt, but I'm here to pick him up."

James's shoulders visibly slump, and it's like he shuts down. If he was another kid, he would probably whine and beg to spend more time with the dog. But he already seems to know he has no agency over his life, so he just accepts the situation and what adults tell him. Sarah must read this, too, because she says, "We have a few extra minutes before we need to pick up Byron from swim practice."

James brightens at this news. Eric has finished putting away the workout equipment and joins us. James turns to me and says, "Can I do the handshake trick again? I want to show Coach Eric."

As James goes through the commands with Finlay, Eric makes all the appropriate praise noises.

"That's amazing, bud!" he says, and holds his hand out for James to give him a fist bump. James grins, and as his little knuckles make contact with Eric's bigger ones, I swear I feel a crack open up in my chest.

I instinctually step away to hide any complicated emotions that might show on my face. Sarah joins me, probably thinking we're giving James some alone time with Finlay and Eric.

As we stand a little apart from them, she says, "Thank you so much for doing this. James adores Eric and even though he's not the sportiest kid, he loves coming to class to see him. And now, with Finlay, the highlight of his week has gotten even better. It's all he talks about at home." She gives me a big smile.

"Of course, I'm happy to do it," I say, feeling myself flush. It's such a small thing compared to what she does as a foster parent.

"Do you have kids of your own?" she asks innocently.

Ugh. My least favorite question of late.

"Not yet. We just got married this year." It's my standard answer these days, while thinking sadly, *And who knows how much longer we'll stay married if we can't resolve the very question you just asked?*

"Well, when you do, I can tell you'll be wonderful parents," she says.

I smile politely at her in response.

She continues, "James is such a different person around you guys. He's always been a quiet kid; and when he came back to us, I was really worried that he'd retreat further into his shell. But," she waves her hand toward Eric and James, "he's so comfortable with you, and it's such a blessing. I see hope."

Following her hand, I look over at James chatting

happily to Eric, and I hope she's right...for James, and for me and Eric.

25

———

In celebration of Finlay's graduation from obedience school, I suggested to Eric that we take him to Montrose Beach Dog Park to test how he behaves with other dogs while off leash. At least that's my cover story. My real purpose for the outing is to bring up the idea of adoption and see how Eric responds.

In between my consulting work and Jordan's client calls, she and I put together an outline of what Eric and I would have to do to become adoptive parents—the pros and cons of adoption agencies versus going through the state, what we could expect, costs, length of wait. I thought about contacting Adeline to get more information, but I figure she's still got her hands full adapting to parenthood. Also, I don't want her maybe saying something to Mark, and then Mark mentioning it to Eric. One can't be too careful.

Jordan let me practice on her, and once she declared I was ready, I made this date with Eric. I had thought about doing a dinner at home, but Jordan said it would probably alert him that I wanted to have a big talk. She suggested bringing the topic up during a drive or a walk. "It's easier to do it while you're next to each other and not facing him. Less confrontational," she explained.

She's the expert, so here we are on the lakefront walking toward the dog beach. I mentally rehearse, repeating Sarah's words to me that Eric and I will make great parents. It strengthens my resolve.

Once we're close to the beach and having already exhausted other conversational topics during the car ride over here, it's now or never time.

"I can't stop thinking about Adeline and Mark," I begin. "They're such a great couple. I wonder how they're doing adjusting to parenthood."

"Yeah. I'm sure they're doing fine. And, like Mark said, I'm sure we'll see them once they have a routine down."

"Right," I reply, hoping he'll say a little more. He doesn't.

"I was thinking we should've gotten them a card or something..." I trail off, nervous about my next statement, and glance over at Eric.

"Hmm..." He seems to be half-listening, distracted.

I touch his arm lightly. "Did you hear me? We should've gotten them a card or something."

"Yes, sure, a card," he says and then suddenly exclaims, "Finlay, drop it!"

I look down and Finlay has a McDonald's burger wrapper in his mouth. Finlay ignores him and so Eric grabs the wrapper from his jaws. He throws the wrapper into the garbage can it fell out of, and Finlay's eyes are sad as he watches his prized possession disappear.

"So much for obedience school," Eric says with a chuckle.

"Right?" I swallow.

Great. Maybe a beach day with the dog wasn't the best idea for a serious discussion. But here we are, and I have to do this. We've waited long enough to have this conversation.

I take a silent deep breath and try again. "So, babe, you know with Mark and Adeline now being parents, and Jordan and Jake as soon-to-be parents, I've been wanting to talk again about how you feel about having a family?"

The words are out there, and there's no turning back. I steel myself for his response.

He slows his pace and looks at me. "I've been wanting to talk to you about this too. Maybe we should sit down?"

"Okay," I say. My palms start to sweat, and my legs suddenly feel like Jello. Sitting sounds like a good idea. Luckily, I spot an empty bench right before the beach entrance.

When we reach it, Eric takes my hand as we step off the walkway and gently pulls me down onto the seat with him.

Still holding my hand, he turns sideways to face me. "So here's the thing. I freaked out, okay? The ectopic pregnancy hit me harder than I thought. Like I said, I had mentally prepared myself for us having a kid, but then I wasn't prepared for the possibility that something could happen to you, and that it could just be me raising a child by myself." He swallows. "You know my mom raised my sister and me alone, and I wasn't ready for that."

I nod. "I know."

That's fair. And, really, it's just the flip side of his earlier fear of not being there for our child. But it's the first time he's articulated his worry about raising a child alone, and I already feel my carefully constructed arguments crumbling.

I'm about to ask, *And now?*

But before I can speak, Eric continues, "But then I talked to Jake."

I hold onto that small word, *but.* "You did? When?"

"After you told me about Jordan's pregnancy, I invited him out for a beer to celebrate. We had a big talk about his situation and fatherhood in general. He's scared, but excited. He said it was ultimately Jordan's decision to keep the baby, but once she made it, he found he was surprised at how happy he was. He admitted he never wanted kids before, and didn't see himself settling down into marriage until later, or ever. But he loves Jordan, and this is what she wanted. And so while this isn't what he had imagined for his life, he said it's even better than what he thought he wanted."

"Awww, that's so great." I love hearing how much my brother loves my best friend. And I can't believe formerly commitment-phobe Jake is the one possibly changing Eric's mind on kids.

"It is." He smiles, then lowers his head and looks up at me. "And, you know, I wasn't really saying I didn't want a family with you. I was just going through something. I'm sorry. I've been selfish, I know. I should've kept those thoughts to myself."

"Never apologize for saying how you feel." Now I feel like I've been a horrible person. "I should apologize for being mad at you."

"No. You had every right to be. I can see how my words did that. But, hey, we got through our first big argument and now we're here together on a beautiful afternoon." As he's speaking, he slides down from the bench onto one knee. "Allison Caulder, will you have a baby with me?"

I laugh, relief rolling off me in waves. "Of course! I never thought you'd ask."

I put a hand on my heart and flutter my eyelids in an exaggerated manner before leaning forward to kiss him. All my arguments weren't necessary, and I wonder if I need to thank my older brother for this outcome. I'm getting exactly what I hoped for, but there is still something on my mind.

"You know, there is another possibility…"

Eric cocks his head.

"I've been thinking a lot about adoption lately," I say.

He sits back on the bench, his forehead scrunched up as he looks at me, waiting for me to say more.

"It's just an option, and nothing is guaranteed. But, you know, me getting pregnant isn't guaranteed either. I look at Adeline and Mark, and well, I don't know…what do you think about maybe adopting?"

He blinks a few times and says nothing.

My palms start sweating again. He just asked to have a baby with me after being spooked twice, and now I'm throwing something new at him. I feel an imaginary Jordan on my shoulder scolding me. I'm a pusher. Why am I pushing this? I got what I wanted. Am I trying to get this to blow up in my face?

Finally, Eric speaks. "Actually, I have thought about it a little. But I thought you wanted to have a baby." His brow is still furrowed.

"The two aren't exclusive," I say.

He nods, and I see his mind working.

"I've done some research, and we could register with an agency like Mark and Adeline or go through the state," I start, ready to download all my research onto him.

Finlay is getting fidgety the longer we sit on the bench, and he nudges Eric with his nose.

"I see," Eric says, slowly. "Here, let's keep talking while we get this guy to the beach."

At the beach, as we watch Finlay run around and splash in the water with the other dogs, I explain some of the differences and options to Eric, and he asks thoughtful questions. My prep with Jordan wasn't all for naught. But the big takeaway is that Eric is back on board for having a family; and as I watch an unrestrained Finlay giddily splashing in the water with the other dogs, I, too, want to jump in pure joy, pumping my fist in the air. But I restrain myself and settle on doing a little happy dance in my mind.

Eric only takes a couple of days to think about our conversation and surprises me over coffee before he heads out to work.

"I like this idea about adoption. We should do it," he says.

"You're sure?" I hold my breath.

"Yes. And I think we should also still try for a child. I like the idea of us having two kids. I don't know what I'd do without my sister. And you probably feel the same about your brother."

My heart swells in my chest, and I hug him. "I like the idea of two, too."

"So, what are the next steps? How do we sign up?"

I laugh at his eagerness. What a one-eighty from before.

"I guess we find an agency. I can see if Adeline would recommend theirs?"

The second Eric leaves for work, I send her a text.

Eric and I are considering adoption, and I'd love to talk to you about the first steps and if you'd recommend your agency. I know you're really busy with parenthood, so no worries if you're too swamped to respond. Hope all is going well!

She responds five minutes later.

That's so exciting! I would love to talk to you. Lucy has her nap around 1:30 (though not always a given). Are you free to chat on the phone then?

I text back immediately: *YES* and *Thank you!* And she says she'll call me then.

* * *

AT JORDAN'S CONDO, I'm having a hard time sitting still as I try to work, watching the clock tick down until my call with Adeline. Jordan is just as excited as I am. Though I try to temper it, not wanting to jinx anything, and say to her, "Trying to get pregnant and adopting, neither of those things are a given, you know."

"It's going to happen," Jordan says, her eyes shining with glee. "It just is. And I can't believe our kids are going to be cousins!"

We both make a ridiculous, high-pitched *eeee* sound and laugh. Finlay joins in, barking and jumping around us in excitement. So much for managing expectations.

When my phone rings, I take it out on the balcony.

"Hi, Adeline," I answer. "Thank you for taking the time to talk to me today."

"Of course. I'm so happy to help."

"First things first, though, how are things going with Lucy?"

"It's been amazing. Exhausting," she laughs, "but still amazing. We're so in love with her. It felt like it took forever, and now that she's here, I can't imagine my life without her."

"That's so wonderful. I'm so happy for you. And we can't wait to meet her!"

"Thank you." I hear her smile through the phone. "And we'll have you over. Right now we're overwhelmed with our new schedule, and so have just been slowly introducing her to family members. But once we're feeling totally settled, I think we'll do a birthday party or something. Anyway, tell me about you guys and your decision."

"I waited so long, and I thought getting pregnant would be easy." I fill her in briefly on how I had an ectopic pregnancy, then my frozen eggs fiasco, and the consideration of my age (leaving out Eric's existential crisis). "Anyway, I'm ready to be a mom now, and I want to explore every possibility."

"I get that. So let me tell you why we went through our adoption agency."

She explains that she and Mark really wanted a newborn baby to raise from infancy. They looked into several agencies and even independent adoption through an attorney. "While an agency adoption can be more expensive, it offers more resources and ours made the process much smoother. Though it can take a while, and in many cases years. So patience is key," she warns me.

"Do you mind me asking why you didn't go through the state route?"

"We thought about fostering to adopt, but it's complicated. The parental rights might not be terminated. There might be other birth family members involved. And with our jobs, the reality is at times we'll have to depend on a nanny, and we didn't want to bring third parties into a difficult situation. With the agency, it's much more amicable because the birth mother chose us."

"That makes sense." I think of the kids at Eric's CrossFit and how little I know about each of their former home situations.

"Though it's all a learning curve." She laughs. "But so worth it."

She gives me the information for the agency they used and promises to send an introduction email to her contact there this afternoon.

* * *

Two weeks later, thanks to Adeline's introduction, Eric and I are sitting on the other side of a desk at the adoption agency's offices. We've filled out the preliminary paperwork online and now have our introductory interview. Even though the meeting is supposed to be informational, it still feels more terrifying than any job interview. As my mind spins, I keep reminding myself that right now adoption is only an idea, another avenue for us. Working with my Girls Run It girls and visiting Eric's CrossFit kids' session these last couple weeks, I couldn't help imagining how one day it might be my kids doing all these activities. So even though these are just first steps, it feels so much more important—I want this. Funny how something that hadn't crossed my mind until recently has suddenly become my mission.

Though Eric looks calm and friendly, as we chat with the agent, each time he reaches over to grab my hand, I can tell he's nervous, too.

The adoption agent explains the entire process to us,

from the background checks we'll undergo and the classes we'll have to take.

"Have you thought about what you imagine your adopted child to be like?" she asks.

Other than wanting two kids, Eric and I haven't talked specifics. We look at each other. "A boy," we both say, our eyes widening at the other's response. But then I quickly add, "It actually doesn't matter."

Eric follows my lead. "Right. We're open to whoever is the right child for us."

"I understand." She smiles as she looks down and makes a note.

For the rest of the meeting, she answers all the questions that have been buzzing around our brains since we decided on adoption. The only downside is when she goes over the costs, the final number could be close to the six-figure mark. Both Adeline and Mark are partners in a large law firm, so I have an inkling of what they make, and which is why she probably didn't warn me. Eric and I are doing fine, but only as well as two self-employed, new businesspeople can be.

The agent sends us home with an application, a list of documents to gather, and instructions for personal letters of recommendation. Outside her office, I find myself trembling a little. "I'm going to call a realtor and get my place on the market."

Eric talks me down. "Hey, day by day," he says. "We haven't signed anything yet. Nothing can happen until after we finish our application. So let's first get started on that, and go from there."

"You're right," I say, feeling my breathing return to normal.

"And, anyway, I bet your parents are probably going to

want your place, now that they'll soon have two grandkids downtown."

"True." I laugh. We reach our car, and before getting in, I look over the roof at him and say in wonder, "We're really doing this."

He gives me a full-on, crinkles-in-the-corners-of-his-eyes smile. "We're really doing it."

And we head home to celebrate by taking Finlay for a walk and then diving into the application process.

26

<hr>

Today I'm meeting Kate and Suzy for an overdue business/catch-up lunch by their office. Since we have regular Zoom calls and are in contact weekly, I have a feeling this will be mostly a personal meal on the company's credit card.

As soon as I arrive at the restaurant, the host takes me to the table where Suzy and Kate are already seated. "Hey, you two!" I say when I reach the table.

Kate says, "Hey," and nods from her seat.

But Suzy gets up to give me a hug, in lieu of a hello. And the first thing she says to me upon greeting is, "You look happy. Are you glowing?"

I laugh. "Sort of, but not in the way you think."

"Hmm…In that case, I was thinking of ordering a bottle of the Sauvignon Blanc, if you're interested?" She raises an eyebrow as she settles back into her seat.

"Sure. That sounds great," I say, as I sit down and pick up the menu.

"So what has you so sparkly today?" she asks.

I fill them in on Eric's and my decision to adopt and our interview with the adoption agency.

"Wow, that's so cool, Allison," Kate says. "That makes perfect sense for you guys."

"Awww, that's wonderful," Suzy says. "And deserves a toast." She raises her wine glass. "Here's to you and Eric and your future child."

We all clink glasses.

"Thanks," I say after taking our first sips. "We haven't officially signed yet with the agency, but we've already started the home study classes. We have to do a lot of paperwork and background checks, so we're gathering everything." And then I look at them with big, pleading eyes and my hands in the prayer position. "And on that note...we're going to need letters of recommendation from friends and family. Just general, 'Eric and I are decent people and would make excellent parents,' blah, blah, blah..."

"Consider it done," Suzy says, and raises her wine glass at me again.

I look at Kate.

"Same," she says. "Tell me what to say, and I'll say it."

I laugh. "Thank you so much! You two are the best."

We order our meals, and they catch me up on the latest PR gossip. Once they've filled me in, we talk business, quickly reviewing our current projects, and then get back to the latest in our personal lives.

"So if you and Eric find out you're getting a baby, are you planning to stay in the city?" Kate asks.

"We haven't talked about that yet, though we have been talking about getting a house. Selling our places for something more family friendly with a yard."

"Ah, an 'if you build it, they will come' situation," Kate says.

I laugh. "Exactly. And in the meantime, I'm sure Finlay will enjoy a yard. And we will too. With the loft, I can't say I'm that excited about taking him outside multiple times a day in the winter."

"Whatever you do, just don't do it in the suburbs," Suzy groans. "Since my oldest was born, I've been counting the days until my kids are out of the house, and Rich and I can move back to a condo downtown. I don't know why a city person like me thought raising my kids there was a good idea."

"Hey, I grew up in the suburbs!" I say. But I get her point. At this stage in my life, I've lived in the city for so long that moving back to the 'burbs would feel like completely uprooting my life, akin to moving to another state. And I couldn't imagine Eric wanting to move away from his coffeehouses or his CrossFit kids.

AFTER LUNCH, which lingers until two o'clock, I mention that I'm going to head to The Cauldron.

"In the Gold Coast?" Kate asks.

"Yes."

"I'll go with you. I could use one of Brian's matcha lattes."

While Brian does make a delicious drink, going a mile out of the way to get a matcha latte seems a little extreme. And I must give her a questioning look because she says, "I'm not headed back to the office after this. I need to run some errands that way, and then I'm going home."

Since it's a warm early September afternoon, and there

may only be a few more before colder weather hits, we decide to walk the mile from the restaurant to The Cauldron. As we're chatting, I say, "Well, for your sake and mine, I hope Brian is in today."

"Oh, he definitely is," she says.

I turn to look at her. "How do you know?"

She smiles at me. "He told me yesterday."

"You were at The Cauldron yesterday, too?" Again, his drinks are good...but still.

"No, more specifically, he told me last night." Her smile grows bigger. And is that a blush forming on her cheeks? Realization dawns on me.

"Hold on..." I stop walking and put my hand out toward her in a stop position. "Are you saying—"

"Me and Brian?" Her eyes sparkle mischievously. "Yep, that's what I'm saying."

"Wait! When? How?"

Kate and Brian?

Kate and Brian!

It's one of those pairings that I wouldn't think of, but once it's out there, they make perfect sense as a couple. They have the same wry sense of humor. Both are serious about their jobs and serving their customers, yet are not exactly people persons. And, well, with their dark hair and eyes, they look cute together.

"It started when we met at the Lincoln Park launch party," she says. She tells me how they struck up a conversation when she ordered her first drink from him. After her second latte, they continued talking and Brian asked her if she wanted to meet up sometime. They exchanged numbers, and a few days later, he invited her to an Indian café known for their masala chai. For their second date, they went out to Kumiko, a Japanese cocktail bar in the West Loop. The night ended at her place, and they've been an item ever since.

"Wow! That's so great," I say.

"Thanks. It has been. We didn't want to say anything at first because we weren't sure where it was going, and we didn't want things to get awkward around you and Eric."

She looks at me with an apology in her eyes. I wave my hand in a "doesn't matter" motion.

Now that the secret is out, Kate can't stop talking about Brian. She gushes about his knowledge of teas and beverages, and I've never heard her so smitten with anyone she's dated. And when we get to The Cauldron, the big grin on Brian's face tells me he feels the same.

I've been pushing him to get on TikTok or any social media platform to do some reels, either showing how to brew tea properly or just sharing some tidbits of his tea knowledge. So far he's been resistant. But I think I now have an ally in Kate to put on the pressure.

"Where's Eric?" I ask.

"He's at the Lincoln Park location," Brian says.

"Oh?" I had planned to work a little here, then Eric and I were going to get Finlay and head to the CrossFit box together.

I take out my phone and see that I missed a text from him while I was walking.

No need to bring Finlay today. Kelly called. James is sick and won't be there. Broken espresso machine at Lincoln Park today. I'm headed there now to see if I can fix it.

Oh. I'm bummed about missing James. And since there's no reason to hang around here, I decide to take off and give the two lovebirds their space.

✳ ✳ ✳

WHILE I WAIT for the El at the Clark and Division station, I respond to Eric's text.

Okay. In that case, I'm going to head home and take Finlay for a walk. And do I have some gossip to tell you tonight!

I add a winky face to my text and press send. With my phone still in my hand, it rings with my brother's number. Phone calls from him are rare, and even rarer in the middle of the day.

"Jake?" I answer. "What's up?"

"Hi, Al. Jordan's water broke, and she called an ambulance," he says, his voice an octave higher than usual. "I'm on my way to Northwestern now to meet her."

"Oh, my god! Is she going to be okay?"

Oh no, oh no, oh no. She's two weeks away from her scheduled C-section, which was already going to happen three weeks earlier than if she had been allowed to carry to term. What does this mean for her baby?

"I don't know," Jake says. "Can you just meet me there?"

"Yes! On my way! I should be there in fifteen minutes."

The second I end the call, I order an Uber with shaking hands. It's a minute away, and so I race up the station stairs to meet it. In the car, I text Eric to let him know what's going on, and that I'm headed to the hospital. Then my mom calls.

"Jordan has gone into premature labor," she says, her panicked tone matching my own worst-case scenario thoughts. "Your dad and I are on the way downtown to Northwestern."

"I know. Jake told me. I'm on my way there too."

"Okay, darling. Call me if there is any more news, and see you soon," she says.

* * *

WHEN I GET to the hospital, Jake is sitting in the waiting room.

"Jake! Why aren't you with Jordan? Where's her room?"

"Hey, Al," he says, his voice cracking. "I didn't get here in time. They rushed her into surgery." He leans over, his elbows on his knees, and rests his forehead in his hands. My normally stoic brother trembles.

I drop down onto the seat beside him.

"I'm sorry," I say. "Did anyone tell you how Jordan was? How long delivery would take?"

"They said when her water broke, she also lost a lot of blood, and that the baby had to come out now."

I still have so many questions, like what this means for the baby, as well as for Jordan. But if Jake knew anything more, he would share it with me, so I don't ask him to elaborate.

I reach out to rub his back, which feels damp, and I guess he must have run here to be with her. My heart breaks for him.

"It's going to be okay," I say.

I hate myself a little for using this platitude because I don't know if it's even true, but I can't stand to see him so scared. I now understand Kate's words of reassurance in the aftermath of my failed pregnancy. I'm saying everything will be okay because I want it to be true.

He takes a deep breath. "I know. She's at one of the best hospitals in the country."

"Yes, she is." I smile a little, remembering Jordan said the same to me when my mom was in the hospital. "So, I guess we just wait."

He nods.

Now that I've been sitting still for several minutes, between the two glasses of wine I had at lunch an hour ago combined with my nerves, I feel a headache coming on.

"I'm going to get some water," I say. "I saw a vending machine on the way in. Can I get you anything?"

Jake shakes his head.

Standing alone at the vending machine, my back to the empty hallway, I burst into quiet tears. I give myself a minute to feel all the fears—fears for Jordan, for Jake, for their baby. Between my mom, myself, and now today with Jordan, I've spent more time in hospitals and with doctors this year than all my years combined. At any moment, life can shift without warning.

I take a deep, steadying breath and make my selection. Then I pull myself together, walk out to the waiting room, and wait.

Much like my dad and I waiting for my mom to get out of surgery, Jake and I don't talk much. I take out my phone to reply to Eric's text, but have no signal in this part of the hospital. I'm honestly kind of grateful; otherwise I'd be Googling risks for premature babies.

After what feels like forever, but was probably only thirty minutes, a doctor comes out. "Jacob James?"

My brother jumps up. "Yes."

"Congratulations. You're a father." The doctor smiles.

Jake's rigid body goes slack, and he makes a noise like a laugh-cry. His eyes shine, and his smile is wide. "Thank you. How are they?"

"Both mom and baby are well. Jordan is in her room sleeping. Because we had to perform a C-section right away, there wasn't time for an epidural, so she was under general anesthesia. Your daughter is healthy, and let out a big cry to let us know she arrived."

Jake and I laugh like hyenas.

"She's in the NICU being monitored, and I'm happy to take you to meet her."

Jake follows the doctor, but I hang back to meet my parents and give him this private moment with Jordan and his daughter.

I walk around the waiting room area, trying to get a signal. And when I do, I text Eric: *Jordan had her baby! Both are okay!*

I sit down again, repeating the good news to myself.

Several blissful minutes fly by and my parents arrive. They bustle in, my mom ten feet in front of my dad, and when she sees me, I stand to tell them the good news.

"Traffic was quick," she says in greeting, then grabs my hands. "What's happening? Where's Jake? Where's Jordan's room?"

"Everything is fine. Jake is with your granddaughter, and Jordan is in her room sleeping."

"Everyone is fine! Oh, thank goodness!" She squeezes my hands too tightly. She then turns her head, looking for my dad, who has just caught up to us. "Pat, Pat? Did you hear that? Everyone is fine!"

"I certainly did," he says, smiling. "Hi, honey," he says to me.

We're all beaming at each other and almost don't see Jake as he walks into the waiting room. He's smiling in a way I've never seen him smile before, as a proud father.

"Ready to meet your granddaughter and niece?" he asks.

27

Looking through the window of the neonatal intensive care unit, Jake points out his daughter to us and, with pride and love in his voice, says, "Meet Ella."

"Hi, Ella." I put my hand to the glass and look at my niece.

She is so tiny and looks so alone in her incubator. She's hooked up to a breathing tube and a heart rate monitor. It all brings tears to my eyes. But she's Jordan's daughter, and I know she's a fighter.

"She's gorgeous, Jakey," our mother coos.

"Thanks, Mom."

My dad puts his arm around our mom and says, "That's Grandma, now."

"Grandma," my mom repeats. "The most beautiful word." She sighs, leaning into my dad's embrace.

I smile to myself, thinking right now that "aunt" is a pretty wonderful word too.

"Are we allowed to go in?" my dad asks Jake.

He shakes his head. "Just Jordan and I are allowed in for

now. But they said that she should only be in here for one or two weeks, and then we can take her home. Because she came early, they want to monitor her and make sure her lungs are fully developed. Also, she needs to be in an incubator to stay warm and help regulate her temperature."

My mother's eyes go wide and before she can ask the question we're all wondering, Jake quickly says, "They told us, though, that everything looks as it should. One month preemies rarely develop long-term health issues."

My parents nod, reassured, as they gaze at their granddaughter.

"I should go and check on Jordan," Jake says. "The doctor said when she wakes up, she'll be in a lot of pain, and I want to be there for her."

"Can I come with you?" I ask.

"Sure. But I'll go in first and let you know if she's up to seeing anyone."

We leave my parents to continue admiring their granddaughter, and Jake and I head back to the room to see Jordan. I linger outside, and then hear a groggy, "Fuck."

She must be awake.

I overhear Jake tell her what happened, and a nurse explains where the painkiller button is and that she'll feel like this for the next few hours.

I then hear Jordan ask, "Is Allison here?"

I take that as my cue.

"I'm here. Congratulations," I say, approaching her bed.

"Did you see her?" she asks. Tears pool in her eyes, and now her voice is soft and filled with love.

"Yes. She's beautiful."

Jordan starts to full-on cry.

"It's okay, it's okay," I say, petting her arm.

"I know, I know. She's going to be okay. That's what everyone told me when I got here and before they put me under." She looks up at me. "I've never been so exhausted and happy and worried, and in so much freaking pain." She points to her watery eyes, and then she makes a noise that sounds like a laugh-sob. "I can't turn this faucet off."

I laugh and hug her shoulders. "You do whatever you want. You just had a baby!"

"Right?" She laugh-sobs again. "Did Jake tell you her name?"

"Yes. Ella. It's a beautiful name."

"Thank you," she says and smiles. "But her full name is Ella Marie James."

"Marie is my middle name!"

"I know." Her smile grows wider, and she looks at Jake, who is also grinning.

"We wanted her to share something with her amazing aunt and godmother."

"*Awww*, you guys!" Now I'm laugh-sobbing, and I go over to give my big brother an enormous hug.

My parents arrive and congratulate Jordan.

"The nurse was checking on Ella when we left," my mom says.

"I should be with her right now." Jordan's smile disappears, and she starts crying again.

"You will be," Jake says, putting his hand gently on her shoulder. "She's right down the hall sleeping."

"I can take you in a wheelchair in a couple minutes when you're ready," the nurse says. "If you're planning to breast-feed, we recommend starting within an hour window after birth."

"Okay." Jordan nods and winces, then turns to Jake. "We should call my parents."

We all take one final minute together, and then my parents and I leave them alone to FaceTime Jordan's parents.

* * *

Since Jordan and Jake will stay overnight in the hospital, I offered to go to their place to pick up a change of clothes and some toiletries. "We'll drive you," my mom says, "I brought some things for them."

Once in Jordan's condo, I discover the "things" my mom has are the same baby clothes I found in the linen closet.

The nursery is pretty much set up in Jordan's old office and is devoid of frills. Jordan didn't have an official baby shower because she claimed the placenta previa made her too tired. But knowing her general aversion to baby showers, I suspect this was a made-up excuse to avoid one, and I let it go.

As my mother folds the adorable onesies into dresser drawers, she comments, "These will probably be too big for her, but she'll grow into them quickly." After placing the clothes in the drawers, she looks around the room, and then pokes her head into the closet, *hmm*-ing to herself.

"I wonder if they need anything else," she says.

Little does my mom know that Jordan and I had been working through a registry checklist, so we have the major items down. But that won't stop my mom from buying *waaay* too much for Ella, and it's only a matter of time until this room is bursting with stuffed animals, artwork, books, and all things nursery-décor related. While they aren't married (yet), I can't help thinking to myself how Grandma Theresa is now Jordan's mother-in-law. *Welcome to my world.*

Jordan already had her "go bag" packed, so I just need to grab some stuff for Jake. I pick out some sweats, another pair of jeans, and a shirt, as well as boxers (which makes me weirdly uncomfortable). I put them in a carry-on bag I found in the hall closet, and we go back to the hospital to drop them off.

* * *

BEFORE HEADING BACK to the suburbs, my parents and I have dinner on the patio at Blue Door Kitchen in the Gold Coast, and Eric joins us. We fill him in on how Ella, Jordan, and Jake are doing and order a bottle of wine so we can toast to the new parents, a quick recovery for Jordan, and to Ella's health.

Then my mom says to Eric, "We haven't seen you in a while. So, tell me, what's new with you?"

"The Cauldron is doing well, and I'm hopeful that we'll have a third location by next year." He takes my hand. "And maybe next year, there will be another grandchild to celebrate."

My mother's eyes go wide, and she looks at me for confirmation.

I grin. "Nothing to report yet." And this might not be the right place or time, but since we're going to need letters of recommendation from my parents, here goes…"But Eric and I have been thinking about adoption."

"Adoption?" she repeats, as her eyebrows knit together.

"In addition to trying," I quickly add, anticipating her

follow-up question. "There's nothing wrong. We want to have at least two kids, and it seems like a good idea."

"Well!" She beams and raises her glass of wine again. "I think that's a *wonderful* idea. Good for you."

"Yes, here's to you!" My dad raises his glass too, and we all clink glasses again.

And because we're in a celebratory mood, I also fill them in on Brian and Kate's romance, to which everyone comments on what a day it is for surprises and calls for another toast.

After dinner, Eric heads back to work and my parents give me a ride home on their way out of the city. I walk Finlay and send a few emails, then put on my pajamas, even though I'm anything but tired. I turn on the TV for some Bravo or some mindless reality show to calm down, but I can't stop thinking of the reality of today. My brother and Jordan are parents. I'm an aunt and a godmother. My parents are grandparents.

I get up to make some chamomile tea, hoping it will help me sleep. While my water heats in the microwave, I wander over to the kitchen table with the intention of scrolling through my phone. On the table is the photo of James and Finlay that I had printed out, and I pick it up. I had put it in a frame and was looking forward to giving it to James today. I guess it will have to wait until next week. In the photo, James is looking into the camera and smiling the biggest smile with his arm around Finlay. Finlay's mouth is halfway open, in what looks like a dog version of a smile. A smile of my own forms.

The microwave dings and I set the picture down to make my tea.

That night, I dream a jumbled dream of kids playing in a

backyard. There's a little girl who I know is Ella (in that way that dreams don't make sense, yet you know who everyone is). Then there's an older James too, and he's pushing another little girl on a swing. They are all laughing and happy like the best of friends.

* * *

WHEN I WAKE, I feel a sense of peace, as if the dream told me everything will be okay with Ella. I look at my phone and can't believe it's already a little after eight, which means Eric has left for work. Yesterday was quite the emotional roller-coaster, so I guess I needed the extra sleep. Hearing me rustle in bed, Finlay comes in and starts trying to lick my face to say, "Good morning." This is my cue to get out of bed.

"I love you too," I say to him, while I throw off the covers.

The coffee is still warm from when Eric made it, and he left me a post-it saying he already took Finlay out this morning. I pour myself a cup, quickly get dressed, and head over to the hospital to check in on Jordan.

* * *

WHEN I ARRIVE, her room is empty, so I head to the neonatal intensive care room. From the window, I spot Jordan sitting next to Ella in her incubator. When she looks up, I wave, and she waves back. She starts to rise, but a nurse sees her, and gently puts her hand on Jordan's shoulder to sit back down in the wheelchair. Jordan points to me, and the nurse wheels her out to where I'm standing.

"Hi, how are you?" I bend down to hug her.

"Hey. I'm good. Ella's doing well," she says.

"That's great. And where's Jake?"

"He went home to shower, check in on work, and get some things for me. But he should be back soon."

She tells me that she needs to stay in the hospital for the next few days to heal and to make sure she doesn't have any more bleeding or complications.

"I don't care that I have to stay here. In fact, I want to stay until it's time to take Ella home. I don't want to be too far from her."

I nod, understanding.

We look at Ella from the window. "I still can't believe she's here already," Jordan says.

"You're a mom, Jor," I say, still in awe of yesterday's event.

She is quiet for a few seconds, and then says in small voice that doesn't sound like her, "Am I going to be a good one?"

"Of course you are! What do you mean?" I say, looking at her confused.

"I mean, I should've been taking it easier. You were right. Now she's here early, and she's so tiny."

"No, Jor, *you* were right. It's not like you were out doing marathons or anything. You were just in your place, moving from the bed to the sofa, or walking around the neighborhood. This was one of the risks."

She doesn't say anything, so I continue. "You're already an amazing mom. Look at you here—"

She puts up her hand and gives a little laugh, probably to stop me from going into cheerleader mode. "I have to tell you, yesterday, I'd never been so scared in my life. But I've also never been so okay with something. I can't believe how much I love her," she says.

"I love her too." Though I've only seen Ella through the window, she already has such a big place in my heart.

"Less than a year ago, I never wanted kids. And now, can you believe I'm a mom?" She repeats it, then stops herself and looks at me. "I'm sorry. That's insensitive. I'm still loopy from everything."

"Oh stop it. That's not insensitive. It's the truth. And we're all in different places than we thought we'd be."

"I never would have imagined this, but now I can't imagine it any other way." She grins. "Thank you for being here." She looks back at Ella.

"Are you thanking me or Ella?" I ask.

"You." But with her eyes on Ella, I can tell she wants to be in the room with her, not standing outside it with me.

So I say, "I have a meeting this morning, so I should probably head out soon." And I leave her to spend time with her daughter.

* * *

THE FOLLOWING WEEK, I bring the framed photo of James and Finlay to CrossFit. I wrapped it in a gift bag, and when I hand the bag to James, he breaks out a wide smile. He pulls out the photo, and if possible, his smile grows even more. "Thank you," he says.

"You're welcome, honey."

"I'm going to keep this forever," he says, his eyes still glued to the photo. Then he looks at Finlay and says, "It's us!"

Finlay thumps his tail and licks James's face, and James giggles.

As James is showing Finlay the framed photo, I'm

looking at him and I can suddenly see this boy as a teenager, then a college student, and growing into a young man. I can also see this framed photo sitting on a mantel with other family portraits. *Our family.*

James. This boy's name. My maiden name. Everything seems to click into place, as if it were fated.

A lump forms in my throat as a wave of emotion hits me. I look up and meet Eric's eyes and see what I need to know there. Last week's dream wasn't only about Ella being fine—it was about our future.

EPILOGUE

We're throwing a birthday party for James at our new house. As of six months ago, James is officially our son.

The adoption didn't happen as fast as we wanted, but the process was as painless as we all needed it to be. Eric and I first spoke to Sarah, who teared up and said, "I was hoping something like this would happen." She said the decision was up to the social workers, but that she could help us out. Because Eric and I had already undergone background checks, had personal references, and some home study under us, we were able to fast-track becoming foster-to-adopt parents. There were a couple bureaucratic bumps that had me sweating it out—a late change in our caseworker and the new one needing to get up to speed, as well as a rescheduled court date to make the adoption official—but overall everyone had the same wish to move things forward.

The ultimate decision was up to James, and we could tell he wanted to live with us as much as we wanted him to. In the beginning, he was exceptionally polite and called us

Allison and Eric, even though it all felt a little awkward, and we were worried about making a false step. The first night James slept at our place, Finlay stayed with him in his room and has continued to ever since. He follows James everywhere, and so we put James in charge of feeding him.

We weren't immediately a family. It took time, and then one day, James introduced me as Mom to one of the kids at his school, and from then on we became Mom and Dad. Because James is older and has memories of his birth parents, we made a Life Book for him with their photos, and even visited where he originally lived. We encourage him to share his memories of them; they're a part of our story and our family too.

He's into Legos, space, and Star Wars, and has become good friends with Eric's nephews, his new cousins, who have also turned him on to video games. With James in our life, Elaine and I have grown closer. (She admitted to me that after watching her brother's previous relationships fizzle out, she had been nervous about getting too attached to ours.) Tonight the boys are all sleeping in a space-themed tent in the backyard, that they can hide out in. And he just received a telescope as a present from my parents, so the boys are excited to use it.

Adeline and Mark are sitting on our outdoor lounge chairs with Lucy. Lucy is on Mark's knee, giggling as he bounces her. Across from them are Darren and his husband, who have been talking to them and us about adoption. Kate and Brian are overseeing the bar on the patio, serving some of Brian's tea concoctions. Their relationship is still going strong, and with Kate's help, Brian is now a TikTok sensation for his tea videos, which I knew he would be. Suzy and her husband are chatting with my parents by the dining table where we've laid out all the food, filling their plates, while their brood plays with the other kids.

And, of course, Jake and Jordan are here with Ella, who is now just over a year old. Jake mans the grill, and Jordan follows closely behind Ella in the yard, as she walks and tumbles in the grass. In fact, the three of them are here a lot, since they live next door.

In between everything else going on, once we decided to adopt, Eric and I also decided to get a jump on house hunting. When we found a new construction with an available house next door, Jordan and Jake bought the other. Jordan and I joke all the time about how we've been each other's adopted family since we met in college, and now we're sisters-in-law, our lives forever entwined.

When the cake comes out and James is told to make a wish, he blows out the candles; and between his laughs and smiles, he keeps his wish a secret. I can't believe what a happy kid he is tonight. I also have a secret, but it's too soon to share and so I'm keeping it to myself for the time being. This is James's day.

Looking around at all these people I love, and what our lives were like only a couple years ago, I can't help but think, sometimes when you let go of what you think your life is supposed to look like, what comes next might be even better —and in our case, even greater than expected.

ACKNOWLEDGMENTS

With each new novel, both the supporting casts of fictional and real-life characters in my writing life grow. I'm so grateful for those who have supported me through all my books and the new connections who helped with this one.

The first people I need to thank are my lovely readers. You're the best accountability partners. You asked me for a sequel, and here it is! I hope you enjoyed it. And if you're a new reader, thank you for taking a chance on this book.

Thank you to the incredible editorial team who helped me shape this story into being–Annie Tucker, Chrissy Wolfe, and Charlotte Hayes-Clemons. Thank you to talented book designer Katarina Prenda for its gorgeous cover. You're all the dream team!

Thank you to my writer community and fellow authors —Emily Bond, Lainey Cameron, Meg Donohue, Jean M. Grant, Cerrissa Kim, Lisa Williams Kline, Anita Kushwaha, Allison Larkin, Maria Murnane, Camille Pagán, and Anastasia Ryan—for your support and insights. A special shout-out to Kari Bovée for our monthly writer calls. C. D'Angelo, thank you for answering all my questions about becoming a therapist; I'm so grateful our debuts brought us together. And thank you, Andrea J. Stein for your friendship and for being my last-minute date at the Independent Press Awards dinner.

Thank you to Jane Green for an incredible writing retreat in Marrakesh and the magical mountains in Morocco.

Thank you to Maryam Ghaffari-Ragan for being my "official" Palm Springs PR rep. Thank you to Beata Osmondson and her book club. (Glad we survived that Lower Wacker adventure!) Thank you to Olivia Luk for hosting me at the American Writers Museum, and Tonia Luk for inviting me to Zoom into her living room with her book club. And thank you, Melissa Amster of Chick Lit Central for the amazing book recommendations over the years and for reading mine.

Family time! Thank you to:

My parents, Catherine and Richard Terry, for always nurturing my love of reading and writing. My brother Ed for sharing the details of dog obedience school (and Louie the beagle, who never met a squirrel he didn't want to chase). My sister-in-law Lori who introduced my books to her book club in Door County. My Aunt Sharon and Aunt Ella for your love and sweet cards after reading *Charming Falls Apart*. You are missed. My husband's family, the Greenwell clan, for being the best cheerleaders. Veronica and Tom Greenwell for your card of encouragement while I finished this one. My husband, Ray, for your patience while I tried something new.

ABOUT THE AUTHOR

Angela Terry is the award-winning and Amazon bestselling author of *Charming Falls Apart*, *The Trials of Adeline Turner*, and *The Palace at Dusk*. She is also a Chicago Marathon legacy finisher and races to raise money for PAWS Chicago —the Midwest's largest no-kill shelter. She resides in San Francisco with her husband and two cats.

For more information on her books, book club requests, and events, visit her at www.angelaterry.com. And for updates, sign up for her newsletter on her website.

Charming Falls Apart **Excerpt**

Chapter One

Please be home, please be home, please be home, I pray while opening the front door to my condominium, keys in one hand as I precariously balance a box of "personal belongings" on my hip while kicking a second box over the threshold. Thankfully, Neil is sitting at the kitchen table.

"Thank god you're here!" I exhale, expecting him to relieve me—both of the box I'm holding and my horrible day. Instead, Neil stays silently rooted to his seat, staring at his phone. He's already changed out of his work clothes, the usual button-down shirt with slacks, and into an old T-shirt and his favorite pair of jeans, making me wonder how long he's been home and if he listened to my voicemail.

Receiving no help from my fiancé, I make my way inside with the door slamming shut behind me.

I unceremoniously drop the first box onto the kitchen table with a *thunk*. "You'll never believe what happened today." Though the boxes should be some indication.

Neil remains uncharacteristically quiet, still focused on his phone and not me—his lack of curiosity and eye contact makes me want to snatch the phone from his hand.

"Well?" I prompt him.

He swallows and finally meets my eye. "We need to talk."

While that phrase is never good to hear, it can't be worse than what I just endured. Our wedding is only a month away; so, lately, that sentence, when uttered, means that something has gone wrong with one of our bookings or our parents or surprisingly demanding guests.

"Sure. Okay," I say, wiping some dots of perspiration from my forehead with my now free hand. "But can I go first? It's been a horrible day, and I can't deal with wedding stuff right now." This is an understatement.

I walk over and deposit myself onto the sofa, kick off my shoes, and throw my arm over my eyes. I wait a couple seconds for Neil to come sit next to me. He doesn't, so I just start talking. "*Ugh.* Where to begin?"

Finally, I hear the kitchen chair scrape back and Neil's footsteps. With my eyes still covered, I feel him standing over me. "No, Allison. I really need to talk to you first. This is important."

I sigh and give in. My news will have to wait.

"Fine. Okay. What's so important?" I say, removing my arm from my eyes and prepping myself for the latest wedding disaster. Since I've been the one dealing with the vendors, it must be a guest issue.

"I can't marry you," he says, his voice sounding oddly strangled.

I peer up at him. "Excuse me?"

Neil clears his throat and, with more determination in his voice this time, repeats, "Allison, I can't marry you."

"What do you mean *you can't marry me*?" I enunciate each word. *What in the world is going on, now?*

"I can't go through with the wedding."

Oh. It's not much of an elaboration.

Not this again, I think but do not say. These last few months, Neil has been stressed out by everything wedding-related—the cost of the invitations, whether we really needed a photographer *and* a videographer, or why I hired a band when his green-haired, multiple-pierced, eighteen-year-old cousin was an amateur DJ—when, really, all he has to do at this stage is show up wearing his suit at the appointed time on the appointed date. All my friends assured me though that this was normal guy-getting-married behavior and to not let it freak me out as well.

I pat the side of the sofa next to me. "Neil, honey, sit down."

When he remains standing, I take a deep breath and say, "I know the wedding planning has been stressful. *Trust me*, there've been times *I've* wanted to call it off, too. But it's almost over. In a month we'll be at the finish line saying our 'I do's.'"

"No. It's not the wedding planning." Neil shakes his head and takes a step back from the sofa. "I can't marry you because I'm in love with someone else."

And for the second time today—

The.

World.

Just.

Stops.

I open my mouth a couple times, but nothing comes out. Since I can't seem to form words, I instead end up staring at him for several silent seconds while my heart beats wildly against my chest and I wonder if today is simply a bad dream or a massive practical joke.

Surely, I couldn't have heard him correctly, but do I ask him to repeat the horrible words that I think I just heard? Turns out, I don't have to.

"I'm so sorry, Allison." His eyes, bloodshot and drooping with contrition, remind me of my old Basset hound, Barry, when he was caught doing something he shouldn't.

He must feel safe that this news has rendered me immobile because he finally sits down next to me. "I'm so, so sorry."

My throat is tight and I'm not sure I can breathe. I search his eyes for confirmation of what is happening and manage to say in a small voice, "You're calling off the wedding?"

"Yes."

"There's someone else?" I ask in an even smaller voice.

He nods.

"Oh." I look away and stare into space at some point above his head.

Quickly and nervously, he starts to explain—as if his explanation will soften the blow. "I didn't mean for it to happen. It just did. I didn't do it to hurt you. I would never want to hurt you." *Funny*, I think, *because you're doing a good job of it now*. "But it would be worse to continue our relationship and lead you on. It's better to break up sooner rather than later with the wedding coming up and before everything becomes more complicated."

His words sound like a speech he has practiced, probably with the "someone else."

I still don't have any words.

"Allison," he pleads, trying to evoke a response from me, but I refuse to look at him. "Al, please say something."

His mind is made up enough to call off our wedding and break my heart. I'm not sure what to say to that. How can you beg someone to stay with you once they've said they're in love with someone else? It seems to be the definition of *game over*.

Finally finding my voice, I manage to whisper, "Who are you in love with?"

Neil is silent. My eyes drift back to his and I notice his eyes have grown wide. Fear.

"Who are you in love with?" I ask again, a little louder this time.

Neil stands up. With words so rushed they sound like one, he says, "I'm in love with Stacey." And with that declaration, he backs up and grabs a bag that has been sitting in the hallway all this time and that I am just now noticing.

Stacey. My maid of honor. *Of course.*

"I'm sorry, Allison. I wish things weren't ending like this."

His eyes meet mine for a heartbreaking second, and I believe him. Until, coward that he is, he breaks eye contact and then turns and hurries out the door—our door—before I can even tell him my big news.

Once the door clicks behind him, I say aloud to no one, "I got fired today." And, with that, the tears I've held in all afternoon come rushing out.

I wake up in the morning puffy-eyed and exhausted and hoping that yesterday was all a bad dream. I look over to where I've expected to see Neil the last five years. But his side of the bed is empty, and there are no head indentations on the pillow, or any indications that he slept there and simply woke up before me.

I turn away and stare numbly at the ceiling for several eternal minutes before reaching for my phone. I check the time: 10:17 a.m. *How can that be?* I fell asleep last night sometime before ten, which means I've slept for more than twelve hours. Still, when I begin trying to move my leaden limbs, I feel like I've been hit by a ten-ton truck, my insides smeared along the Kennedy.

My phone rings, breaking the silence with Beyoncé's latest, which forces me into action by answering to shut it up.

"Good morning, birthday girl," my friend Jordan enthuses while I inwardly groan.

Oh, right. I'm thirty-five today. Somehow I forgot all that with the news of losing my job *and* my fiancé in the span of a few hours.

"Good morning," I reply groggily.

"You sound awful," says Jordan, and I can feel her frowning over the phone. "Did you already start celebrating last night?"

"No, nothing like that." Though this morning is resembling a bad hangover. "I'm just waking up."

"Well, I won't keep you. Just confirming that we're still on for Adobo Grill at eight tonight?"

Oh my god—my birthday dinner tonight. After yesterday, there is nothing to celebrate and the absolute last thing I feel like doing is going out. But begging off would require an explanation and since my grief-filled brain can't form an excuse fast enough, I dully respond, "Uh huh."

"Can't wait to see you and celebrate!" Her cheerfulness sharpens my heartbreak.

"Same here," I say, not meaning it.

"Ugh. You sound terrible. You better get some coffee in you, girl."

"Yes, I'll get on that."

"Love ya! See you tonight." Jordan hangs up taking her cheerfulness with her.

Yes. Coffee. It can't cure all my problems, but it can cure at least one. I'm so drained I'd probably go back to sleep if I didn't have to figure out the next chapter of my life. Of course, this realization makes me want to pull the covers over my head, which I do, and never come out.

Argh.

But that's not who I am and it's not who I plan to become and I give myself a sad pep talk. Okay, these are just some setbacks. Some major setbacks, true, but I've never been one to give up. I can't let Neil get the best of me. I realize though that once I get out of bed there are painful steps to take. There is a wedding to cancel. There is job hunting to do. There is a birthday dinner to attend.

There is the fact that I am thirty-five years old and my life has crumbled around me.

What do I do first?

It's Saturday, my long run morning. Normally, I hate skipping a workout since I used to always be training for something—the Chicago marathon or the occasional sprint triathlon—although the last few months, it's all been for seamlessly fitting into my wedding dress. So though it's the last thing I feel like doing, considering the uncontrollable downward trajectory my life took yesterday, I *also* feel that I should stick to whatever constants I still have in my life. Mustering all my strength, I push the covers off me and roll out of bed. I pull my meticulously highlighted blond hair into a ponytail, throw on the requisite running gear, lace up my shoes, and am out the door before I can second-guess myself.

* * *

The late morning May sun does little to lift my mood as I head toward Lincoln Park, promising myself that for an hour, I'll try to forget that I'm Allison James—the thirty-five-year-old, unemployed, former fiancée.

As I make my way to the end of Dearborn nearing the Lincoln Memorial, there's a group of people that on closer inspection turns out to be a bridal party getting their photos taken. I look to where the smiling maid of honor is standing next to the smiling bride and fixing something in the bride's hair. Tears sting my eyes and my chest threatens to explode and I want to shout at the universe, "Oh, come on!" as I veer toward the lakefront to avoid them.

It was my maid of honor who inadvertently introduced me to Neil. Stacey had invited me to a Cubs game when one of her friends secured a box (even though, in my opinion, it's usually more fun in the bleachers), and Neil was a friend of the friend who had the box. Neil was the type of guy Wrigleyville attracts. He was good-looking in a clean-cut way with closely cropped light brown hair and warm brown eyes that crinkled slightly when he smiled. He was fit, but not obsessively so. He golfed and occasionally played volleyball at the lakefront in the summer, though he admitted he preferred watching sports to actually doing them. We ended up sitting next to each other and spent the entire game talking about everything—movies, music, *The Amazing Race*, favorite Chicago spots, our jobs (he worked in sales for a sports marketing company; I was a PR account manager), our friends, our families, and even childhood pets (his was a female turtle named Steve). I was completely taken in by his friendly demeanor, lopsided grin, and honest face (how ironic, all things considered). When I accidentally swallowed my beer too quickly and got a terrible case of hiccups, he tried helping me with all the tricks in the book. "Hold your breath. Here, we'll have a contest." Yet, he kept making such ridiculous faces while he held his breath that I would end up laughing and hiccupping even more. Then he tried to scare me, but trying to do so at a rowdy baseball game was near impossible. The only thing that seemed to cure them was when he asked for my phone number.

Our relationship progressed easily and quickly, and within a year we were living together in my condo and planning our future. From the first date until yesterday, everything about our relationship had felt so simple and right—so how could it have all gone wrong?

And, Stacey, of all people? I could understand it if maybe he went for someone completely different, but Stacey also works in PR and is physically another version of me—five foot seven, blond (although even more bottled than I am), and a gym-honed size four.

And he couldn't have possibly chosen her because of her personality. The woman is insanely demanding. Whenever we go out, she wants to pick the restaurant or bar and usually picks one with no consideration for others' finances. God forbid if any service is less than stellar because she's a stingy tipper (*when* she tips) and always wants to complain to the manager. She was one of those customers I feared when I worked in retail during high school. Though it was exactly for these reasons that I asked her to be my maid of honor, hoping her forceful personality would help keep the wedding day schedule on course. Sure, she's funny and fine in conversation, but aren't all PR people? That's our job.

So the only thing I can think of, and the thought makes me ill, is that she must be really, really good in bed. I would give her that. Not that I don't have my own tricks, but Neil and I were together for a long time. Things got comfortable. The sexy chemises I always wore to bed at some point turned into flannel pajamas (but in my defense, Chicago winters are brutal!). The stress of wedding planning took up a lot of our free time, and our most in-depth discussions became centered around issues such as which font looked best on the save-the-date cards. But everyone knows that's just wedding planning and every couple goes through it. So why didn't we survive? What was wrong with us? Or more to the point—what is wrong with *me*?

This last thought sucks the air right out of me, and I stop running. Spying a nearby bench, I collapse onto it, rest my forehead on my hands, and let the tears silently spill.

I am not a demanding person. All I asked from life was to have a nice job I was good at, find a nice guy to settle down with and have our nice family, and then to live our nice happily-ever-after preferably in a suburb with good public schools. Since many of my high school and college friends have surpassed me in almost all these areas, clearly, the flaw is with me.

Suddenly I feel someone sit next to me, and a voice says, "I'll be your boyfriend if you want?"

I look up to find a teenage boy smirking at me. Judging from the eye-liner and black clothing, I assume he must be an art student at Columbia or the Art Institute.

Well, okay, maybe I demand a nice guy in my age bracket.

Feeling ridiculous to be caught out crying on a park bench, I smile politely at him before standing and taking off in a slow, sad jog toward home to get started on the depressing task of piecing my life back together.

* * *

Lost in my thoughts on my way home, I run into a chalkboard sign on the sidewalk and almost fall over. *Great*, I might as well add a broken limb on top of everything else falling apart in my life. I straighten up the sign and see that it's advertising a new coffeehouse that opened a couple days ago in my Gold Coast neighborhood.

Need a wicked brew? Step into The Cauldron.

Still in need of my morning caffeine (and a cure for this emotional hangover), I could use a wicked brew.

As soon as I open the door, I appreciate the welcoming vibe. The décor is simultaneously cozy and industrial with exposed brick walls and a fireplace on one side. Everything is very Restoration Hardware—dark wood tables and metal chairs are mixed in with comfy, worn leather sofas and chairs tucked into corners and lots of vintage-looking lighting. By the counter, there is a glass display filled with pastries, sandwiches, and salads. A guy who looks around my age stands behind the register.

"Good morning. How are you?" he says.

Good manners force me to lie. "Fine, thank you. You?"

"Great! I woke up this morning, the sun was shining, and I'm alive. What can be better than that?"

I smile and nod politely at his new-agey comment. Between that and his surfer-like, naturally blond hair and light blue eyes, I decide he must be a transplant from California.

"So what can I get you this morning?" he asks.

"I'll have a large latte with almond milk and a banana, please."

I grab a banana from the basket on the counter while he rings me up. My gaze wanders over to the pastry case, but I seem to have lost my appetite along with everything else. And, anyway, I have rules about this. Six days a week, I eat ultra-healthy. Then on the weekend, I'm allowed one meal of whatever I want. I never break my rules, not even for a breakup or job loss. If I start breaking the rules now, I can't imagine what new chaos will erupt in my already disastrous life. Best to stick to the program.

While I wait for my latte, I walk around the place, idly looking at the various books and magazines on display. Seems like a great place to hang out in peace. Unfortunately, that's not something I have the luxury of doing today—I have a wedding to cancel and a job to find (and more tears to shed).

"Excuse me, miss? Here's your latte." The guy from the cash register sets down a paper cup on the table where I'm sitting.

I jump a little at the sound of his voice. I was so lost in my thoughts that I didn't even notice I'd sat down. Composing myself, I smile up at him. "Thank you."

"I meant to call your name, but I forgot to ask."

"No worries. It's Allison." I wrap my hand around the warm cup and stand.

"Thanks for coming in, Allison. I'm Eric. Hope to see you again."

He has a kind smile. Exactly the type of smile I need today. "This is a cute place. I'll definitely be back."

"And, here, take this too." Eric hands me a small bag. "It's on the house."

"Oh! Um, thanks. What is it?"

"A lemon blueberry scone. It's my mother's recipe."

"Wow, thank you. That's really nice of you. I look forward to trying it."

He breaks into a grin, and then I really must go because I'm not sure how much kindness I can handle in my fragile state without melting down in public again.